The

MW01047073

Neal F. Litherland

ISBN:

DEDICATION

This book is dedicated to all the writers out there who read their rejection letters, and get back to work. There is no harder part of the job, and if you can face those, then you can face anything.

Don't stop. Keep writing.

ACKNOWLEDGMENTS

I want to thank my beta readers, my plot pickers, and everyone who took me out for a shake and told me not to give up on these stories. That they'd find their home eventually. I took your advice to heart, and decided they'd waited long enough.

Contents

Introduction

I spent my childhood consuming books in almost any form I could find them, but some of my favorites were short story collections. Whether it was the infamously terrifying *Scary Stories to Tell in The Dark* series, or collections by Bruce Coville and Isaac Asimov, I always kept a book of short stories near to hand when I was a young reader. They were sort of like a fiction buffet, giving me a dozen different stories from just as many authors, each one with its own, unique sense of style, feel, and taste.

Despite the number of anthologies I'd read, though, I never really asked where they came from. All I knew was that when I went to a bookstore or the library, there were always shelves full of these little bite-sized stories. Then in 2012 I came across a small romance publisher who had put out an open call for short stories for an upcoming anthology.

That was when the light bulb went off. I'd been writing short stories for years (mostly as extra credit projects in school), but now that I'd found the front door to a paying market I was off to the races. I had three short stories accepted in as many months, and for the next couple of years I did my best to make sure I was writing at least one new short story every month for submission to an open call.

A lot of these short stories were accepted, and they've appeared in anthologies like *SNAFU: A Collection of Military Horror*, *Sidekicks*, *Noir Carnival*, and *American Nightmare*. And while I like to think I had a pretty solid acceptance record, there are still plenty of stories I wrote that just weren't quite right for the anthologies I submitted them to. While a few of those stories eventually found new homes when I submitted them to other open calls, there have always been a few orphans lying around that just never seemed to make the team.

That's why I figured it was time to build them all a home, and get them out there so that readers who've enjoyed my other short fiction can see what it is I've been keeping in the drawer and waiting for a rainy day.

These stories run the gamut, from the ghosts of Vietnam that still haunt an old veteran, to the secrets that lurk down the alleys of Chicago's mean streets, to the things that dwell in the backwater parishes of Louisiana with a hunger for blood and lullabies, these pages are filled with the odd, the strange, and the occasionally macabre. While I'm going to share a little bit about each story's conception below, you might want to read them first, and then come back here. As they say on the Internet, danger, there be spoilers ahead!

Also, keep in mind that some of these stories are older than others. As such, it's possible the publishing companies I originally wrote them for are no longer in business, or that I've since forgotten what the theme of the original anthology call was. That's why some of these are going to be more detailed than others.

Dressing The Flesh: This story has the most clearly remembered origin for me. Several years ago Tor had an open call looking for stories to fit into the *Nightbreed* universe. Both the film, and the novella *Cabal* by Clive Barker, are favorites of mine. While this story didn't get picked (and it was adjusted to be a stand-alone piece once Tor turned it down), it's had several close calls with magazines and horror anthologies over the years. But it seemed to always be a bridesmaid instead of a bride.

Champion For Hire: Originally written for a semi-regular sword and sorcery anthology collection titled *The Barbarian Coast*, this fantasy take on *Yojimbo* was going to be my contribution to the second book. Sadly the publication seemed to have up and vanished by the time I went to submit it, and this particular tale remained untold… until now, that is.

Dead Man's Bluff: This one is a bit of a cheat, since it was originally written for and published for a brief time on Yahoo! Voices before that site closed down. It has never appeared in print, however, despite several submissions. A weird little Western, it hasn't managed to find a new home despite a few different publications giving it thoughtful consideration.

Bloody Bones: When I came across an open call asking for stories of fey (seelie, unseelie, and the gray area in between), this story hit me like a runaway freight train. While it wasn't to the taste of the original publisher, as I strongly suspect they were looking for stories where the fey's presence was felt much more strongly throughout the piece, it remains one of my favorite dark dramas. Hopefully you feel the same once you've read it!

Assault on Olympus: Written for SNAFU publisher Cohesion Press, this one almost made the cut, but got edged out at the last moment. SNAFU: Armageddon was looking for unique end of the world scenarios, and instead of zombies, nuclear fallout, or even Cthulhu, I thought I'd go in a different direction… metahumans. If you've ever wanted to see a military horror story about superheroes, then today is your lucky day.

Mark of The Legion: I've been holding onto this story for so long that I don't actually remember what the original call for it was. But what I wound up with was a glimpse into a world I'd never visited before, and a curiosity regarding the Foresworn Legion, whatever empire they serve. I may have to come back here at some point, and figure out what's actually going on beyond the scope of this story.

Hero's Wake: The second superhero tale in this collection, the original call was for stories that showed us the lives of metahumans behind their costumes. To that end, I figured I would give my readers a glimpse of how these heroes mourn the passing of one of their own. When they're among each other, and they can be who they really are. No gimmicks, no made-up names… and we find that, deep down, even those with extraordinary powers are really just people.

Heart and Soul: This one is a bit of a special case, as the publisher I wrote it for shuttered its doors before this story could be accepted or denied. However, it's the second story set in my world of Chicago Strange (the first being *Little Gods* published in *The Big Bad II* for those looking for continuity), and it is the first appearance of the dowser Gerald Caul. The seed for a bigger project called The Caulbearer Cases, that's still on my list of potential future endeavors.

Suffer The Children: I wrote this story for an anthology titled *Streets of Shadows*, but didn't get chosen for it. I'd had the character of Malachi floating around for a while, and published a previous story about his adventures titled *Skin Deep*, but I wanted to showcase how both he and my style had changed since then. This tale is the result.

Eyes, Hands, and Heart: When I came across an open call for a collection of steampunk Grimm fairy tales, I had to wrack my brain to come up with something that would be outside the norm. After all, there were bound to be dozens of steam-powered Red Hood armor suits, and monocle-wearing animals going to Bremen to become musicians. The one Grimm story I couldn't get out of my head was *The Three Army Surgeons*, and if you know that story, well, my re-telling has a bit of a twist to it.

Jungle Moon: A relic of my early writing career, this was one of the last short stories where the bulk of the tale is told through dialogue rather than action. Still, I think it is the best version of that setup, which is why I felt it should be included here.

Nerves: Much like *Jungle Moon*, this story is also one of those tales where two characters sit in a room and talk. And while I was leery about essentially doing the same trick twice, the ending of this one got so many of my beta readers when I first put pen to paper that I felt almost compelled to share it with all you fine folks.

Happily Ever After: A fitting final story for a collection like this, *Happily Ever After* was one of the only stories I wrote first, and then tried to find a market for once I had it complete. While it never quite found a place to sit before now, hopefully everything you've read by the time you reach this one will give you a sense that there is something lurking behind that title.

And now that we've gotten all of those out of the way, please, enjoy the following tales! Or, if you're coming back here for the break down after you've already read the rest of the book, I hope you had fun, and that one or two of these tales put a shake into you that's going to be a long time coming out.

Dressing The Flesh

February had teeth. It wasn't like the slow, glutted cold of January, or the playful, chilly nips of December; February was hungry. It was a vampire month that took no prisoners, and gave no quarter. It tore through overcoats, raked cheeks, split lips, and seared eye sockets. It was a bitter beast that howled down the alleys on every lake breeze, and wrapped itself tight around those unfortunates who had no brick bastions or rented rooms to hide in. Some of them made it through, hollow-eyed and shivering. Some of them died, reduced to nothing but cold meat when their seasonal lover had sucked away the last of their warmth.

The street tribes had their rituals and protections against the ravenous cold. Wadded newspaper stuffed into pant legs and coat sleeves was popular. Some swore by the Times, others preferred the Red Eye, but everyone agreed that the fresher the paper was, the better it kept in the heat. A few asphalt survivalists curled up in dumpsters, letting the miasma of rotting garbage warm their bones. Others camped on steam grates and sewer drains, letting the Windy City's exhausts keep them safe. Burn barrel sing-songs and prayers over clutched candles did for others. Shared bottles of hooch and snake oil bought with rumpled bills and dirty coins were legion. In the end, none of it truly mattered. The only way to survive was to hide.

Ace knew how to hide. He'd had a lot of practice since he left the only home he'd ever known, and his family had scattered to the winds. He haunted rooftop redoubts, slunk through sewers, and secreted himself in the thousands of shadows in the concrete honeycomb of Chicago. A million eyes passed every day, and not one of them saw him unless he wanted to be seen. He had remained invisible... until Tagg found him.

Lisa Taggart was an inner city dust devil; beautiful from afar, but dangerous to get caught up in. She had a passion for secrets, and that hunger drove her insatiably. It was why she'd sat down next to him six months ago, and started talking. He'd been half-starved and alone, a rural refugee lost in the big city. She'd taken his hand and smiled, pulling him into her wake before he could even think about it. Before his mother's voice, still clear in his memory even after her long absence, could tell him to stay away from her. He hadn't let go since, and the two of them had been nearly inseparable.

She'd probed his secrets, and smiled when he'd kept so much of himself back. She'd taken him to places only she knew about; places even he hadn't suspected existed. She had shown him rainwater grottoes where runoff fell in cascading waterfalls, and led him along hidden highways where midnight markets offered to buy and sell anything and everything. She had settled a dusty hat on his head, and frowned with the careful consideration of the artist as she made him try on a dozen sets of dark glasses before declaring the final pair satisfactory for his sensitive eyes. She had cajoled him into the houses of the crucified god, and held his hand as he bit his cheek bloody while men and women in black looked him over before offering him a meal. She'd given him his street handle when his true name had proven too exotic for her tongue to pronounce. She'd lain in his arms and listened to the silence of the witching hour, neither of them saying anything. She had called him her mystery, and it made him smile.

Tagg talked about the cities she'd known. The greatest places in the world, each with their own tastes and textures. Each with their own unknowable places and hidden byways. She told him street level legends, and the fireside tales passed down by hobo elders and strung-out prophets. He asked if she believed in monsters, and she told him a thousand myths couldn't be wrong. Monsters were the best secrets, she said, and she would keep looking for them until she found one. He asked what she'd do when she did, and Tagg had smiled her private little smile. She said she wouldn't know until she was face-to-face with one. They sought, they saw, they moved, and he was content.

Then the storm had come.

Tagg had braved the frozen, daytime streets on a beg-and-borrow for coins and food, but she hadn't come back before the blizzard. Snowed in beneath an unused access grate, Ace waited with all the patience he could manage. When the storm abated he drew a small, charcoal mark high up on the wall, telling Tagg to meet him at Saint's Basement in case she came back and found him gone. Then he went casting for her.

He looked in the shelters, asked around the stations, swung through a dozen box towns, and talked to a hundred brothers and sisters of the outstretched cup. He asked street strutters and tourist trappers, flesh merchants and fast talkers if they'd seen a girl with a rainbow streak and worn down boots smoking salvaged cloves. According to the chatter Tagg been hither, she'd been thither, but no one could tell him where she was right then. Every time he got a hot tip, it went cold by the time he turned up. He checked in with their favored shelter, hoping that she'd gotten his message and was waiting for him there. He found all sorts of regulars sharing cups of thin coffee and bowls of thick soup, but nobody had seen Tagg. Once Ace had looked everywhere else he could think of, and there was no more avoiding it, he turned up his collar and headed for the Butcher's Breezeway.

The place had sat vacant for years; a crooked shunt in the meat of the city's south side. In another life it had been part of a slaughterhouse complex, and the ghosts of blood and shit still lingered around the sagging hulks of the outbuildings that had been left behind. The cracked paths were lined with trash and dirty snow, and frigid mud clung to the sway-bellied center of the main lane where concrete had buckled. The steel doors were layered with urban hieroglyphs too; gang crests like the flags of conquering kings that had once ruled here, before their empires collapsed beneath their feet to be replaced by newer, younger blood. There were stoops along the lane as well, set low to the ground and deep enough that the wind whipped right past without looking too hard at who was crouching in the doorways. Despite rumors the place was haunted, Tagg had sworn the Breezeway was a safe, sheltered spot she'd happily bunk down in for a few nights if she had to. She hadn't been anywhere else he'd looked, and Ace couldn't think of anywhere else she might be.

Ace moved slowly, quietly shuffling through the mud. He kept his head down, the constant breeze knifing through his coat. He prodded a midden heap with the toe of his shoe, but only a single, half-starved rat poked its head out. He looked in the shadows of every stoop, and even glanced through the boarded-over windows. There was nothing inside the buildings but a single splotch of ash where someone had built a campfire, but it was just as cold and dead as everything else.

He was debating whether to stay or go when Ace heard a sound that didn't belong there. A low rumble, almost a purr, like an animal on the hunt. Running lights slashed across the sides of the abandoned outbuildings, and Ace cursed as he ducked into the furthest stoop from the road. The lights paused, then cut out. A moment later a car door creaked open. A foot crunched on gravel, and the door closed. Leather creaked, and something flapped in the wind. Light bloomed, swinging back and forth through the ruins. A man stepped into the alley. A big, dark shape behind his torch, he wore a long coat with a watch cap pulled down over his ears.

"Hello!" He called out, bass voice echoing in the crisp air. "Is anyone there?"

Ace slid deeper into the shadows, moving slowly so as not to draw the man's eye. He wasn't a cop, that much was clear, but he wasn't from the street either. The wind carried a touch of English leather, dusty wool, and an off-brand soap that still held a hint of strong lye. The man took a tentative step into the alley, looking down to make sure he didn't step in any of the half-frozen filth.

"My name is Father Baxter," he called out. "If there's anyone there, I'd like to offer my help. A hot meal, a shower? A room for the night at least. Just to get you out of the cold!"

The Father came another step down the alley. He walked like everything around him might break, or like the ground might give way without warning. He looked clumsy and unsure, but his eyes stayed on the move. Ace bumped something with his foot, and it fell onto the next step with a hard, metallic clink. The holy man stopped no more than fifteen feet away, his Roman collar a splotch of white in the dimness. A gold crucifix glittered just above the top button of his overcoat. Ace scrabbled in the darkness until he found what had fallen. A scuffed Zippo lighter, with a red heart on one side, and the queen of the suit on the other. Scars had been carefully carved into the corners of her mouth, and every heart had been painted white. It smelled like bubblegum and butane. Ace would have known it anywhere; it was Tagg's lucky lighter.

"Hello?" the priest called again, swinging his light to cover the mouth of the stoop. "Is someone there?"

Ace stood up slowly, and fumbled the lighter into his pocket with half-numbed fingers. He came out with his hands up and held away from his body. He was just another lost boy; a ratty stray with swarthy skin and wild eyes, wary of any hands extended in his direction. Especially friendly ones. The man in black looked him up and down, then smiled a big, square-toothed smile.

"What's your name son?" he asked.

"People call me Ace."

The priest took another of his deliberate steps, and offered a hand shrink-wrapped in black leather. "Baxter."

Ace shook the big man's hand. The priest's grip was strong, and the leather was cool against his palm. Ace let go, and hunched against the wind. If Baxter was uncomfortable, he gave no sign of it. Ace waited. Baxter waited. February crouched on the eaves above, and it waited too. Finally the priest raised his hands to his mouth, and blew on them.

"What brings you out here, Ace?" he asked. Ace shrugged one shoulder, and tucked his hands into his pockets.

"Just looking for a place to wait out tonight," he said.

"There wasn't anywhere better than this?" Baxter asked, glancing at the looming, bulging walls.

"Everyone's trying to get in on a night like this," Ace replied. "First come, first serve. I wasn't quick enough."

"I see," Baxter said. He turned up his collar, and tugged his cap down even further. His cheeks were a ruddy, stung red by the cold, and his eyes were starting to water at the corners. "Is there anyone else with you?"

Ace shook his head. "One man show tonight."

"My offer stands," Baxter said. "Or if you'd rather, I could take you someplace else? I know of a number of shelters that always have room for one more when the weather gets bad."

Ace ran his tongue over his teeth, and sucked a little spit from the inside of his cheek. "I'm looking for someone. A white girl, seventeen or eighteen. Her hair is a washed-out rainbow, and she has a scar on her right cheek. Her name is Tagg."

"Tagg?" Baxter said, his eyebrows winging up and hiding under his hat. "Lisa Taggart? She was here last night. I gave her a room."

"Is she still at your place?" Ace asked, taking an involuntary step closer.

"One thing at a time my young friend," Baxter said, laying a hand on Ace's shoulder. "I believe she left me an address and a phone number for the place she was going. I had planned on calling when I got home, but thought it best with the weather being what it is that I come through and make sure there was no one else here I could help. A good thing I did, it seems."

"Where's your place?" Ace asked.

"Not far," Baxter replied. "Perhaps three miles or so?"

"All right," Ace said. He inclined his head, then added a grudging. "Thank you."

"It's no trouble," Baxter said, walking back the way he'd come. Ace followed, and tried to ignore the feverish thing writhing in the pit of his stomach. He wrapped his hand around the lighter in his pocket, and squeezed until it hurt.

Baxter's car was sleek, and the leather seats felt almost alive with warmth as Ace slid inside. The priest flipped on his lights, then backed carefully out of the quadrangle. The undercarriage scraped the curb, and the whole car bobbed. The night slid by outside, and the cold slid off the glass like water. They passed one block, then another, the wasteland falling away. Traffic lights stood like watchful sentries at mostly empty intersections, and late night storefronts blazed phosphorescent in the dark. Homes slept beneath white nightcaps, with the flicker of late-night make believe behind their curtains like prime-time dreams. Ace watched it all, his gaze flicking along the street signs at every turn and twist. They slowed, and Baxter swung the wheel left, sliding into a freshly plowed driveway.

The house looked much like any other house in that part of the Back of the Yards. A squat, brick structure, it had the wide windows and jutting porch common to days when people had to suffer through summer heat unaided. The garage looked newer than the house, though not by many years, and it was cast from the same, blocky mold. It was the sort of place workmen had once been given to sleep, raise their families, and to wash the sweat and filth of the day from their skins. A black letterbox was affixed to the front door, and above the door itself was a small, brass plaque. Its one-word declaration said simply *Knockerman*.

"If you'll wait on the porch please, Ace," Baxter said, opening his door and getting out. "I've got to put this thing away."

Ace got out, and climbed the five steps to the porch. Baxter hauled open the garage door, and drove the dark sedan inside. Its purring ceased a moment later, and the door swung back down. Ace looked to his left, his right, and across the street. None of the other homes had cars in evidence. Several houses were still glutted with snow from the storm. No night lights flashed in his neighbors' homes, and no dogs barked. Even the wind had gone quiet, with so much open room to run. It wasn't empty, but the little neighborhood echoed. Ace turned back as the front porch lamps bloomed. Locks clicked open, and Baxter opened the door. He had a bundle of newspaper under one arm.

"Sorry for the chill, but it's an old place," the priest said, closing the door behind Ace and stepping past him into a room that was one part den and one part office space. "I'm just going to light a fire."

Baxter knelt down in front of the fireplace and started stuffing yesterday's sheets between a few half-burned logs. There was no ash in the grate. He muttered to himself as he worked, crinkling and tearing sheets before pressing them home. Ace shifted his weight, and the floorboards creaked. Baxter broke one match, then another, grunting as he tossed the kindling into the fire. The third match caught, and tongues of fire licked blue with cheap ink. He dragged a grate in front of the burgeoning blaze, and nodded with satisfaction.

"There now, that's done," he said, turning toward the desk in the corner. "Now then, where did I put that notepad...?"

Baxter stepped behind the desk and tugged a chain on a small, green-shaded desk lamp. He pulled out one drawer after another, and leafed through papers with his leather-clad fingers. He shuffled the stacks on the scarred wooden top, frowning as he set one pad aside after another. Finally he opened a small box, and unfolded a creased, dog-eared sheet. He offered it to Ace, smiling broadly.

"Here now," the priest said. "This should be it. Whether she's actually there or not I can't tell you, but it's what I have."

Ace took the sheet and studied the loose, sloppy scrawl. The address was somewhere north of Touhy Avenue, but he didn't know anything else about it. The numbers were crooked, but they were all in the right place.

"Thanks for this," Ace said.

"It's no trouble, son," Baxter said, stepping back over to the fireplace. He unhooked an iron poker, and hunkered on his heels. "There's a phone in the kitchen, through the entryway there. She's nearly as old as the house, but she worked as of this morning."

"Thanks," Ace said again.

The kitchen was a cramped affair, with chunky cabinets and a tile floor so clean it felt slick underfoot. A stainless steel refrigerator stood against one wall, oddly modern in a home from the last century, and next to it hung a heavy phone made of old, black plastic. Ace took it down, pressed the handset between his shoulder and ear, and punched the number. He gnawed at the inside of his cheek, willing someone to pick up on the other end. There was the click of a machine switching on, and just as a recorded voice began to speak in his ear, the world exploded in painful, white light. The phone clattered against the wall, and somewhere a voice was telling him what time it was.

Ace lay on his back, all of his bones turned to water. He didn't remember falling, but it was the only explanation for how he'd wound up on the floor. The ceiling lamps were bright, but as far away as distant stars in the night sky. He felt light-headed and chill, like when he'd snuck out to sit atop the tombs and stare at the northern lights in that home he'd known so long ago. His mouth hung open, and he absently noted a strand of drool running from the corner of his mouth. He tasted pennies, and wondered if he'd bitten himself bloody when he fell. Something pulled at his leg, and he wondered what it was. He tried to lift his head to look, but his neck had all the strength of soiled sackcloth. A moment later something eclipsed the stars, and Baxter looked down at him. The priest was talking and smiling, but there was something different about him. He was the same, but twisted, like the moon turned black by the sun.

"What..." Ace managed, the single word slow and smudged as he tried to refocus his eyes. Baxter stopped talking, and his eyes widened. He stood up, towering over Ace. He held the poker in one hand. The end was twisted slightly out of true.

"You have a hard head, boy," Baxter said, his voice rolling out of his chest. The flat head of the poker touched Ace's cheek; it was cold, and left a long smudge of ash on his face. Ace flinched as the iron drew back. It swung in like the tide, and darkness rolled over Ace.

***

Someone called his name. His real name. It was a whisper in the blackness, rough against an unfamiliar tongue, and it tugged at his ear. He

7

tried to turn away from the whisper, to burrow into the comforting darkness all around him. Wakefulness wouldn't let him go, though, and it dragged him out of the hole he'd fallen into. Back into the waking, aching world.

He smelled blood first. Faint, fresh scents on top of the older stains that lingered like coats of varnish. Next was old steel with a hint of rust, and brick dust gone damp with perspiration. Aged wood and fresh oil mingled with the mist of evaporating water gone cold and stagnant beneath the ground. Under all that was sour sweat, and a faint trace of bottom-shelf bubblegum.

"Tagg," he muttered through lips gone dry and tacky. Her name reverberated in his head, shaking his skull and threatening to make it burst. Ace sucked in a deep breath and held it, clenching his teeth until the sensation subsided. "That you?"

He opened his eyes slowly, first one then the other. His vision swam in and out of focus, but he saw more than he wanted to. A heavy, steel rod hung with dangling chains swayed above dingy, white tiles. On the other side of those tiles was a wall-sized rack of butcher's blades, each shaped and sharpened to fulfill a single, bloody purpose. A closed door that muted the rumble of a generator lurked against a nearby wall. The acrid stink of burned gasoline lingered lightly in the air. There was a vanity with a tarnished mirror, and a tall armoire sitting side by side, both of them antique, and out of place. A black hose with a cheap, plastic spray head was coiled against the wall like a sleeping serpent. Black drains with stained, rotten teeth dotted the floor. And in the center of the room sat a thick, stained block of wood with deep grooves and gouges worn by generations of enthusiastic chopping. Ace turned his head slowly, clenching his jaw against the pain. Tagg sat in a cage next to him. She was naked, with dried blood on her upper lip, and her dirty hair hanging in her eyes. She was shaking, reaching through the skinny bars from her cage and into his, her fingertips resting against his wrist. She said his name again, the two syllables dribbling from her lips like tears.

"I found your lighter," Ace said. The words hurt less, but he stayed where he was a little longer. Tagg squeezed his wrist, and gave him a watery smile.

"Are you all right?" she asked.

Ace closed his eyes, and focused. He took a deep breath, and let it out. "Do you mean aside from being naked and caged up in a basement?"

"Yeah," Tagg said. "Aside from that."

"He hit me in the head with the fireplace poker," Ace replied. "I should have known. He knew your real name. No one knows your real name."

"Just you and my mother," Tagg said. "Asshole read my diary. First day he sat right there and read it to me, waiting for me to piss myself. When I did he gave me the hose."

"He isn't really a priest, is he?"

Tagg snorted, and shook her head slightly. "Some hustler's eye you've got."

"What else did he do?" Ace asked.

Tagg shook her head again. "It isn't important."

She tried to pull her hand back. Ace turned his wrist and held her. He opened his eyes, and looked at her face in the dimness.

"What else?" he asked.

Tagg swallowed, and looked away from him. Her tongue rasped over her lips, but before she could answer a door opened and a light came on. An arched doorway lit up, and a pair of heavy work boots came down the stairs beyond. They were followed by the hem of a black cassock, a glittering crucifix, and finally Baxter's bluff face. He still had his hat on, pulled almost down to his eyes. He smiled, and it was a barbed, poisonous expression; the true face of the man beneath the cassock

"You're tougher than you look, boy, I'll give you that," Baxter said, chuckling as he turned on the rest of the lights. Bright lances stabbed at Ace's face, but he didn't turn away. "Out all day looking for your little friend in this weather, and I still had to ram that sweet spot on your skull two or three times to put you out. And here you are, up and about before I can even put my work clothes on."

Tagg slowly slid her fingers back through the bars, curling more tightly in on herself. Ace lay where he was, breathing slowly. The big man flicked on the vanity's lights, and opened the armoire. A collection of clothes hung there. There were blue uniform shirts with badge patches next to tweed jackets with fraying cuffs. There were white polos with crossed axes and helmets, and a small sampling of work shirts with oil stains and grease spots. Discarded skins meant to fool his prey, and hide what he truly was.

"My grandfather told me, when I wasn't much older than you, that the companies running the slaughterhouses were a joke," Baxter said, his fingers busy with buttons and zippers as he tugged and peeled at his camouflage. "They gave a man a house with a garage, but didn't pay him enough to put a car in it. They made him work meat all day, but wouldn't give him enough to buy any of his own. So the old man got his own meat. Snuck it right in through the back door, brought it down here and did what he did best."

The big man slipped the cap off his head, and carefully hung the cassock on an old-fashioned wooden hanger. He gently tugged the collar free, and hung the crucifix on a tiny hook. He pulled at his gloves, setting them down on the vanity. Ace's eyes went wide.

Baxter's body was a canvas of the carnal. Blue whorls of jailhouse ink bleeding into black talons and barbed wire. Faces of demons with bloody maws, and beautiful women shucking their skins like inconvenient blouses. Chains and whips writhed over corded muscle, and defaced horrors devoured the meat and tendons that lay just beneath the skin. The ghoulish feast writhed with every twist and flex, the sprawling mural nearly alive as he carefully put away his sheep's clothing.

"He brought me down here when I was a boy," Baxter continued, his voice wistful. "He put a knife in my hand and showed me every cut. Told me how to spill blood, and taught me how to slice with the grain. He showed me where the sweetmeats were too, and he always gave me the choicest bits of anything I killed."

Ace sat up slowly, wary of his head. He glanced at Tagg. She stared at the phantasmagorical tattoo, searching for its hidden meaning. He hissed, and Tagg cut her eyes toward him. Baxter laughed, looking over his shoulder.

"Something to share with the rest of the class?" the big man asked.

Ace smiled, a painful, tight expression that didn't show his teeth. "Just trying to decide which of those knives I'm going to cut you with."

"Is that so?" Baxter chuckled, shaking his head slowly; an amused uncle who wasn't going to rise to a child's bait. He took down a stubby, punch grip blade with a half moon curve. He brandished it, and set it on the cutting block. "This is the one you'll want to use. It gets in deep, and flays back the skin. Does your work for you."

"You don't say?"

"I do," Baxter said, putting a thick, stained apron on. He tied it behind his back, then stood on the balls of his feet and took a box from the back of the armoire. He set it on the vanity, and removed what was inside. "Oh, I do."

When the butcher turned back to the cages, he wore a different face. Tanned a mahogany brown, a heavy snout pushed from below beady, black holes. The ears were cropped, and notched from long wear. The cheeks were sunken, and flaps of old flesh hung round his thick neck like a headsman's hood. He laughed, a muffled, snuffled sound from beneath the swine's head as he picked up the gutting knife and crossed the floor. He pointed the curve of the blade at Tagg's cage, then at Ace's, reciting in a high-pitched voice as he did.

"This little piggy went to market," he said. "And this little piggy stayed home. And this little piggy had roast beef, and this little piggy had none..."

When he reached ten, the knife pointed right at Ace. Ace looked into the eye holes of the grotesque mask. He couldn't see the butcher's smile, but he heard it as the big man reached for the lock.

"Are you sure you want to do that?" Ace asked.

The snuffling sound came again, and hot, sour breath puffed through the mask's nostrils. "Don't be scared," the butcher said, swinging the door open. "We're all just meat, in the end."

"Yes," Ace said, closing his eyes and taking a deep breath of the charnel house air. "You are."

Ace let go of the boy he'd been, and remembered what he was. His skin bubbled, blackened, and charred. His flesh whirled, twisting in currents of his inner heat like cinders in a sand storm. The coals in his belly, banked for so long, roared. The butcher stepped back, and threw up an arm. The thing in the cage rose from the ashes, flickering, slithering, his substance fluid as he slid through the spaces between the bars and stood before the skin stealer. He drew another breath, and swelled even larger.

There were names for his kind. They were old names mostly; old words from old peoples. More names than his mother or his father had been able to teach him. Daemons some had said, and others devils. Some had called them angels, and prayed to them for deliverance. In the empty places and the ruins they had been feared, and men had stayed away. Some had tried to bind them as servants, to enslave them as man enslaved all things. They had burned bright in the darkness, like the moon herself. The tribe of smokeless fire. He could have told the butcher those things; spoken to him with the roar of communion. The only language men like him spoke was blood, though.

Fortunately, it was a tongue Ace was familiar with.

The swine king came, swinging his blade. The burning cloud slid one way, then another, dancing like a candle flame in a downdraft. The butcher was old though, and sly. He feinted and swung back, burying the curved knife into the brightness of the burning thing's belly. The blade had been iron once, but it had known fire's embrace, and would do the creature no harm now. The cinders parted, and the blade slid between them. The butcher swung again, and again, but the blade slipped through seamlessly. His other options exhausted, the butcher did what all beasts did in the end. He ran.

The living inferno gave chase, howling a crackling laugh. It slid closer, pacing the man, then wrapping itself around him. It ground against his back, searing the scenes of torment inked on his flesh to charred, black meaninglessness. Skin split, and steam hissed through the rents. Hot tallow bubbled out after, dripping like the meat's own magma. The creature lapped up the fat, and sank burning fangs into the muscle beneath. It grabbed the masked man's mantle, and kissed it. It married the skins of man and beast together, the two seared into one. The butcher made it up one step, a second, and fell into a smoldering heap.

Azhar stood over the dead man, staring down at him. His real face was a thing of brutal beauty; impassive and burning at the same time. Beautiful things couldn't last, though, for that was part of their magic. His father had told him so when Azhar had been young, and he asked why their home had been razed by the elders, and they were cast out to wander the deserts of man again.

He walked back into the abattoir. With every step he swallowed cinders, and wrapped his sacred fire in flesh once again. When he stood before Tagg's cage, only his eyes showed what he was. He closed them, and when he opened them again they were the same as they'd been before. Dark, watchful, but a boy's eyes all the same. He wrenched the lock off her cage, opened the door, and stepped back from her.

Tagg stared at him. She slowly unwound herself, and crawled weakly out. She stood, swaying like a girl in a dream. She touched him, lips slightly parted. She felt no heartbeat, and showed no fear.

"What are you?" she asked.

Azhar smiled a little. "It's a secret."

"Tell me," she said, raising her gaze to his face. "Tell me everything."

He told her. As he spoke she came steadily closer, a moth circling the flame as he talked of tombs and torchlight in worlds she had never known. He blasphemed, and told her the true myths of his people. When his story ran out, she shut her eyes as if she were jumping from a high place. She slid her arms around him. He put his arms around her too, moving slowly in case she tried to run. She didn't.

They were quiet for a long time, standing there in the dead man's basement. She ran her hands over him, tentatively at first. Her skittishness faded, and Tagg looked up. The expression on her face was both determined, and afraid. She looked impossibly young.

"Show me again?" She asked.

Azhar smiled, and showed her.

Champion for Hire

Sandekkar was a city in crisis. The walls still stood strong, and guards manned its gates and parapets alike. An experienced eye noticed how loose the watch's swords sat in their scabbards, though, and the loaded crossbows kept close to hand. Behind the walls the city took on a furtive air; like a rich man fallen on hard times who was trying to keep his poor fortunes a secret. Merchants plied the streets, and businesses stood open, but there were few customers about. Doorways and railings sported copper skulls, silk nooses, or painted serpents like signs of fealty, and everywhere both men and women wore steel at their hips. With the assassination of its former lord, the City of Slaves had gone from an iron fist to a nest of vipers, each trying to claim the empty throne. Sandekkar was ripe for bloodshed, and the smell drew cutthroats, drifters, and soldiers of fortune who were all eager to sell their skills for a handful of gold.

Einar drew looks when he entered the main gates from the Long Road. It wasn't his heavy shoulders, nor the ropes of muscle cabling his arms. The city had her share of brutes, some several times bigger than the hulking northman. It wasn't his tangled thatch of sun-bleached hair and beard either, as Sandekkar was a place familiar with men and women of all colors and tones. What drew the gazes of the city's residents were the hard, blue eyes with crows' feet in their corners, and the massive sword he carried over one shoulder. The great blade and the man who carried it were both old campaigners, and they wore their scars where all could see.

Einar strode through the Traveler's Quarter without slowing. That part of the city was filled with peddlers and pilgrims, wayfarers and wanderers. To a man they could all load up their wagons or heft their packs, and be gone within the hour. They had no interest in the current unrest of the city except to stay apart from it while making a tidy profit. He skirted the wealthier neighborhoods as well, where liveried soldiers and hardened mercenaries stood outside manor homes in rank and file. Einar's name was great where he came from, but he had no illusions that he cast a shadow this far to the south. His steps followed the sea breeze, and by mid-day was on the streets of Low Town.

The district was a gutter overflowing with the scum of a dozen kingdoms. It was a place where Pharish foot pads, with their copper skins and almond eyes, cut purses with a grace dancers would envy. A place where Kastigan corsairs swaggered along the boardwalks, their greasy beards and long braids a complement to their harsh, growling accents. Wharf bouncers stood on shaded porches, and doxies of every stripe strutted and catcalled passers by. Taverns and public houses butted shoulders with run-down apothecaries, and slant-stooped money changers. Low-rent rooms sat atop several structures, and balconies leaned drunkenly over the street like architectural overbites.

At a glance, Low Town looked like any other waterfront drain. Loud, coarse, and ugly, the neighborhood was unashamed and unabashed at itself. It was wrong, though. The buzz of humanity was muted, and furtive. Laughter was cut short by some, and forced out louder by others. People walked with their hands near their hilts, and their eyes on the ground. A dozen buildings flew red flags, and a dozen more bore black banners. Einar had seen it before; soldiers wore their commander's colors when battle lines were being drawn. What he didn't know was which war chief had claimed which colors, and which of them would prove the better paymaster.

"You there, outlander!" a voice called. "Come here!"

Einar turned, and saw three men taking their ease in front of an inn built from old ship timbers. Two of them leaned with their backs against the wall to either side of the door, and the one who'd spoken leaned forward off the porch with one arm resting against a wooden post. He held a bottle in his free hand, and by the sound of his voice it wasn't his first of the day. All three men had the weathered skin and thick thews of cargo haulers, but the heavy cudgels and curved daggers on their belts spoke of a different trade entirely. There was no banner on the inn's door, but each man wore a tattered, black band knotted around his right arm. Einar considered them.

"Are you deaf, or just stupid?" the drunk called, spitting into the dirt at Einar's feet. "I said come here."

"I heard you just fine," Einar said, taking a step toward the trio.

"So you can speak," the man said. His companions sniggered, and the man on the left lifted his own bottle to his lips. "My friends and I were wondering, what do you need such a large sword for?"

"It's a tool of my trade," Einar said.

"And what trade is that?" the drunkard asked, sneering before swigging again.

"Champion."

All three of them laughed. Einar frowned, but said nothing while the riffraff guffawed. As their laughter grew louder, the street grew emptier. Travelers slipped down alleys or turned onto cross streets, eager to be away whatever was about to happen. By the time the black-banded brigands had finished, Einar stood alone in the late afternoon sun.

"A champion," the leader said, putting a falsetto trill into his voice. "What kind of coward fights with a sword like that, eh?"

"Some men's tools are bigger than others," Einar said with a shrug. "It's nothing for you to be ashamed of."

The man to the left of the door sputtered, coughing cheap wine onto the dusty boards. The other door guard goggled. The third man stared, as if the northman had started barking at him.

"What did you say to me?" he demanded.

Einar smiled, showing square, white teeth. "I think you heard me well enough, friend. Or are you deaf, as well as ugly?"

The leader dropped his bottle, snatching at the butt of his cudgel. His stubby fingers were stupid with wine, and it took him a second longer than it might have had he been sober. In that lost moment Einar stepped onto the inn's porch, cupped the side of the man's neck, and heaved. The leader's head slammed into the support beam hard enough to shiver the timber, and he went down like he'd been poleaxed. With no lost motion Einar stepped over the leader, driving a heavy right hand into the second man's face. The guard's head smacked the solid wood wall, rattling his brains and rolling his eyes up to the whites.

"Inbred swine," the last man spat. He threw his empty bottle aside, snatching his knife from its sheathe. "I'll take that out of your hide!"

He slashed, and the dagger's edge dug a shallow trench across Einar's brigandine. Metal screeched against metal, and Einar grabbed the man's knife wrist. The knife fighter let go of the knife, catching it in his free hand as he drew back for another blow. Einar drove his forehead down into the daggerman's face, and blood spurted as the smaller man's nose broke. The man with the black band shook the stars from his eyes, trying to stab Einar. Einar shifted his weight, and threw his opponent bodily into the street. The daggerman sprawled, the knife went flying, and before he could scramble to his feet Einar leaped after him. The northerner brought his boot down hard; ribs cracked, and the sprawled head cracker let out a howl choked with blood.

"What in the thousand hells is going on out there?" a voice boomed from inside the inn. A moment later the doors swung open, and a fourth man stepped out into the light.

The newcomer cut a fine figure. He was dressed in whipcord trousers, and a billowing white shirt that was free from the sweat and dust so common to a hot day. He was swarthy, dark-eyed, and had a sweep of thick, black hair tied back with a black leather cord. He wore his black band on his right arm, just like the others. He was short even for a southerner, and carried himself with a theatrical air. His short sword's sheathe was hand-worked leather inlaid with gilded thread, but the hilt was worn and looked often-used.

"Well now," the swordsman said, giving Einar a wide, friendly smile that didn't come within a league of his eyes. "Just what have we here?"

Einar took his boot off the fallen man, turning to face the new threat. "Are these friends of yours?"

"These are my men," the newcomer said, stepping down off the porch. "Men under the protection of the Prince of Thieves."

"Prince?" Einar said, shrugging off his traveler's pack. "That sounds serious. And who might you be?"

The southerner stopped, one foot almost off the ground. His smile vanished. "Who am I?"

"That's what I asked," Einar said. "Who the hell are you?"

"You back-birthed barbar bastard, you don't even recognize-"

Einar slung his pack in a hard, underhand throw. The swordsman skipped back, flinging his right arm up defensively. He drew with a speed born of long practice, but Einar's fist closed over the swordsman's hand before he'd cleared half a length of steel. The southerner strained, snarling as he pulled at the iron grip. Einar squeezed tighter, bore down with his shoulders, and wrenched. His opponent's face paled with pain, and he hissed as something popped. Einar shoved, and the other man fell into the dust cupping his broken wrist in his free hand.

"You son of a bitch!" he hissed, scrabbling for his hilt with his other hand. "I'll make you pay for this."

Einar's answer was the sound of steel on leather. The monstrous blade rasped free from its sheathe, and the cutting edge shone sharply in the sunlight. Einar pointed the tip toward the prone enforcer, who stopped trying to draw his own sword. The fallen man narrowed his eyes, measuring the distance between him, the sword, and its wielder. He slowly held up both hands.

"Take off the baldric," Einar said.

"What?"

"Did I stutter?" the northerner asked. "Take off the baldric."

"Why?"

Einar cocked the sword back, taking a two-handed grip on the hilt. "No more questions. Remove the sword belt, or I split you open."

The southerner growled, and half rose from where he sat. He took another look at the blade, and at the warrior who wielded it. The small man relaxed, awkwardly unbuckled the clasp with one hand, and lifted the belt over his head. Einar nodded, but never took his eyes off the man.

"Drop it. Then stand, and step away." The man did as he was told, cupping his damaged sword hand and wincing every time he tried to move it. "Collect your men, and get out of my sight."

The leader went from man to man, helping them to their feet with his good arm. They leaned and stumbled, panted and winced, but in short order the four of them were out of the dirt. They glared at Einar with eyes hot as coals from hell's own forge. Einar gestured off toward the other end of the street.

"Go."

The four of them left, shambling. The leader paused, bending as if to collect his sword.

"Leave it."

"What?" the gang's leader asked.

"Leave it," Einar said, each word loud and deliberate.

"It's my sword."

"Not any more it isn't."

The toughs bristled, but retreated when Einar took a step closer. They were brave when they thought they had advantage, but swollen heads and bloodied mouths had taught them caution. The leader pushed out his chest, tossing his head like an unbroken colt.

"You're a dead man, outlander!" the swordless swordsman spat. "The Prince will hear of this."

"I'll be here," Einar said. "Run along, cur, and tell your master."

Einar watched until the toughs rounded a corner. He waited the length of one, long breath, then another to see if they'd circle back. They didn't. People stuck their heads out of cover, peering around shop curtains and over swinging bat wing doors. A few brave souls ventured into the street, and when the sky didn't fall others joined them. Einar sheathed his sword, and picked up the discarded baldric with its short steel.

"That was handily done, northerner."

Einar turned, and saw an old man standing on the inn's porch. Gray-bearded and bald-headed, his slightly stooped frame sagged in the middle. Despite his kindly appearance, he held a punter's iron in his hands, and looked like he knew how to use it. He grinned, showing gaps where several of his teeth had once been.

"Do you have a name?" the old man asked.

"Einar." Einar retrieved his pack, and glanced up at the gray beard. "Will I find a warm welcome on deck?"

The old man laughed, and leaned on his punt like it was a walking stick. "Been to sea at some point, have you?"

"A time or two."

"You'll find no steadier berth than the Squall's Rose in all the harbor." The old man said, chuckling at his own joke as he gestured toward the doorway. "I'm Altan. Come aboard, Einar, and welcome to you."

The inn's common room was wide, and dim. A handful of tables filled the space, and a long bar made from a ship's railing stretched across the far end of the room. Storm lamps held candles in tiny, glass prisons along the walls, and a captain's wheel hung from the center-beam like a chandelier. Above the doorway the legend *Squall's Rose* was carved into the timber, lovingly painted in gold leaf. The place smelled of pitch, spices, and sea salt.

"What are you drinking?" Altan asked, stepping behind the bar.

"I haven't much coin-"

"I didn't ask if you had money, I asked what you were drinking." The old man took down a tarred leather jack, wiping it down with a rag. "Light or dark?"

"Dark," Einar said, setting his pack on the floor. He tossed the short sword atop the room's center table, and rested his own blade against the table's edge where the hilt would be near to hand. He sat, facing the main door. "If you'll join me, of course?"

"Of course," Altan said, his voice serious. "It's bad luck to let a man drink by his lonesome."

Altan drew them each a drink, then pulled a chair up to Einar's table. He handed a jack to the northman, and held his own up. "To the troubles of the city."

"To coming out on the other side with as much gold as a man can carry," Einar said. The two men touched the rims of their cups together, then drank. The ale was thick, bitter, and sat like a stone in the gut. Einar drained his, belching appreciatively. "That's good."

"I know, I'm the one who brewed it," Altan said. "Care for another?"

"I would."

Altan drew a second draught, and handed it to Einar. "My thanks."

"Taken and accepted." Einar took a slower drink, chewing the brew before swallowing. "Who were those men?"

"Whoreson jackals on an errand from Gadran Lorne, our infamous Prince of Thieves," Altan said, drinking deep. "Fortunate you came when you did. Things were about to turn ugly."

"Fortune works in funny turns," Einar said.

"Spoken like one who's ridden the wheel," Altan said with a laugh. "The lickspittles are no nevermind, but you'd have been better off killing Jonwinn. He might dress like a noble lady's whore, but Lorne didn't make him his right hand because of his pretty face."

"You can always kill a man later," Einar said, swirling his ale. "You can't take it back once you have."

"Truer words."

"What should I know about this man, Lorne?" Einar asked.

"He's a petty thief with a hole in his belly," Altan said. "There's nothing too low for him, long as there's meat at the end of it. The only reason no one killed him when Drann sat on the throne was because he kept himself small, and ate up the crumbs left by the bigger thieves' guilds on the wharf."

"What changed?"

Altan shrugged, and took a longer drink. "The Slaver King died, and with him went the old order. Knives in the dark became the doings of the day, and Lorne's petty crew of burglars weren't shy about dealing in blood once the demand for it went up. He sucked up every gutter snipe and waterfront rat he could find, and after he bullied and beat most of the dives in the district under his boot heel he found himself running half of Low Town. He does muscle work mostly, but he'll do murder, whoring, fencing, and anything else he can get his grubby fingers on if there's coin in it. Every building with a black banner is territory he's claimed."

"Who claims the other half?"

Altan had his mouth open to answer when the porch boards creaked. The door opened, and a woman walked in. She was long and spare, with the high cheekbones of a courtesan, and the sultry grace of a fireside dancer. A beaded shawl was wrapped around her shoulders, and it clicked in time with her steps. She smelled of jasmine, a subtle scent mixed with the clean sweat dotting her dark complexion. Her eyes flicked to the sheathed steel on the table, then settled on Einar. She smiled, an expression fit to stir any man's blood.

"You are the man who defeated Jonwinn Fords?" she asked.

"Word runs swiftly in this town," he said. "My name is Einar."

"My mistress bids you welcome to Sandekkar, Einar," she said, dipping into a low curtsy. She slipped a hand inside her dress, and withdrew a small, leather pouch which she held out to him. "A gift."

Einar took the bag, and opened the drawstring without taking his eyes from the woman. A half dozen gold marks spilled into his palm. He bounced the coins thoughtfully before returning them to the pouch. "Your mistress is generous."

"She would be pleased to hear you say so." She smiled wider, as if the compliment had been given to her instead of her employer. "She requests I escort you to her that she may thank you in person."

"Where is she?"

"She awaits your presence at the Setting Sun."

"Tell her I will come in my own time," Einar said.

The messenger's smile slipped. "She will not be pleased to hear that."

"Your mistress's pleasure is your concern, not mine."

She curtsied again, though not as deeply as she had before. "Shall I tell her when she might expect you?"

"This evening," Einar said.

"Very well. Simply ask for the mistress of the house when you come."

Her message delivered, she turned and left without another word. Einar watched her go with no little appreciation. He glanced at Altan, who snorted and drained the dregs from his mug.

"You're favored, my friend," Altan said, his tone belying the words. "It's not often the Queen of Killers sends a runner for someone."

"The Queen of Killers?" Einar asked with a raised eyebrow.

"Did you perchance notice the long daggers yonder lovely had snuggled up over her hips?"

"There was a third in the small of her back," Einar said. Altan nodded, working sour spit in his mouth.

"The thieves' guilds were rumors before the Lord's passing, but the assassins' guilds were barely whispers," Altan said. "They were discreet. The smell of power and the promise of riches was like a fever, though. Poison's flowed like wine, and bad blood clogged the city's drains. Some decided to quit the game and take the Long Road, but a few remained. Reina Morningswell was one of them."

"She's an assassin?"

"Among other things," Altan said. He leaned closer to Einar, his voice pitched low as if someone might overhear. "Ostensibly she's nothing more than a brothel keeper. But that red manor she lives in is a fortress, and it's said there's a death for every pleasure behind its doors. Like a spider in her web, she's barely ventured out of that armored whorehouse since Drann's demise. It hasn't stopped her from killing every rival she or her red locusts could lay hands on, though."

"Ah." Einar swirled his ale, weighing the coin purse in his free hand. "These two have been at war, then?"

Altan shook his head, and got up for another tankard. "Nothing so grand. Low Town is a small rung on a big ladder, and both of them know if they exhaust themselves and their people fighting in the streets then someone bigger will just and snap up the whole quarter once they're bled dry. Someone who can afford trained soldiers, and who doesn't have to make due with head breakers and spine twisters."

"So what's their play?"

"A battle of champions," Altan said, taking a long swallow from his fresh jack and leaning his elbows on the bar. "The duel is tomorrow night.

One fighter from each camp. The loser takes the Long Road, and the winner lays claim to Old Town proper along with everyone in it."

Einar bounced the coin purse in his hand again, frowning thoughtfully. "Jonwinn was the prince's champion?"

Altan laid a finger along his nose, and winked at Einar. "Fords is one of the finest swordsmen in the city. He was the only man in Lorne's company who stood a fighting chance against Aspis, and Lorne knows it. What's more, the Queen knows it too."

"Aspis?"

"The Queen's champion." Altan shuddered. "Her son, but no one knows who his father was. He has a taste for blood like some men have for wine or lowland leaf, and he's not shy about quenching it. Worse, he likes to use envenomed blades so that first blood tends to be the last blood."

Einar nodded. "Where is this duel happening?"

"The only neutral ground in Low Town." Altan rapped his thick knuckles on the heavy wood of the bar. His expression was that of a man knocking on his own coffin.

"It's a good place for it," Einar said.

"Tis." Altan reached beneath the bar and pulled out a bottle of something stronger than ale. He poured. "I didn't have any choice. They came to me and said that if I didn't assent then they'd simply put my Rose to the torch."

"Seems you made the only choice you could."

Altan drank, grimacing as the pop skull burned its way down to his gullet. "I bought time, nothing more. There's a saying in Sandekkar, 'every slave master cracks the same whip.' No matter who wins tomorrow, the lash will come down all the same."

"I don't like slavers."

Altan laughed. It was a tired, wistful sound. "I'm afraid you came to the wrong city then, friend."

Einar nodded, and he kept nodding as if he'd forgotten he was doing it. He tucked the purse away, and leaned back in his chair. He pressed his feet flat to the floor, focusing on the door and the street noises beyond it. Altan finished his drink, then wiped the jack along with the rest of the bar. The street in front of the Squall's Rose remained empty. No one came in for a drink, or simply to pass time out of the sun. Einar sipped his brew, and waited. Before he'd emptied his second jack, there was a commotion outside the inn. Moments later the door opened, and two men entered.

They were a study in opposites. One was big and pale, with a heavy, barrel chest and arms knotted with muscle and scars. The other was short and gangly, with the long nose and sallow skin of a wharf rat. The big man wore a chain shirt crisscrossed with weapon belts, while his smaller companion wore a silk robe over his expensively dyed shirt and trousers. Einar slowly lifted his cup, and drained it dry.

"You're bold, northerner," the silk-swathed scoundrel said.

"It's one of my better qualities," Einar said. "I see your dog delivered his message."

The rat-faced man laughed. It was a harsh, unpleasant bark, like his throat had forgotten merriment's proper tone. "Few men would call Jonwinn Fords a dog, and live to tell about it."

"I'm proud to count myself among them," Einar said. "You are the Prince of Thieves?"

"I am." Gadran Lorne swaggered into the room, thumbs hooked behind his belt. "And who in the seven hells are you?"

"Einar."

"Well Einar, you have put me in a precarious position," Lorne said. "On the one hand, you beat several of my men bloody, and may have crippled one of them. A man of my standing can't let that sort of thing stand."

"And on the other hand?"

"On the other hand, you beat several of my men bloody, and may have crippled one of them. Anyone who can do that without even pulling steel is not a man to be taken lightly."

"I am that."

"So I see," Lorne said, baring his teeth in a yellowed grin. "What I have for you is a proposition."

"I'm listening."

"It's a simple thing, really," Lorne said, pulling out a chair and seating himself across from Einar. "Jonwinn was to stand for me in a fight tomorrow night. If you took his place, and won the duel, I'd consider your debt well paid."

"I'm sure you would," Einar said. "But my sword's for sale. You want it, you need to pay for the privilege."

"How about I have my men in the street come in here, kill you, and drag your body behind an ox cart instead?"

"You could do that," Einar said with a shrug. "Maybe they'd kill me, and maybe they wouldn't. Either way, you still need someone to take your man's place in the fight."

"Truth." Lorne reached a flask out of an inner pocket, taking a long sip. "What's your price?"

"Two hundred marks," Einar said. "Half when I put on your black band, the other half when I win the fight."

Lorne said nothing for a long moment. He took another sip from his flask, holding the liquor in his mouth for a time before he swallowed. He nodded once, and rested his hands on the table.

"All right," he said. "You come with us now, and I'll have the first hundred in your hands. You'll stay as my guest, and tomorrow night you fight."

"I have a room for the night already," Einar said. "As you said, I left a lot of your men bloody today. There might be accidents if I sleep under your roof."

"I can control my men," Lorne said, his lip curling up in a sneer.

"I don't doubt it. But why give a letch a key to the whorehouse?"

Lorne leaned back in his seat, chewing on his bottom lip. Thoughts flickered in the depths of his flat, black eyes, but they were little more than shadows. He nodded again, grabbed the sheathed short sword off the table, and stood.

"We'll be here tomorrow at first light then," Lorne said. "I'm being generous with you, northerner. Don't disappoint me."

"Bring my payment, and I shan't."

Lorne paused at the door, turning back to Einar. "One more thing. I know the so-called Queen of Killers sent one of her strumpets to sweeten you up. Stay away from her, or I will hear of it."

Einar shrugged. "There are plenty of brothels in Low Town, should I feel the need."

Lorne turned on his heel, his minder no more than a pace behind. A moment later Einar and Altan were alone in the Squall's Rose. Einar stood, and stepped to the bar.

"You play dangerous games, friend," Altan said.

"Are there any other kinds worth playing?" Einar asked.

"If you win the fight he'll have you stabbed in the back as soon as everything's settled," Altan said. "There's no sense in paying you once you've won."

"Worse men than him have tried." Einar fished two marks out of the pouch, and set them on the teak.

"I don't have change for gold."

"I didn't ask for any," Einar said. "All I ask is a room, and some wash water."

"This can be done." Altan took the gold.

"Good," Einar said, grinning as he retrieved his sword and pack. "Why are you smiling?"

"Because, my friend," Einar said, clapping Altan on the shoulder. "It's not every day that a whore gives *me* gold."

Low Town changed when the sun went down. The day shades flew up like sleeper's lids, and bawdy tunes hummed in the close, night air. Lamps were lit above taverns and alehouses, the wicks sprinkled with copper and salt flakes so the fires danced with all the colors of an alchemist's snuff box. The shadows stretched long, smoothing the tired wrinkles from the jades' faces and the peeling paint from smoking dens. Wine flowed freely, and even the black and red banners faded into little more than checkerboard beauty marks in the tide of debauchery.

Einar emerged from the Squall's Rose a very different man. Gone was the ragged, dusty traveler with stooped shoulders and gritty eyes. In his place stood a warrior with steel in his spine, and iron in his guts. The brass nail heads of his brigandine glinted in the lamplight, and the hilt of his sword stood up over his right shoulder. The blade was sheathed, but the man who carried it was not. He stood on the porch for several moments, eyeing the crowd as it passed. Most paid him no heed, bent as they were on their own, private debasements.

He headed north, then east, visiting two taverns, and a small inn that had been a horse stable in another life. Einar kept a steady eye on his back trail, and soon noticed three men dogging his steps. They wore black bands, short knives, and long faces. Once he knew who he was looking for it was a simple matter to slip them, ducking through side doors and walking through the muck of a single back alley. Once he was sure the watch dogs were no longer on his trail he walked west, boots thudding on the paving stones of Dagger's Way. He reached his destination before the Harbormaster's bell had run the tenth hour.

The Setting Sun was aptly named. Every shingle on every gabled roof, every wall, every curtain, every hanging lamp, and every flower in the gardens was red. Though patrons walked along the footpaths arm in swaying arm, and the sounds of song slipped through the night air from open windows, the place was not as docile as it seemed. Einar took note of the heavy, iron bands on the open gates, and spied sharp pottery shards set into the top of the wall. He saw shapes in the shadows, and caught the movement of watchful figures at darkened panes. The house had teeth.

Einar mounted the steps, and pulled a scarlet cord. A bell rang, and a honey-haired girl with a full figure wearing a red robe that left very little to the imagination opened the door. She smiled at Einar, and her eyes smoldered when she gazed up at him.

"You're a new face, handsome," she purred. "What can I do for

24

you?"

"I'm here to see the mistress of the house," Einar said, returning her smile in kind and admiring what she was displaying. "On her invitation."

"So you're the one she's been waiting for," the blonde said, stepping back and gesturing him inside. "Follow me."

"With the greatest of pleasure."

The Setting Sun was the same within as without. Plush, crimson carpets ran along stone-flagged hallways, and red rooms offered pleasures in a hundred, scarlet varieties. Women and men circulated, garbed with a careful carelessness that showed off lean muscles, rounded hips, and which hinted at firmer delights. Dragon smoke perfumed high-ceilinged chambers filled with supine shapes dreaming lotus dreams. Well-appointed parlors lined in burnished cherry wood were lined with bottles and casks of every kind of drink that could be drunk. Other quarters rang with the sounds of lovemaking in all its varieties. Some doors were closed, but many were not. It looked like a sinner's heaven, if one could ignore the slender blades the courtesans concealed, or the calculating glances seen from the corner of the eye.

Einar's guide stopped at a closed door no different from any other in the dozen hallways they'd passed. She rapped sharply three times, waited a beat, and then knocked a fourth time. A sharp click came from the lock, and the door opened an inch. Without touching the knob she pushed the door open further, and waved Einar forward. He came, ducking his head beneath the lintel.

There was nothing remarkable about the room, and that was what made it remarkable. The floor and walls were stone, the ceiling nothing more than bare beams. A cold fireplace sat in one wall like an empty socket. The only furnishings were a pair of high-backed chairs, and a small side table between them. A brass pitcher and three cups were the table's only accouterments. Both chairs were occupied. A man lounged in the right seat, and a woman sat in the left. The woman sat with her shoulders back, her head high, and her hands folded in her lap. The man slumped half-in and half-out of his seat, his chin resting on his hand and his heavy-lidded gaze fixed on the middle distance. He was shirtless, with slender bracers at his wrists and soft, calfskin boots wrapped around his feet. She wore an elegant dress that fitted her from neck to ankles, giving testimony to the body beneath. Both were handsome, with the same olive complexion and dark, curly hair. Both had eyes like polished jasper. She was older, he younger.

"My, my, he is a big one," the man said, his voice as boyish as his looks.

"He is," the woman agreed. "Thank you Sarassa, you may go now."

Without a word Sarassa stepped back into the hallway. The dark-haired lady pressed down on a stone with her foot, and the door swung shut. The lock snapped into place, and the young man picked up one of the three cups. He swirled its contents idly, looking Einar up and down. The woman did the same.

"You are the Queen of Killers?" Einar asked.

The young man laughed, nearly losing his grip on his wine. "He's brassy, mother. Can we keep him?"

"Hush, Aspis," she said. If the title upset her she gave no sign. "I'm Reina Morningswell. Your name is Einar, is it not?"

"It is."

She nodded, dipping her chin very slightly as she picked up her own cup. "Why did you refuse my invitation today when I sent my runner for you?"

"I was fresh from the road, and not in any state for company," Einar said. "Also, I've been selling my sword arm for a long time. If someone sends me a gift wrapped in a pretty package they either want to make sure I don't hear another offer, or they want to put a knife in my ribs. Sometimes both."

"And did you hear another offer?" she asked.

"I did."

"What did the so-called Prince of Thieves promise you?"

"If I fight as his champion in the duel tomorrow night, then he will graciously forgive me for bloodying his men in front of half of Low Town. I told him I'd stand for him if he paid me two hundred marks, half up front and half after the fight."

The Queen pursed her lips, sipping from her cup. "You're a confidant man, offering to step into a battle you know nothing about."

"It's what I know how to do."

"Suppose I offered you twice that price not to fight?"

"It's always easier not to fight," Einar said. "But I want to know what's in it for you."

"With Fords out of fighting condition, Lorne has no one who could carry the day for him," the Queen said. "All you would have to do is stay your hand, and my champion would cut the other man to ribbons. Whoever steps into the ring."

Aspis licked his lips and grinned. The expression held all the warmth of a shed snake skin.

"Suppose I didn't?" Einar asked.

The Queen raised an eyebrow at him. "Suppose you didn't what?"

"Stay my hand."

"You would rather accept less gold for more work?" Aspis asked, smirking.

"Forests and trees," Einar said. "If I fight for Lorne and win, then I'm part of a winning side. His men aren't skilled, but he has a great deal of them. If you abide by the agreement and stand down, then he'll have enough power to make a bigger play with, or against, the other districts. More territory, more power, and one step closer to the throne. If I stand aside and give you free passage, then all I have is a toll when you move on."

Aspis glanced at his mother out of the corner of his eye. The Queen took a long sip of her wine, and favored Einar with a slow smile. It held even less warmth than her son's had.

"You're not as stupid as you look."

"Stupid rarely lives to be as old as I am."

"Still," the Queen said, setting her cup back on the table. "That is a great many ifs."

"It is."

"I could provide you a few more," she said, leaning forward slightly. "What if I gave you four hundred marks as well as a commission in my house, and you could still collect your bounty from Lorne at the same time?"

"I'm listening."

"Of course you are," the Queen said. "You've done this kind of thing before, haven't you?"

"In the north," Einar said.

The Queen waved a hand. "The names for things change, but the ceremony is always the same. In Sandekkar each side chooses a representative. They choose a time and a place. The champions fight to the terms of the duel, and when one is victorious, the two parties both drink. The winner to success, the loser as a last goodbye. Everyone from back alley blood letters to the lords and ladies on high observe the custom. Refusing the drink is often seen as grounds for the whole challenge beginning anew."

"Interesting," Einar said. "But I don't see how that puts gold in my pockets, or victory in your hands."

The Queen smiled, and reached behind the pitcher. She held up a small bottle filled with a clear liquid. She uncapped it, proffering it toward Einar. "Smell this, but don't let it touch your skin."

Einar came forward and sniffed lightly. "I don't smell anything."

"Nor would you taste anything, but rest assured you would know all the same." The Queen closed the bottle, setting it back onto the table. "Yaranari venom is very difficult to obtain. Purifying and distilling it so that it can be used without any tell tale warning signs is even more so. There is no protection, no antidote, and if used properly it is deadlier than any dagger."

"Ah," Einar said. "You would have me poison Lorne's cup?"

"I would," the Queen said. "The glasses are filled before the duel, and each fighter carries the cup to his respective side. You and Aspis can give a good show of things, and then you take a knee. The duel pauses, and we'll ask if you yield. Do so, and when Lorne drinks the day will be won."

"How can I trust you?" Einar asked. The Queen laughed, a beautiful, brittle sound like ice-glass cracking. It was all the answer Einar needed.

"All right," he said. "I want half my gold now."

"Of course," the Queen said. She wrapped the bottle in a blood-colored kerchief, and held it out. "Sarassa's already been instructed. She'll have the amount waiting for you as you leave."

"Bring the rest with you tomorrow." Einar took the bottle, tucking the heavy glass away into his belt pouch.

"Of course," the Queen said with another of her empty grins. "I always pay my dues in coin of the realm."

"Northerner," Aspis said, just as Einar turned away. "Won't you have a drink with us?"

Einar paused, then retrieved the third glass. He raised it, his expression serious. "To victory."

Aspis laughed, throwing his head back. He touched his glass to Einar's, and winked. His mother inclined her head. They drank.

The main room of the Squall's Rose had been mostly cleared. The tables had been pushed back, and a circle of thick sawdust was drawn through the center. Einar sat at a corner booth eating warm porridge when Gadran Lorne entered the inn with a dozen of his men hard on his heels. Lorne's face was calm, but a twitch in his left eye gave him away when he sat down. Einar took another mouthful, slurping the thick gruel off his spoon. Lorne's men spread out, and the Prince of Thieves drummed his fingers on the table. Einar continued eating as if they weren't there.

"I told you to stay away from the whore queen," Lorne said.

"So you did," Einar said, not looking up.

"And you defied me."

"I did."

"You back biting shit smear," Lorne snarled, leaning over the table. "I ought to-"

Einar casually backhanded Lorne hard enough to split his lip. Lorne's head snapped back, and he sat down hard. A dozen blades hissed as they cleared leather. Einar ate the last bite of his breakfast, and tossed the spoon into the wooden bowl. Lorne touched his mouth, and spit blood onto the floor.

"Give me one reason not to kill you right now."

"You still need me to fight for you," Einar said, leaning back in his chair. "Aspis is an animal. I wouldn't give your men here good odds against him if they could fight him together, much less one at a time."

"What do you know about it?"

"I met the man," Einar said. "I took his mother's invitation to hear her offer for my services. She was willing to pay me a damn sight better than you are, but steel can only be bought once. I took the chance to see what kind of man Aspis was, and to see what I'd be stepping into the ring with."

"And?"

Einar shrugged. "He's young, he's fast, and from what I can tell he favors a blade that only has to cut once. He's overconfident, though, and I think that will be what does him in."

Lorne dabbed at his swelling lip with his sleeve. His hackles were still up, but he'd put his teeth away. "Anything else you think I should know?"

"Just this," Einar said, taking the kerchief-wrapped bottle out of his pouch and setting it on the table. He gingerly pulled the edges back, revealing the bottle and its clear liquid. "She wanted me to poison your cup with it. That way, whether the duel is won or lost, you still die."

Lorne reached out, but didn't quite touch the bottle. He clenched his jaw, and his nostrils flared as he stared at the little bottle of innocuous death. He drew his hand back, and swallowed hard.

"My apologies," Lorne said. He waved to his men, and they put their weapons away.

"Accepted," Einar said. "As long as they come with my gold."

"You heard our champion, Valker," Lorne said to his bodyguard.

Valker nodded. He drew out a length of black cloth, and tossed it to Einar. Einar wrapped the cord around his arm, flexing carefully to be sure it wasn't tight enough to weaken his grip or loose enough to foul his swing. Once the band was on, Valker dropped a sack onto the table. It was heavy, and the coins inside clanked as they spilled over one another. Einar took the gold, and tucked it into his pack.

"You aren't going to count it?" Valker asked.

"Never count your gold until you've been paid in full," Einar said. "I still have a job to do."

"Damn right you do," Lorne said. He smiled, the expression painful, bloody, and vicious. "I can't wait to see the look on that trumped-up trollop's face."

"Nor can I."

Lorne's cadre dispersed, straddling chairs and leaning against the walls. In no time at all the rattle of dice cups, and the turn of cards filled the room. Prayers and curses soon followed, along with the clink of copper and the richer notes of the occasional silver piece. Einar remained where he was. So did Lorne. Valker stood guard, watching the room just as if there was something to see.

Hours passed, and with them came the crowd. It began as a trickle, with some of the curious arriving under the premise of getting a drink or a meal. They nursed ale and made small talk, idling over to places with a good view of the ring. As mid-day came and went the trickle became a steady stream; idlers and laggards mixed with braggarts and beggars. By the time the sun kissed the horizon most of the inn was filled with onlookers and spectators, as well as those who made their assorted livings from crowds. Wine and ale ran in rivers, and the place was loud with the sounds of anticipation. Then the doors opened, and as one the voices went still.

Reina Morningswell walked into the Squall's Rose one hip at a time. The Queen of Killers wore a simple, scarlet wrap that left her legs flashing and her shoulders bare. Her hair was piled atop her head, and long needles as deadly as they were beautiful held it in place. Rubies glinted on her fingers, and in the valley of her breasts. She paused, smiling as a dozen members of her household filed into the inn as well. They were just as beautiful as their queen, all in red and just as dangerous. The crowd melted back from her as they would have from a tiger. Aspis strode up next to his mother, his unruly hair slicked tight to his skull. He was dressed in darker tones than the matron, and his skin gleamed with a light sheen of oil.

"I trust we haven't kept you waiting?" she asked.

"Not long," Lorne said, slithering out of the booth and straightening his vest. "It is a lady's prerogative, after all, to leave men waiting on her pleasure."

Aspis sneered, resting his hand on the pommel of a wickedly curved weapon too long to be a knife, but too short to be a proper sword. Its twin hung loosely on his other hip, swaying slightly as he shifted his weight. He was about to speak when his mother brushed her fingers against his shoulder, and walked around the edge of the circle.

"Let us have this over and done with," the Queen said, sweeping toward her people in a swirl of red cloth. "We've wasted too much time already."

"My sentiments exactly," Lorne said, a grin on his face and murder in his beady, black eyes. "Come on."

Lorne walked to the edge of the circle, and sat in a high-backed chair. Morningswell lowered herself demurely into its mate on the other side of the circle. A table sat next to each of them, the surfaces clear but for a single, empty goblet. The champions picked up the cups and walked around the circle, careful not to step inside. Altan placed a silvered pitcher on the bar, and each of the fighters poured a full measure of wine. Aspis with casual grace, Einar with a carefully measured tilt. They each returned to their respective sides, resting the glasses on the tables. The inn was hot, close, and except for the creak of wood and a few nervous coughs, quiet.

"The terms," Morningswell called out into the empty room. "First blood, or until one yields."

"Only if your boy scours his blades before we begin," Lorne shot back. "Otherwise I say it's yield, or to the death. It would be the same difference either way."

The corner of the Queen's mouth quirked. "All right then. Until one yields, or to the death."

"The winner claims all of Low Town," Lorne said. "The loser will have until sunrise to leave the district, and all of Sandekkar."

"Agreed," Morningswell said. Aspis licked his lips, picking up a touch of sawdust and rubbing it between his hands. Einar did the same.

"I'd try for death," Lorne hissed to Einar. "That boy will cut your cods off if you give him the chance."

"Don't worry," Einar said, unsheathing his sword. "You'll get what you paid for."

Einar had barely stepped into the circle when Aspis charged. His blades flew in a flurry, slashing and jabbing, aiming for Einar's arms, his face, his hands; anywhere his flesh was exposed. Einar twisted, interposing his steel at the last moment, shoving back against the assault. He dropped his guard, and when Aspis stepped in Einar butted the younger fighter in the face. Einar pressed his advantage, throwing an elbow and then a shoulder into Aspis's midsection. The slender fighter's armor was meant to stop the blade of a sword, and Einar's heavy, meaty blows drove the wind out of the dark-haired youth. Aspis reversed his grip, smashing the pommel of his weapon into Einar's jaw.

They drew back from each other, weapons raised and breath coming harder. Einar spat blood onto the floor, and Aspis held himself gingerly, half bent over as a single trickle of blood ran from his left nostril. Both of them grinned, lips pulled back as they circled and tested one another. Aspis feinted, but Einar kept his feet planted. Einar jabbed his point forward, but Aspis caught the bigger weapon with his two smaller ones, pushing it out of the way as he side-stepped. Every pass brought them closer; a deadly dance of twitching muscles and razor-sharp edges.

Einar swung, and his sword whistled as it bit through the air. Aspis ducked, tucking into a forward roll and coming up under the bigger man's guard. His short blades scissored, and Einar dropped his sword as he threw himself backward. He stumbled, and went to a knee. He paused, and drew in breath to yield when he looked into Aspis's eyes. They were bright, and alive as Einar had never seen them before. It was the only warning he had.

Aspis swept his weapons down like hatchets, aiming to bury them deep. Einar threw himself to the side, landing hard on his shoulder. Aspis tried to check his rush, but stumbled as both blades bit deep into the hardwood floor. Einar scrambled, puffing as he flung himself up from the floor and snatched up his fallen sword. He spun, bringing it up just in time to catch the next blow. The momentum of the swing stopped Aspis's advance, throwing him back.

"You are good," Aspis said, chuckling breathily as he scraped one blade along another. He stepped to the side, and Einar mirrored him. "But you're old, and you're slow. Better give up now, while you still can."

Einar lowered his guard, and half turned to look back at the Queen of Killers. She sat as she had before, with her hands in her lap and one leg crossed over the other. There were spots of color in her cheeks, and her lips were flushed bright, blood red. Einar kept turning, pivoting on his rear leg. A blow glanced off Einar's back with and angry, metallic hiss, and he brought the great blade around with all his weight behind it.

Aspis was fast, with all the speed and reflexes of youth. He was a killer, sure as any beast that strode the forests or the plains. But he was eager, and when he saw his opponent's back he leaped with everything he had. That was why Einar's blow caught him across the small of his back, tearing through the light armor before shearing into the muscle and bone beneath. Aspis fell, his throat locked so tightly that only a high-pitched keening sound escaped his lips.

Einar coughed, and sucked in one deep breath after another. Aspis writhed, hissing and snarling, clawing at the floorboards. His legs refused to obey his command, and blood pooled beneath him. He glared at Einar with cold, reptilian loathing. The blood slowed, and Aspis's face slackened. Whatever lived behind his eyes departed, leaving behind an empty, broken husk.

The silence persisted for a single heartbeat. One cheer sounded, then another, and before long the quiet collapsed. A steady roar of animalistic glee rang from the rafters and reverberated in the floor. There was no approval in it, nor was there any malice. It was the sound of beasts the world over, acknowledging a victor. Einar had heard it many times before, and it was always a comfort knowing he lived to hear it again.

"Silence!" the Prince of Thieves called. The crowd ignored his words, but in time the noise died away to a whispered roar. Lorne bowed his head to the Queen of Killers, the courtly gestured ruined by the greasy, gap-toothed grin he wore. "The duel is decided. Low Town is mine."

"Yes," Morningswell agreed, her tone frosty. "It appears that it is."

If Lorne heard the cold snap in her voice it didn't seem bother him. He simply showed more teeth, and raised his glass. "To the victor goes the spoils, eh?"

The Queen of Killers said nothing, but she tipped her head slightly in acknowledgment. Both of them lowered their goblets, drinking while they held eye contact. Lorne belched and smacked his lips, laughing. The laughter choked off, though, and Gadron Lorne clawed as his throat. His face turned red, then purple. He gagged, falling out of his chair. He started coughing, and blood flecked foam flew from his lips. Reina Morningswell smiled as she watched, but the smile soon faded. Her chest hitched, and her face drained of color. Her wide, staring eyes fixed on Einar, and she reached toward him. She tried to stand, but her legs buckled. She collapsed, sprawling into the spreading pool of her son's blood. In moments three corpses littered the floor instead of one.

Horror struck the celebrants dumb, turning the Squall's Rose into a living tableau. Screams of "poison" and "murder" shattered the stillness, and suddenly everyone was moving at once. The onlookers broke for the doors, bellowing and hammering at each other as they streamed into the night. Lorne's men, now leaderless, sat stunned until Valker drew a short sword and a wicked dagger, barreling toward the remainders of the late Queen's red retainers. The assassins scattered, the thieves hot on their heels. Within moments the Squall's Rose was empty except for Einar, Altan, and Low Town's recently deceased nobility.

"Remind me never to make an enemy of you, Einar," Altan said into the empty common room.

"Never make an enemy of me."

Einar wiped the blood from his blade, sheathing it. He knelt down next to the Queen of Killers, and ran his hands across her cooling skin. He plucked the rubies from her fingers, and the necklace from her throat. He didn't spare so much as a glance for Aspis. He kicked Lorne's body out of the way, and sat down in his recently vacated chair. The seat was still warm.

Altan poured them each a mug, then drew up a chair. The two men sat just outside the dead circle in the empty inn. All around them half-filled tankards and glasses sat like abandoned babes, waiting patiently for their parents' return. Einar fished out one of the ruby rings, and rolled it across the table.

"For the silver pitcher, and the goblets," Einar said. "They looked like they cost a pretty."

"They did," Altan said, tucking the ring into a pouch around his neck. "Though not this much."

"Consider the rest a gift," Einar said. "For doing what I asked."

"Killing that filth is gift enough," Altan said, taking another swallow. "Still, it leaves a bad taste in my mouth."

"That can be washed out," Einar said. "And better a bad taste than no taste at all."

"Truer words."

Altan stood, and closed the doors. Einar lifted his glass and looked into its amber depths. The man who looked back at him was old, scarred, and bloody. He didn't look like the sort of man who would poison the well, but appearances could be deceiving. Einar looked at the circle. He saw the boy who would gladly have killed him while he slept, the woman who would have slipped poison into his meals with a smile, and the man who would have repaid victory with murder. If he'd helped a single one of them to victory, his life would have been forfeit. With all of them dead he was a free man, and a man that every tongue in the city would be wagging about by dawn. There would be other paymasters. Perhaps even honorable ones. He'd been told that such existed.

Einar chuckled, and looked back at the man in his glass. They smiled at each other. Neither of them had lived as long as they had by being good men. One man drank the other down neat, and swallowed hard. He stood up, walked to the bar, and poured a second glass. Then he sat back down in the dead man's chair, opened up his pack, and began counting his gold.

Dead Man's Bluff

Luck has a sound. If you listen closely, you can hear it in the New Orleans box shuffle. There's a certain cadence, a rhythm broken only by the cutting of the deck, that's unmistakable if you know what you're listening for. Faking that was hard, but not impossible if you put in the time and dedication to learn how. James Garnett had practiced since before his voice had started to crack, and in his hands the deck was true as a wife, and honest as gold. It was a masterful performance, and like any accomplished stage show, when it was done right no one ever noticed.

The man who'd taught him to deal crooked diamonds had been a great apostate of luck. Luck was for fools and farriers, his father had said, and unless his son wanted to hang horseshoes for the rest of his days then he'd best learn to sharpen his cards until they could draw blood. His father had demanded absolute perfection, and in time Garnett had learned to deliver it without fail. His father had yelled at him when he made mistakes, and occasionally given him the back of his hand, but he had never once damaged his son's fingers. Even on nights where he'd gone to bed with a fat lip, or a swollen eye, Garnett's hands were always safe from his father's punishments. It was for his own good, his father had told him on the nights where he'd drunk enough to loosen his usually closed mouth. Luck was an awful mistress, and if you played her false one too many times, she would come for you. And when she came her wrath would be swift, and terrible. Best to keep her sweet as long as you could, and to know when it was time to move along.

For his part, Garnett had scoffed at the idea that he might be cursed just for dealing a few fools the hand they deserved. But as he'd grown older and wiser, he'd begun to wonder about his old man's rambling sermons about Lady Luck, and if there really was something out there keeping score of his back-handed deals. He wondered how, time after time, even his best-laid plans seemed to unravel just as his fingers brushed the brass ring, driving him on to the next town to start all over again.

It was in Gallows Hill, identical to dozens other small cow towns that dotted maps of the West like a frontier rash, that Garnett was sure he'd found a place to recoup some of his losses. A herd of longhorn steers had come through recently, and the drovers mixed with what few town folks there were at a saloon called the Hangman's Laugh; a dowdy place where the beer was cloudier than the glasses, and the floorboards were the only things that were straight and narrow. There were drinkers and diners aplenty in the bar, though, and that was what mattered. Men who had earned their money with sweat and grit, and who were now buying themselves a little pleasure with it. Many of them, flush and idle, were more than happy to play a hand or three of poker. Especially if Garnett was buying the first round to get the friendly game going.

He started off losing, but Garnett always made sure to win when it counted. He spun yarns, told jokes, and made sure that even when a man lost the game, he still had something to laugh about. A few dour fellows were immune to his charms, but their chairs never stood empty for long once they'd walked away from his table. There was no trouble in his corner of the place, and enough of his money trickled back behind the bar that he doubted the house would take the side of anyone who was sore over a losing hand.

Garnett had been alone at his table for nearly half an hour, and he was nearly ready to pack it in for the night, when the bat-wing doors eased open, and a figure stepped out of the evening darkness. It resolved into a pale young man in an old-fashioned high collar. He wore a long, black coat, and a flat-crowned hat. He looked like bad luck, dressed up in his Sunday-go-to-meeting. He glanced around the room, and his gaze settled on Garnett's table. He crossed the room, his heels knocking on the hardwood floor. Garnett had a smile waiting for him, but it curdled on his lips. The boy's eyes were steady, and unblinking as they regarded the gambler. They were also an unsettling shade of green; the luminescent burning copper in a Chinaman's firecracker.

"Evening," Garnett said, clearing his throat. "Can I help you, friend?"

"I'm looking for a game," the young man said, his voice a strangled whisper. He touched the green felt of the tabletop, dragging the tip of one finger across the cloth. "Have another hand in you?"

Garnett suppressed a shudder, and summoned his winning grin again. "I may. If you'll have a drink with me, and tell me your name?"

The young man smiled, thin lips pulling back from straight, white teeth. He offered his hand. "Fawkes."

"James Garnett," Garnett said, shaking the proffered hand.

Garnett caught the bartender's eye, and nodded. The bald man poured two glasses of the coffin varnish the saloon passed off as real whiskey, and brought it to them on a platter. Garnett took the glasses, and handed one to his new companion. Fawkes peeled off his coat, and hung it on a wall hook along with his hat. He took the glass, and the two of them clinked before they drank.

Once they'd drunk their drinks, and the barkeep had refilled their glasses, the real performance began. Garnett dealt Fawkes several good hands, letting the green-eyed gambler get comfortable. Then, once he'd set the scene, Garnett slowly started to stack the court against his young opponent. A few Jacks here, a few Kings there, and the chips that Fawkes had won began to trickle back across the river to Garnett's own stacks. Fawkes just smiled, and ordered another drink for himself, and for Garnett.

"Brought that shuffle a long way, didn't you Jim?" the pale young man asked in his cheap tobacco voice.

The question blew down Garnett's spine, and just like that, the cards began to fall over one another like dead soldiers in his hands. Garnett laughed, trying to repair the damage to his shuffle, but he'd lost the feel of the cards. So he clacked his teeth, and dealt blind.

"No one calls me Jim except my mother," Garnett said, glancing at his cards.

"Is that so?" Fawkes replied, tossing a few more chips into the pot. "Odd, that. Ah well, I suppose there's more than one Louisiana gambler who handles a deck as well as you do that's come out West."

"A fair number of them, I would wager," Garnett said.

Garnett lost that hand, and lost it badly. Once the cards were gathered, Fawkes held out his hand. Garnett frowned, but held the cards out. Fawkes took the deck with his left hand, and he did something that was hard for Garnett's eye to follow. With a smooth flick of the wrist and a slide of his fingers, he cut the cards once, twice, and a third time before he offered the cards back to Garnett.

"I don't shuck another man's deck," he said, humor dancing in his sea glass gaze. "You keep the cards. I don't need to deal you, Jim."

Garnett took the deck back, and realized his hands were clammy with sweat. His mouth had gone dry as trail dust, and there was something niggling at his mind. Something that he should remember, but the thought was shy, and wouldn't come. So Garnett put his performer's smile back on, and shuffled the deck again. From that hand on, though, it seemed like he couldn't win. Aces deserted their posts, full houses stood empty, and once he dealt himself the cards he'd meant to give Fawkes. It wasn't every hand, but it was enough to bleed Garnett of the winnings he'd managed to amass since he'd sat down that afternoon.

When Garnett came up for air, he saw that the saloon had died like a snake with a broken back. There had been some music when they'd started playing, and there had even been some other games going on around the room, but the life had bled out between the cracks when he hadn't been watching. He took a sip of his drink, swished it around in his mouth, and swallowed. It was time to bring the game to a close.

When Garnett picked up the cards again, he was careful to skim them over his fingertips. As he shuffled, he felt for the subtle curves, and barely there pockmarks that told him what faces lurked on the other side. This time there weren't any mistakes. There were no wandering loyalties, and the cards danced the box social just the way he told them to. The cards slid across the felt, smooth as buttered silk, and twice as sweet.

"Headed back East?" Fawkes asked, tossing his ante into the center of the table.

"I wasn't terribly set on one direction over another," Garnett said, anteing up as well. He looked at his hand; aces full of jacks, with the two court pages wall-eyeing one another. Just as he'd known they would be. "What about you? Heading that way?"

"Yes," Fawkes said. "I've got business with a man."

As Fawkes spoke, he rearranged his cards on the table with a single finger. The cards curved in a sickle moon, like a huckster's fortune telling. Once the cards had been arranged to his liking, Fawkes tossed three of his blue chips into the pot. Garnett had seen some strange gambits in his time, but he'd never seen a man bet blind in a game of bluff before. Garnett paused, and glanced at his cards again. Then he matched, and raised.

"Who's the man you're looking for?" Garnett asked. "Always happy to help, when I can."

"A fellow by the name of Ruby," Fawkes said. "Jim Ruby."

"Gentleman Jim Ruby?" Garnett asked. "I've heard the name, but I also heard that he died. Something about a falling out with Johnny Ringold, and his black-hearted bunch?"

"No, Ruby isn't dead," Fawkes said. He matched Garnett's raise without so much as glancing at his own hand, then added another stack of chips with a casual push. "Had the words straight from Ringold himself."

"I thought he was dead, too?" Garnett asked, looking at the pot. He could have stopped right then, taken his earnings, and called it a night. He had more money than he'd come to town with, and it was enough to see him on to the next burg. But he had never been a man to walk away from good odds, especially when he'd tilted them in his own favor. So he pushed the remainder of his chips into the pot.

"Ringold? Oh yes indeed, dead as Latin," Fawkes answered, pulling his lips back from his teeth again. The expression transformed his face into something unpleasant; a rattlesnake smile that was all poison and pain. "Ringold, Harlan Jackson, Mickey Connors, and Adam Fredricks. Terrible ends for them, one and all."

As he spoke each name, Fawkes dropped a stack of chips into the pot. They crashed and slid, the sound echoing in the mostly empty bar. His head was tilted slightly to one side, and in the dim light of the kerosene, his eyes seemed to burn. Like the corpse lamps that hovered over the still waters of lost swamps, and tempted late night travelers to step off the trail. That look made Garnett's mouth go numb, and his throat clenched tight. The thought he'd been trying to remember came to his mind again, flicking around the edges of his memory like a moth fluttering at a lamp. It was a dark shape, like a half-remembered dream of something shameful. Garnett licked his lips, then laid his cards face-up on the table.

"Shall we see what it is you have?" He asked. As the one hand laid down his cards, Garnett slid the other to the hidden pocket in his waistcoat, drawing out the pepperbox pistol he always carried there. A little insurance, just in case some unpleasantness should result from a friendly game gone awry. Or in case he caught someone else cheating, which broke the first rule his father had ever taught him.

Fawkes kept smiling, and he turned his cards over one at a time. His movements were smooth; a simple turn that Garnett had seen somewhere before. He smelled the dead ghost of old incense, and licked dry lips as he watched, mesmerized. One by one the hand was revealed, and Garnett felt the trap drop out in his guts. Hoyle's painted ladies stared up at him; the four queens clustered around the ace of spades. There was something different about the high card, though. The ace was upside down, the tip of the black spear pointing at Garnett's chest like an accusatory finger. The edges of the card were blackened, as if it had been in a fire, and the face was a miniature masterpiece that had been painted with careful brush strokes. He had seen that card before. Five years ago, on the day that he and all the others had been well and truly cursed.

"How did they die?" Garnett asked. His voice didn't shake, and there was no sweat on his brow. He took a steadier grip on his pistol, swallowing the rest of his drink so Fawkes would be looking at the hand with the empty glass in it. "The others that you mentioned, I mean."

"Their luck just ran out," Fawkes replied, leaning back in his chair. His smile remained on his face, and he made no move to reach for the pot. He took a long swallow from his own glass, his eyes never leaving Garnett's face. "Fredricks was thrown by a spooked horse, and the fall broke his neck. Connors was prospecting when a rock fell on him, and crushed his ribs. The body was found a week later, and by then it was in a miserable state. Jackson fell asleep with his cigar still lit while hiding out in a farmer's hay stable. And I think you know how Ringold went, don't you Jim?"

"Shot, wasn't he?" Garnett asked, cocking the pistol as he spoke, raising his voice to cover up the sound of the hammer. "In the back, I was told. Five times. Terrible thing to do to a man."

"It is," Fawkes agreed.

The two men said nothing for a time. Garnett shifted in his seat, and Fawkes sipped at his glass as casually as if he were at home in his own parlor. As if he couldn't feel the budding storm brewing in the taproom. He held Garnett's eyes, and after a time Garnett began to nod. He kept nodding, as if he wasn't truly aware he was still doing it.

"The witch," he said. His voice was raw, like someone had ripped it out of him and put it back in wrong. Fawkes nodded once. "Are you a ghost?"

Fawkes said nothing. He slid a hand up his throat, and unbuttoned his collar. The fabric folded down, and Garnett leaned forward to look, despite himself. Faux tilted his head back, stretching the skin of his throat. There was a rough scar there; the brand of a rope that had been cinched tight, and left to swing. Garnett couldn't look away from it, fascinated by the tiny, puckered whorls in the skin. He remembered now. The house in the hills that none of them knew was there. The fortune teller who lived in it, and who had laid the cards for each of them. The woman that Jackson had taken, and then passed around to the others. He remembered her green eyes, burning with a devil's fire. She had spoken her curse, and Jackson had struck her. He kept doing it, laughing with breath that smelled like an all-sorts barrel. Then Garnett remembered the boy, pale and dark-haired. How he'd tried to run, and how they'd drug him back with a rope. How they'd left him standing on his tip toes on a three-legged stool, wearing nothing but a noose as the house burned around him. There had been no other witnesses to what they'd done.

"No," Fawkes said with a smile as he saw the whole scene flash across Garnett's face. "I'm just lucky."

"Nobody's that lucky," Garnett snarled. He raised the gun, holding it at arm's length. Fawkes saw the gun, but he didn't move. He just tilted his head to one side. His neck popped, making him look like a man still hanging from a noose.

"Don't do it," Fawkes said, his voice low and soft. Garnett pulled the trigger, and the gun exploded in his hand.

All it took was a second. The hammer fell on a jostled load, and the powder sparked to the other chambers. The whole mechanism flew apart like a demon's sneeze; hot lead and sharp steel gouging the tabletop, and digging into the floor. Garnett's hand was gone; a blackened ruin of bone and slag with raw, red meat showing through charred flesh. His mouth had been opened to scream, and it had stayed that way. The hammer had flown free, and pulped the gambler's silver tongue. Slivers of hot lead popped his eyes, the thick goo running down his face like thick, egg-white tears of contrition.

The thing that had once been Gentleman Jim Ruby, the keenest sharp in the deck, tried to get to its feet. The man's body knew it was dying, even if the spirit wasn't ready to admit it. The shattered hulk crashed to the floor, choking on its own blood and bile before the flesh shuddered, and went still. A last breath rattled past the broken teeth, and Jim Ruby was no more.

The green-eyed gambler lifted his drink in a toast, and knocked back the blackberry whiskey neat as pips. He stood, clearing the green felt like a priest wiping off an altar once the service was over and all the attendants had shuffled out the front door. The young man with the hangman's smile picked up the ace he'd brought all the way from that backwoods cabin where he'd been raised, and placed it squarely in the center of the table. He touched his face, rubbing at a small cut from where one of the pepperbox's errant bullets had whizzed past, and let a drop of his own blood fall on the center of the spade. It sat there, round and perfect, darkening the varnish. Finally, he placed every red chip he'd earned atop it, and left them there as he collected the rest of his winnings. Just for good luck.

Bloody Bones

Stuart sat on the chopping block, and caught his breath. He hung his head, gulping thick summer air and trying not to drown in it. Sweat dripped from the tip of his nose, and trickled down the ridge of his spine. It soaked his hair, staining his cut-off shorts in damp patches the shape of his palms. The sun was a palpable weight on his back, even though the shadows were coming out from their hiding places beneath the trees. He could see the abandoned Harradan Road, which was little more than two ruts through the dirt leading into the willows out across the tumble-down back fence. A breeze brought the cool scent of the day's end, and it was strong enough to make his sunburned skin break into gooseflesh. Behind him, the spring on the screen door squalled.

His aunt Sophia stood on the back stoop, looking down at him. A handsome woman, life had licked away the rime of her youth. Her blond hair was tugged into a severe ponytail, and a few, thin strands corkscrewed around her face like fraying rope. Her skin was pulled tight across her bones, and in her faded yellow sun dress with her stained apron she looked like a lemon just starting to turn bad. She put a cigarette in her mouth, and lit it with a kitchen match.

"Stuart, you finish your chores yet?" she called.

"Yes ma'am," Stuart managed.

"Go wash then," she said, blowing a stream of smoke. "Put some shake into it! Supper's ready, and you're keeping everybody waiting."

Stuart picked up the ax as well as his shirt, and headed for the shed. He carefully replaced the ax on its pegs, then crossed the yard again and bent over the hose next to the garage. The rubber felt like a rotting garden snake, and it leaked something fierce, but the cold water sluiced the sweat and dirt from his arms, hair and face. He scooped a dollop of the heavy, pumice soap his uncle took from work, and scrubbed. He ground it into his scraped knuckles and over his hairless forearms, grimacing as he did. If he didn't wash well enough he'd be sent back out to do a better job while everyone else ate. He took off his shoes, patted himself dry, and tugged his damp shirt on over his head.

As soon as he stepped into the mud room he smelled supper; a soupy mixture of thin red sauce, marinated ham, and burned bread basted in garlic. Stuart's gut clenched, and his mouth watered. He padded through the kitchen, still slick from the intercourse of cooking, and down the back hall. The laminate was warm and sticky under his bare feet, and it curled up in places like yellowed notebook paper.

They were seated around the too-big table with its gray, fading cloth. Grandpa Paul sat at the head in an old, gilded chair Stuart's grandmother had found at an estate sale before Stuart had been born. With his leathery skin and narrowed eyes, his grandfather looked like a crocodile holding court. Uncle Roger, Stuart's uncle-by-marriage, sat at the old man's left hand. Roger leaned his elbows on the table, and stared at the meal he wasn't allowed to eat yet while he worked a wad in his cheek. Next to him was his daughter Gertrude. She was growing into her mother's looks, and picking up her father's habits. She chewed a pretty pink plug, tucking her too-short top into her skirt on account of it being family night. Aunt Sophia sat next to her daughter, with little Matt fussing in her lap. He turned his head back and forth until he saw Stuart and smiled toothlessly at him. Stuart slid into a chair across from his aunt, right next to Matt's high chair.

"Good of you to join us," Roger drawled, hawking and spitting thick, brown juice into a sloshing Pepsi can.

"I'm sorry," Stuart said.

"You surely are," Roger fired back, showing his stained teeth.

"Everyone, let us say Grace," Grandpa Paul said. They all bowed their heads, but Stuart kept his eyes open. "Dearest God, thank you for your bounty, your forgiveness, and your love. Amen."

"Amen," the others echoed. Roger snatched the bread basket, taking half a dozen slices, and Gertrude grabbed the plastic noodle bowl. They doled food out for themselves, for each other, and for the others. Stuart watched the bowl move from one end of the table to the other, followed by the sloshing sauce pot. Gertrude gave him a thin, alley cat grin and stretched her gum out before putting it on the side of her plate.

"You finish, boy?" Grandpa Paul asked, tipping the sauce pot over his plate.

"I got the grass mowed, re-stacked the old bricks in the side patch, and I cut most of the cord wood and got it stacked up," Stuart said.

Grandpa Paul stuck the tines of his fork into the drowned mountain of half-cooked noodles. He looked down at his plate as if what he was doing was particularly hard, and required all of his concentration. He raised the dripping oval, gave it a once-over, and slurped it into his mouth. He chewed deliberately, his thick, square teeth like hooves slopping through churned muck. He swallowed, and licked his lips.

"Most of it," Grandpa Paul said offhandedly. "Just how much is most of it?"

"There's the two end anchors left," Stuart said quickly. "A-and about three rows in between them, sir."

"Three rows," Grandpa Paul said, nodding as if he liked the sound of that. "That's a lot of work for twelve, boy. But didn't I tell you this morning to get it all cut?"

"Y-yes sir," Stuart said. He swallowed a mouthful of sour spit, and nearly choked.

"Maybe you think I'm being unfair, is that it?" Grandpa Paul asked.

Stuart shook his head. "No sir."

"You probably want to take some time and enjoy, now that summer's here," Grandpa Paul continued, as if he hadn't heard. "But everyone does their part in this house Stuart. You don't have any schooling to attend, and I expect you to get done what I tell you to get done."

"I could do it tomorrow-" Stuart said, but stopped at the look his grand-sire gave him.

"Don't you blaspheme in my house, boy," he said, leveling the business end of his fork at Stuart. "It's bad enough your mama ran off with a godless good-for-nothing, and left you here for us to carry. I don't need you sweating on the Lord's day and bringing more shame to this home. Do you understand me?"

"Yes sir," Stuart said. He dropped his eyes, and stared at the stained cloth just to the left of his plate. For a long moment nobody moved. Then Grandpa Paul tossed the mostly empty noodle bowl at him, and Stuart scrambled to make sure it didn't tip over the edge.

"All God's children share, Stuart," Grandpa Paul said, digging his fork back into his dinner. "But in my house you carry your weight."

Stuart nodded, and carefully scooped what was left of the noodles onto his plate. He slowly scraped the sides of the saucepan, and managed just enough of the thin sauce to tint his meal pink. There were two slices of bread left in the basket, burned black on the bottom, but he took them anyway.

Supper passed. Roger talked around thick mouthfuls of food about how a good friend of his had been passed over for a job at the auto yard where he worked. Said the job went to some guy because of the color of his skin, and because he was willing to do the job for half of what any self-respecting white man would take. Gertrude talked about how there was a bonfire going on that night, and about how she really, desperately needed to go. Aunt Sophia didn't want her to, but Gertrude pouted and Grandpa Paul dropped her a wink. He haggled with his daughter and granddaughter until it was agreed that Gertrude could go as long as she stayed the night with her friend Henrietta. In return, Gertrude would watch the baby so her parents could have a night to themselves. Stuart offered to do the dishes so she could leave earlier, and his grandfather narrowed one eye at him. You couldn't dig out of a hole with the old man, especially once he'd made it very clear just how deep you were in. Supper ended the same way it always did; with Matt pushing at his tray and crying that special cry that meant it was time for bed. Sophia took her little one off to his room, Grandpa Paul and Uncle Roger stepped out onto the front porch, and Gertrude bounded up the stairs to put on a fresh coat of gloss. Stuart collected the plates, and walked them into the kitchen.

Stuart scraped the leftovers, such as they were, into a Tupperware container. He put it in the fridge, wedging it into the crowded bottom shelf. His stomach was far from full, but Roger always took the food to work the next day. If there was less than he'd expected, Stuart would be left holding the baby. He drank a glass of cold water to quiet his rumbling belly, and filled the deep sink to the water line. He scrubbed the mismatched plates and silverware, rinsing the suds and using an old, ragged towel to dry them. By the time he'd finished, the first shoots of indigo were blooming in the sky. The pots and pans came next, followed by the cookie sheet. Once they were all put away Stuart wiped down the oven, and the counter tops. He took a plastic shopping bag out of a drawer, and dug through the garbage pail. He pulled out the thick, heavy ham bone his aunt had finished skinning for the meal along with several, smaller rib bones that still had gristle clinging to them. They'd been in his uncle's lunch pail, forgotten until he came home. Stuart hummed a meaningless, meandering song as he tied the bag closed. The soothing tune rumbled out of his chest, and wormed its way into the tired, aching weave of his muscles.

"What's that song?" Gertrude asked from behind.

"Huh?" Stuart spun, dropping the bag. Gertrude leaned in the archway, a new stick of gum between her teeth and her lips shining a plastic pink. She'd slung on a denim jacket that emphasized rather than concealed her adolescent blossom, and dangling faux-silver sparkles hung from her ears. Stuart knelt down and picked up the bag. "I don't know. I must have heard it on the radio."

"I like it." Gertrude gave him a small smile, and stepped into the kitchen. She slipped a hand out from behind her back, and passed Stuart a small, folded-over paper sack. "Thanks, Stu."

Stuart looked up at his cousin, and Gertrude flushed. For a moment it looked like she might say something else, but her mother came down the stairs and Gertrude dashed around the corner to ask for a ride. Stuart picked up the plastic bag, shoving it out of sight around the mudroom door. He stuffed the paper sack down his shirt, licking his lips. He gave the counters one more wipe down before he drained the sink, and set the sponge on the block to dry. The front door opened, and Roger's work boots clomped in. They were quickly followed by Grandpa Paul's rocking, uneven steps. The girls went out, still talking over the terms of the evening's outing as the door shut behind them. Roger went upstairs to watch over Matt, and Grandpa Paul made his slow way towards the kitchen. Stuart snatched up the dry plates, and started putting them away.

The old man stood in the archway. He didn't say anything, just lifted a brown, unlabeled bottle to his lips as his eyes followed his grandson. Stuart replaced everything he'd dried, then wiped his hands on the dish towel and hung it across the crooked bar nailed to the particle board wall. Grandpa Paul remained silent, his features carved from sour mahogany. He didn't praise, nor did he chastise. He drank the rest of his beer, and held the empty bottle out. Stuart took it, rinsed it, and walked it to the return bin in the garage.

When he came back inside the old man had retired to the den. Stuart cocked his head, and heard the low growl of the evening news. He picked up the plastic bag, hid it against his left side, and walked past the open archway. He needn't have bothered; Grandpa Paul was in his recliner, the remote control held like a scepter in one hand as he turned through the half dozen channels they picked up way out here. Even when the bag crinkled, the old man didn't shift his eyes. Stuart opened the door to his bedroom, and slipped into the dimness.

Stuart stood there for a long moment, adjusting to the familiar space. The blocky pool of shadow against his far wall grew sharper, turning into his low, scarred dresser. The rumpled mat of darkling moss became his mattress, with its old, stained quilt on top. On one side of the mattress was a milk crate doing double duty as a night stand. The faded digital clock and a goose neck lamp sitting on top looked tired and forlorn. His school bag sat on the other side of the bed underneath the window that looked out into the back yard. Fingers of cinder light crawled around the shade, and danced over Stuart's one shelf. It held an old bible, a farmer's almanac, and a snow globe with a covered bridge inside. There was a carriage in the globe too, but after too many shakes it had tumbled into the creek below. The horse still stood on the path, patiently waiting for his masters to make their way back to his side.

Stuart closed his eyes, and took a deep breath. Underneath the mustiness, behind the curtain of scents his life had laid over the room, there was another smell. It was the ghost of scented candles, and a girl's first-date perfume. His mother's scent, he knew. Stuart drank it in deep, and let go with reluctance. Some day it would be gone, and he wanted to be able to remember it when he couldn't smell it anymore.

Stuart sat on his bed, and fished the paper bag out of his shirt. Inside were two cookies. The scent of mingled oatmeal and chocolate made

Stuart's mouth water, but he folded the top over and slipped the bag into the front pocket of his backpack instead of devouring them. He carefully pushed the plastic bag down into the main pocket, and zipped the bag closed. He'd packed everything else that morning, and it was ready to go. All that was left was for the sun to go down, and the rest of the house to go to sleep.

Stuart waited. He played solitaire with a dog-eared Bicycle deck in the fading pool of sunlight on the floor. When it got too dark to see, he turned on the lamp and opened the Almanac. According to its browned pages the moon should be new, and sunset was at 8:15. The summer should be warm, and it would be a good time to plant beans and other legumes. He wondered for a moment how accurate the almanac had been back then, and just what that summer day so many years ago had really been like. Stuart put the book back on the shelf, and as he did the constant thrum of one-sided conversation in the next room shut off. Grandpa Paul's chair squeaked, and he grunted as he slid out of it. Stuart listened while the old man shuffled to the stairs.

He stood there a long time, trying to catch every creak and groan of the house all around him. His grandfather settled in bed. His uncle snored, a sound like the low droning of midges. It was irritating, but quickly faded into the background unless you listened for it. His aunt was notable only by the absence of her sound, and baby Matt was the same. It was only when the one was making noise that the other could even be heard. Stuart listened until the display on his clock read midnight. He slung his backpack on, and carefully opened his window.

Heat rose from the clipped grass like a fresh baked pie, and it was spongy beneath Stuart's bare feet as he slid onto the lawn. He closed the window behind him, and looked around at the night. Crickets chirped, and a few fat, desperate fireflies still winked in the dark. The sky had stars in it, but there was little more than a bare crescent of moon hanging in the sky. It made him think of the Cheshire Cat's smile, and the whipping Grandpa Paul had given him when he'd caught him reading that book. Things like that weren't allowed in his house. Stuart smiled back at the moon, then slipped through the house's shadow to the garage where he stepped into his old, broken shoes. He ducked behind the shed, jumped the back fence, and ran into the deeper darkness of the Harradan Road without so much as a backward glance.

Stuart didn't stop running until he felt the trees reaching out for him, and the air took on a close, overgrown taste in his mouth. He drank deeply of the wild flavor, then reached into the side pocket of his bag and took out a small, dark cylinder. He broke the glow stick and shook it, hanging it around his neck on an old, thin shoelace. He walked through the tunnel of foliage, hidden from the prying eyes of the sky, and screened from anyone that might glance toward the disused road. Stuart hummed his little song as he walked, and the trees bent closer to listen.

After he'd walked a mile or so, the ruts in the road vanished, and the old gravel smoothed away to rich earth. The trees stepped back, and starlight filtered down through the canopy. The undergrowth grew thicker, with brambles and thorn bushes encroaching on what had once been the land of man. Stuart felt them catch at him, tugging at his backpack as he went by. He grunted, carefully untangling himself so there would be no tell-tale tears that would lead to questions of where he'd been, and what he'd been doing. Then he was past the thorny guardians, standing at the Bridge to Nowhere.

It's proper name, or the closest thing it had to one, was the Abattoir Bridge. An unused train trestle built when the railroad expanded, it had been claimed during the great buy-outs by the car manufacturers in their attempts to strangle the iron roads. It had been a popular back road for a time, but then the main highway project had come through and sucked up most of the traffic. When a slaughterhouse took up residence down the river, the creek below the bridge had run red. Old folks said it had been so foul that buzzards formed hungry storm clouds all up and down the little waterway, swooping down to fill their gullets and collapsing onto the charnel banks when they got too fat to fly. Over time the bridge had fallen into disrepair, with the boards in the middle dropping out entirely, and the rest of the structure rotting outwards like an infected tooth. Rusty signs bedecked with creepers warned people the bridge was out, and to stay away from it.

Stuart walked closer. Old cigarette butts poked out of the tall grass, and used condoms were draped over bushes like neon snake skins. The river still stank, and the water ran black as it burbled beneath the broken span. Stuart strode along the bridge, and the timbers coughed as he passed. They were still strong, but they wheezed as he went out further; as if the bridge was panting at him to stop before it dropped him. He stopped, and sat down with his feet dangling over the edge. He swung them lightly, back and forth, humming another refrain of his song as he looked down at the dark world below.

He had discovered this forgotten place that night he'd tried to run away. It was a place where even the rubbish had lost its color, and the scrawled veins of graffiti had faded to rusty nothingness. He closed his eyes, and listened as the wind sang a duet with the water. He breathed deeper, and a rushing, copper scent invaded his nose. Something shifted below him. The water eddied, and splashed, and a shudder went up through the bridge. Stuart settled his pack in his lap, unzipped the main pocket, and took out the bone bag he'd stolen from the house. It was joined by a second, a third, and a fourth. The older ones reeked of congealed fat and rotting gristle, once he parted their plastic skins.

"I'm sorry I took so long," Stuart said, speaking softly as he ran twine through the handles of the bags. "It's summer vacation, and I've had so much to do. Grandpa Paul's been getting me up before the sun, and he'll probably start doing that again come Monday."

Stuart lowered the bags down hand over hand. Soon they were little more than dirty white blobs in the darkness, rocking like a pendulum as the wind tugged at them. Then the rocking stopped, and the twine pulled taut. It stayed that way for nearly a minute before going limp again. He drew the line back up, coiling it around his palm and elbow. The end of the twine was a hard little knot, with fraying wisps poking out the other side. He tucked it back into his pack, took out the brown cookie sack, and set it between his thighs. The first bite sent a chorus of sweetness through his mouth, and the cookie was barely damp when he swallowed. He'd eaten most of the first cookie before he unzipped another pocket, and took out a book.

The book was older than Stuart, and significantly worse used. Its covers were faded, and shiny with scotch tape. The spine was broken, the pages inside a loose sheaf whose edges had been darkened by generations of fingers. The three word title was ghostly in the green ghoul light of the glow stick; *Grimm's Fairy Tales.* Stuart broke his second cookie in half, put half in his mouth, and gently tossed the other half down between his feet. He took a bite of his half, made himself chew slowly, and swallowed. Below him the bags tore open, and the short, sharp cracks of splintering bone rang clearly in the night. They were followed by a low, grinding sound. It made Stuart think of millstones in the fairy stories. He found the page where he'd left off last time, and started reading.

"Once upon a time there were three goats," Stuart began. The story flowed from the page, and over his lips. Spoken aloud, it seemed to hang in the night air with a palpable weight. It was a story he hadn't heard himself since he was in kindergarten. The grinding noises grew quieter as he read, and there were fewer and fewer of them. Soon there was nothing but the water chatting with the bank below his feet. "And they lived happily ever after."

Stuart closed the book, and set it on top of his pack. There was another crunch from below, followed by a sound like the foundations of a house settling. Stuart smiled, and readjusted himself so he was laying down on the bridge with his head hanging over the edge.

"It's your turn now," he said. "Sing me a song."

Stuart closed his eyes, and listened. The song came; a deep rumble that echoed in the hollows of his heart, and made his pains feel far, far away. That sound held all the power of the earth, and all the fleeting beauty of a rainbow. The boy listened, and the song painted him a story. It told him of places he'd never seen, and things he'd never done with an eloquence beyond what the finest poetry could hope to manage. Stuart rolled over on his back, and stared at the darkness behind his eyes. He smiled up at nothing, and felt a weight he'd barely been aware he was carrying slide off of his shoulders. He stayed like that until the witch light of the glow stick went dark, and the song finally stilled. He left, but promised he would be back.

    ***

June dragged on like a tired old mule walking the same, rutted route every day. In the morning Grandpa Paul gave Stuart a list, and every evening he checked it. Some days Stuart managed to finish everything. Most days he didn't. Uncle Roger worked late, and sometimes when he finally came home he parked crooked. Once or twice he almost caught Stuart sneaking out of his window, but Roger was in no condition to tell his nephew apart from any other bouncing shadow. Gertrude was absent most days, but she was typically home by dinner time. There was usually another girl or two in tow, and they swept through the house like freshman furies. They scooped up anything edible, and blew on by in wild gales of laughter that smelled like strawberry lip gloss. Aunt Sophia watched her shows, and cooked meals. Twice a week she'd go into town to do some shopping, and once or twice she took Stuart with her to carry heavy things.

Stuart didn't mind June very much. Uncle Roger brought home a side of venison from a friend, and Stuart hid the bones behind a tree stump near the back fence. For a week or so there was so much food that even Stuart had a full belly most nights. Stuart continued his hikes to the bridge, and read from his stolen school book like a Saturday night Scheherazade. He always brought bones with, too, because he knew that was just as important as the story.

It was July when things got difficult. As soon as the calendar turned the page it was like a divine hand pulled the lampshade off the sun. The days were somehow brighter, and the heat even hotter. The air was so thick it felt like a damp washcloth pressed over Stuart's face. The first weekend the air conditioner wheezed, and died. Uncle Roger tried to fix it. He pulled

Stuart over to hold the thing up while he tinkered, and sent him running to get tools from the shed when his tinkering didn't work. After two days all of the residual chill had bled out, and the house began sweating like a living thing. Aunt Sofia set up fans in the windows at night, and kept the blinds down during the day, but it was all just so much ritual. Even soaking down the siding and wetting the roof didn't change how hot it was. If anything it felt even hotter. The second weekend of July Grandpa Paul stopped sleeping.

It didn't happen all at once. The first few days Grandpa Paul just stayed up later than he usually did, sitting bare-chested in the den. When Stuart prepared for his weekly sojourn, though, the television never went quiet. Stuart ventured out to go to the bathroom, and Grandpa Paul sat bathed in the black and white glow of vampire reruns. He glanced up when Stuart's door creaked, and Stuart rubbed his eyes as if he was still half asleep. The den didn't go silent until Stuart's window was gray with early dawn light. Stuart curled up on the mattress, and wrapped his arms around a belly full of disappointment.

That pattern held for weeks. By the time the second month of summer had drawn to a close Grandpa Paul would wake Stuart up, give him his chores, and then go to bed as his grandson got to work. Stuart looked for a chance to get away, but the old man sat sentinel every night until the dawn. The bones piled up in their hiding place, and Stuart's heart grew heavy. He tried to sing to himself, but the sun baked the song out of him. It shrank the cool, dark place inside him where the song lived, and soon the tune was like a memory of a memory. Like the smell of his mother's girlhood perfume, which he couldn't smell any longer for the heat baking the room.

It was the first Saturday of August when Stuart finished tearing down the back fence. He'd been swinging and stacking splintered wood in the rear yard since the sun had come up, and he was picking splinters from his hands when he trudged to the garage to wash up. His skin was tight and uncomfortable in a way only sweaty, sunburned skin could be, and the cold hose water wrung a gasp out of him. The sky was thick with clouds, and the breeze panted hot with the promise of rain. Stuart washed carefully, dried himself with a ragged towel, and put on the clean shirt he'd left there that morning. He kicked his shoes into a cubby next to the stairs, and opened the kitchen door.

A cold wind slapped Stuart across the face. He stood frozen in the doorway, his mouth hanging open. There was a deep thrumming in the house, like the whole structure was clearing its throat. The sound made his flesh prickle all the way to his scalp even more than the chill air. It was a

51

thoroughly modern sound, completely unlike the halting, shambling roar of their old air conditioners. Aunt Sofia came around the corner, and Stuart got a second shock. She was wearing her cucumber green summer dress, the one with a sheen on it that she usually wore only to church. She looked at him, and put one hand on her hip.

"Close the door Stuart, you're letting all the cool air out," she said. He did as she asked. Sofia looked him up and down, and her forehead drew into a creased frown that always made her look twice as old as she really was. She had her church pearls on too, and she fingered them nervously. "Go change, Stuart. Those clothes are dirty."

Stuart nodded, and stepped past his aunt. The kitchen was fragrant with the smell of pot roast, boiling vegetables and melting butter. The smell made his belly gurgle, but it also raised the hackles on his neck. They were good scents, but they didn't belong there. They were too rich, and too expensive for the mean little kitchen with its mismatched knobs and hodgepodge doors. The smell was like how his aunt sometimes put too much makeup on to hide a bruised cheekbone, or how Roger would swish mint wash around his mouth when he got home with whiskey between his teeth. Stuart turned back, but his aunt was bent over the oven and paying him no mind.

"Aunt Sofia," he said softly. "What's going on?"

"Your Uncle Stephen was good enough to send someone to fix the air conditioning," she said distractedly, tugging on a pair of oven mitts. "He's coming to eat, and he'll be staying the night. Now go change Stuart, supper's almost ready."

Stuart went. He floated down the hall, and as he passed the dining room a wave of conversation spumed over him. He didn't turn to look, just opened his door and stepped into his room. It was still hot on the other side of the hollow core door, and the air was heavy as he gulped it down. Stuart had his bag in hand, and his three changes of clothes packed before he realized what he was doing. He stopped, and stared into his frayed, stained school bag at the sum of his worldly possessions. He looked at the mostly empty dresser that smelled like old glue and cheap wine. He glanced over at the one bookshelf, and his eyes lingered on the mostly melted snow globe. At last his gaze settled on the window shade; a shadowy door glowing red like a closed eyelid at dawn. There was still time. All he had to do was step through, and he could be away before they noticed.

Away. Stuart closed his eyes, and the word echoed in his ears like a magic spell. An exotic word that could conjure him someplace else if he said it with the proper intonation, and just the right amount of belief. He'd barely managed to catch hold of the idea of Away, though, when it ripped down the middle. Red and blue flashing lights shone through the gap, and memories spilled out. He remembered the sheriff's deputy pulling him out of the ditch, and taking him down to the station. He recalled with perfect clarity trying to tell them why he'd run off, and how the men in county brown told him to be quiet until a guardian came. The feeling of Grandpa Paul's hand on his arm, tight enough to bruise the muscle and grind the bone as the old man signed him out of the station. He remembered the striped back he'd gotten behind the wood shed, and how his grandfather had told him to stop telling lies about his uncle. The stripes had been nothing compared to the other, deeper pains that had sent Stuart running in the first place. He saw in his mind's eye how every convulsion of his bowels had become a dreaded agony, and how every shit had left him gasping for a week after the night he'd run. He remembered the bloody ring around the toilet. His family blamed Gertrude. She never said anything, but sometimes when she looked at him, Stuart knew she knew what had happened to him.

Stuart looked up, and a shadow peered at him from the depths of his closet. It was a thick, heavy-shouldered thing with bright, gimlet eyes and wild hair. It held a sack of darkness, like a stage magician getting ready to pull his next trick out of a hat. The song came out of the sack. It was a deep, strong rumble that throbbed in his bones, and matched the pounding of his heart. Stuart opened his mouth, and the song flowed through him. He felt the story rushing in his veins, but this time it was different. This time he knew the characters, and he knew their actions. He knew, too, how the drama could play out. His hackles lay down, and his heart slowed. Strength flooded him. He met the shadow's gaze, and the shadow looked back at him from the cracked and cloudy mirror. It looked curious, as if wondering what Stuart was going to do next.

A car pulled up outside, and gravel crunched beneath the tires. The engine died, and a car door opened and shut. His aunt opened the front door, and a masculine voice greeted her. Stuart smiled, and the dark boy in the mirror smiled back. Stuart threw his bag in the closet, and changed his clothes. His reflection did the same, putting on the too-tight Sunday suit that stretched across his back and clung to the skinny stack of his ribs.

"Stuart, what are you doing in there?" Gertrude bawled, banging the flat of her hand on his door. "Hurry up!"

"Coming," Stuart called.

They were waiting for him in the dining room, dressed in their occasional formals. Grandpa Paul with his slicked back hair and somber suit, Uncle Roger in his high-collared, button down shirt, and even Gertrude in a soft, out-of-focus blue dress. They seemed like strangers at first glance; another family from a different life he'd never led. Even the dining room around them was different, from the lacy cloth over the table, to the polished platters that held their steaming meal. Only little Matt, squirming and struggling in his miniature brown suit, seemed truly unchanged.

Everyone sat in their usual tableau; the only difference was the man seated at Grandpa Paul's right hand. Even sitting he was tall, with oiled blonde hair and ears that held tight to his skull. He was dressed in crisscrossed shades of green, and with his narrow shoulders and long arms he looked like a particularly cultured serpent. Uncle Stephen looked up when Stuart stepped into the room, and gave him a wide, white grin. What Uncle Roger called his let-me-sell-you-some-Jesus smile.

"There you are Stuart," he said. "You had me worried. I thought for a minute you'd run out on us."

Uncle Roger snorted a laugh up his sleeve. Grandpa Paul chortled, and his shoulders stretched the seams on his jacket when they shook. Aunt Sofia frowned, and buckled Matt into his place. Gertrude smiled dutifully, but she looked down at her plate when she did it. Stuart smiled, but didn't say anything. Uncle Stephen pulled out the chair next to him and slapped the seat.

"Sit yourself," he said. Stuart sat. Stephen smiled at the room and held his hands out, palms up. "Before we begin, shall we pray?"

"Like he really gives a damn," Roger muttered under his breath. It was unclear if he was talking about Stephen or the powers that be, but when Grandpa Paul glared at him Roger took his father-in-law's hand, as well as his daughter's. Gertrude grasped her mother's hand, and Matt watched the whole, grown-up ritual curiously. Stephen took Grandpa Paul's hand, and turned to Stuart. Stuart hesitated, but finally took the offered hand.

"Now let us pray," Stephen said, bowing his head. The others followed suit. Matt looked at Stuart, who lowered his head and stared at the table. "Dear God, we thank you on this, your day of rest, for all that you made of our world and of us," Stephen began.

When he prayed, Stephen barely opened his mouth. It was as if he was trying to strain the backwater Parish accent through his teeth. He lowered his voice as well, giving the impression he was a bigger, softer-spoken man than he was. He continued thanking god for the crops he gave them, and for all the great and good things he chose to lavish his children with. He thanked god for his forgiveness, and as he did Stephen gently stroked his fingertips along the back of Stuart's hand. Stuart flinched.

"Amen," Stephen finally said.

"Amen," the others echoed, reaching for the meal. Stephen held Stuart's hand a moment longer, then released it and held out his plate to be filled.

"Good of you to finally make it out this way," Grandpa Paul said, slicing into the roast and slurping a strip of meat into his mouth. "They keeping you busy?"

"Very," Stephen said, buttering a roll. "We just finished the first summer boys' retreat. All the deacons pitched in, but even with ten of us it took quite a bit of doing."

"Just boys?" Roger asked, chewing a mouthful of green beans. Stephen smiled again; his big, white smile.

"For the first year," he said. "Probably for the second too. We might open a girls' program if there's interest, but we'd need a lot more volunteers for it."

"I volunteer then," Roger said, swallowing and sniggering. "You can have Trudy for the summer."

"Daddy!" Gertrude said, putting enough emphasis into the word that the syllables bulged at the seams. Roger rolled his eyes, and put another forkful of vegetables in his mouth.

"If I didn't have to hear that for three months, I'd consider taking out a loan to help get the thing running," Roger said, leaning forward and speaking in a slurred stage whisper.

"I'll hold you to that," Stephen said.

Conversation came and went like the tide. Grandpa Paul thanked Stephen for his help, and Stephen maintained it was nothing. Roger asked about his brother-in-law's job, and Stephen confirmed he was putting in more time with his accounting firm than ever before. He hinted management had taken notice, and there were rumors of a promotion. Sofia smiled, and told him how proud she was in between trying to feed Matt and make sure he didn't get anything that stained on either of them. Stuart kept quiet, and ate in small, measured bites. He wasn't hungry, but knew if he didn't eat he'd draw attention to himself. He was so focused on disappearing that when Stephen laid his hand on Stuart's shoulder, he almost choked.

"It's too bad you couldn't come with, Stuart," Stephen said. "It would have been a lot of fun."

"Boy has his chores," Grandpa Paul said, gesturing with a fork at his grandson before stabbing another thick slice of roast. "Boy wants to learn more about Jesus, he can read the good book like everyone else in this house. Isn't that right?"

"Yes, sir," Stuart said. Stephen left his hand where it was a moment longer, then turned back to his own plate. A moment passed, then another as Stephen chewed and swallowed thoughtfully.

"Have you been keeping up on your reading, Stuart?" Stephen asked. Stuart nodded, but didn't look up. "Good, that's good. Your mother-"

"Is of no consequence," Grandpa Paul said. His voice had lost all its fondness. It was cold, hard, and sharp; a knife drawn out of its kidskin sheath and held at the ready. No one said anything. No one looked at the patriarch. Stuart held his breath. Grandpa Paul slashed another hunk from the roast, and the rhythm of forks, knives, and spoons picked up right where it had left off.

In time there was nothing left but greasy pots and empty plates. Matt squirmed, rubbing at his eyes and fussing. Sofia slid him out of the high chair, and walked him toward the stairs. Roger hooked a thumb in his waist band, and upended his beer. Gertrude started stacking plates, and Stuart got up to help. The corners of Grandpa Paul's mouth turned down, but he didn't say anything as Stuart shuffled into the kitchen and set his arm load on the counter. Stuart hung his jacket on a hook, rolled up his sleeves, and filled the sink. Gertrude brought the rest of the dishes in, and picked up the drying towel. Stuart barely noticed the congealing grease and thick, clotted butter he wiped out of the crevices of the serving wear. He stared out the small, dark window at the small, dark path of the Harradan Road. The shadow boy overlaid the coming night outside, and stared back at Stuart with cagey, knowing eyes.

"What are you smiling at?" Gertrude asked.

"Hmmm?" Stuart glanced over. "Was I smiling?"

Gertrude shrugged, but she didn't ask again. Stuart washed, and she dried. He hummed the song quietly. The vibration numbed his lips, and put a tingle in his nose. The dishwater had turned a sick shade of gray, and he'd nearly finished cleaning by the time he heard the men head to the porch. Two pairs of heavy boots, followed by the short, sharp slap of dress shoes. Stuart stopped humming, and handed the last plate to his cousin.

"I'm gonna get ready for bed," Stuart said.

Gertrude looked at him for a long moment. There was something in her eyes, one part empathy and one part anxiety that was too old for her face. She opened her mouth, but her words got stage fright. Finally she shook her head, and turned away from him. Stuart took his jacket, and on his way past the counter palmed one of the steak knives.

Stuart slipped back into the darkness of his bedroom, and changed into black jeans and a ragged, black tee shirt. He quietly raised the shade on his window. Drifts of shadow lay on the grass, and the sky was heavy with clouds. He slowly pushed up his window, and jammed thin, wooden blocks under each side. Just to be safe. He clipped his small flashlight to his belt loop, and crawled beneath the covers. The wind blew, and beckoned through the open window.

"Not yet," Stuart whispered into the gloom. "Soon. But not yet."

Hours dragged by. Rain fell in short bursts, but never stayed long. Roger smoked half a pack of cigarettes, and drank two more bottles of beer before trumping up the stairs. Grandpa Paul made up the hide-a-bed in the den, chatting with Stephen all the while. Stuart couldn't hear what the old man said, but his voice was unmistakable through the walls. They said goodnight, and Grandpa Paul went upstairs. The metal frame of the hide-a-bed creaked, groaned, and finally settled. Wind blew, and the bedside clock buzzed. Stuart lay in bed listening, his mouth dry and his palms damp. He heard the sound he'd been listening for one minute after midnight; a slight creak of the bed frame, and a soft footfall on the living room floor.

Stuart shifted, and pulled the blanket up to his chin. The wind picked up, and any other sounds were lost. He stared at his bedroom door, and ran his tongue over his teeth. After an eternity, the door knob turned. He shut his eyes, and took long, slow breaths of night air. He made himself relax, the way a cat relaxed before it pounced.

"Stuart?" Stephen whispered. Stuart didn't move, or speak. Stephen crossed the threshold and shut the door behind him. There was no lock. "Stuart, are you awake?

Stephen crossed the small expanse of floor, and stood over the bed. He smelled like English Leather, and below that a sharper, riper scent of meat that had gone sour, and started to rot. It was a feverish smell, and it almost made Stuart choke. Soft fingers stroked over the blanket, trailing up Stuart's leg. They paused at his hip, squeezed slightly, and continued over his chest.

"Wakey, wakey Stuart," Stephen said, his voice practically drooling as he pulled back the cover. "It's time for you to-"

Stuart's arm whipped out from under the covers, and the knife cut off whatever his uncle had been about to say. Stephen hissed, clutched at his hand and stumbled back. Stuart kicked the covers off, scrambling head first over the window sill. Stephen snatched at him, but his hand was bleeding and his grip slid off Stuart's ankle as the boy hauled himself into the night. He sprawled, and the air whooshed out of his lungs. He clawed at the dew-damp grass, and stumbled half a dozen steps towards the woods. He chanced a look back at the window, and saw his uncle staring out at him. Stephen's eyes flashed like those of a cat, and he smiled. It was a small, thin thing that pulled tight against his teeth without revealing them. It drew his thin eyebrows down, and hooded his eyes. It was his true smile; the one that he didn't show to any of the others. Stephen lowered his head, and slithered out the window. His left hand was dark where he gripped the sill, but none of the strength had left it.

Stuart ran. His bare feet dug furrows in the dirt, and his hair blew back from his sweaty face. His belly clenched, and his ribs ached, but he didn't let that slow him down. He pelted toward the Harradan Road. He lowered his head, the bellows of his breath and the heady roar of blood in his veins too loud to know whether Stephen was still coming after him or not.

Stuart slowed his pace a dozen heartbeats into the cloying shadows of the abandoned road. He opened his mouth, and took shallow breaths of the green air. The ache in his guts tightened, and then slowly relaxed. He strained to see, but the only thing that stood out was the mouth of the Harradan Road; a train tunnel of dark blue against the surrounding blackness. He strained his ears, but didn't hear a thing. The knife's grip was slick in his hand, as if the wood had been smeared with soap. Carefully Stuart took out his flashlight. He had his thumb on the button when something grabbed him.

"Gotcha you little bastard," Stephen snarled. An arm slid around Stuart's torso, and trapped his limbs against his trunk. Stuart strained, and felt some give, but the grip was tenacious. Fingernails dug into Stuart's bare arm, and a slick, oily thing snatched at his wrist. He screamed and dropped the knife, along with his flashlight. He writhed, bucked, and fought against the coils trying to hold him tight. Damp silk pressed the back of his neck, and a heavy bulge ground against the small of Stuart's back. It jumped and pulsed against him, swollen and excited. "Fight all you want. It won't change anything."

The air grew thick as blood in Stuart's throat. He couldn't breathe, and lights began flashing behind his eyes. He went limp, and Stephen grunted. The grip around Stuart held for a moment, then broke. He spilled free, and tumbled into one of the deep ruts of the road. The hard earth bruised his shoulder and banged his knee, but he was free.

Stephen cursed, and grass whispered against his palms as he ran his hands over the ground. Stuart rolled away, and put his foot in a wheel rut. He walked quietly, dragging his toes through the dirt and limping like a blind man. He'd made it a hundred yards when light sputtered to life behind him. He kept walking, eyes straining to pick out the shapes of the trees. Behind him, Stephen started walking, sweeping the small light back and forth across the path.

"Stuart, don't do this," Stephen said. He didn't raise his voice much, but it carried down the path all the same. He paused to glance behind some trees, then kept walking. "Please, Stuart. You're going to get hurt out here. Neither one of us wants that. You know I don't want that."

Stuart closed his ears. He listened, but the words were hollow, nonsense noises like the cawing of a crow, or the far-off barking of stray dogs. The wheel ruts grew shallower, and Stuart lengthened his stride. He hitched from side to side, rolling like a sailor fresh off a boat. A root stabbed into his foot, but Stuart clamped his jaws shut and kept walking. Branches caught at his clothes, but he was careful not to break them as he passed. Then the flow of chatter stopped, and Stuart heard something that chilled his blood. Stephen laughed. The light approached faster.

"Come on now, stop this foolishness," Stephen said. He was still laughing as he closed the distance. "You're bleeding Stuart. It isn't bad yet, but if you keep walking on that foot then it will be by tomorrow. How are you going to explain that to Grandpa Paul?"

The wheel ruts ended, and for a moment Stuart stood completely still. The flashlight bobbed closer, bouncing as his uncle began to jog toward him. Panic dug into Stuart's muscles and froze him solid. He breathed deep, and the smell of the river invaded his nostrils. He didn't think. He ignored the pain in his foot, and the looming barriers of trees. He forgot about being quiet. All that mattered was getting to the bridge, and he ran toward it with everything left in him.

Stephen called out, but Stuart couldn't hear him. He ran with his arms protecting his face, snapping through dry branches and crashing through prickly bushes. He burst out of the forest, arms swinging and legs pumping. He leaped over the low-slung chain, and pounded over the loose, rotting boards of the Abattoir Bridge. He didn't stop until he'd reached the crumbling edge of the center span, panting, gasping and bleeding.

"There's nowhere else for you to run, Stuart," Stephen said.

Stephen stepped over the chain. In the dim light his face was a shadowy thing full of teeth, and a wet, glimmering hunger. His tongue snaked over his lips, leaving them glistening as he came closer. He held the flashlight in his bloody right hand, and kept his left hand half-hidden behind his thigh. He smiled his tight-lipped smile again, taking a long, ragged breath. He was halfway to Stuart when the bridge shuddered, and something shifted down below. Stephen stood stock still, arms outstretched like a tightrope walker without a net. He held the bloodied knife in one hand. Stuart grinned, and tilted his head slightly.

"Who's that clip-clopping across my bridge?" Stuart asked.

The words had barely left his mouth when something big reached from beneath the bridge. Something with claws that streamed brackish, bloody water as it took hold of his uncle in a hand big enough to encircle his torso. It swept Stephen over the side, and the knife fell from his slick fingers. Stuart's uncle screamed once, and the light went out as it fell in the water. There was a wet crunch, followed by a tearing, rending sound. The sounds lengthened and repeated; the slick grind of millstone teeth singing in terrible harmony. Stuart sat down, and dangled his feet over the side of the Abattoir Bridge. He rested his chin in his hands and smiled. There were over two hundred bones in the human body, his science teacher had said last year. Stuart listened, and counted them one by one.

Assault on Olympus

There were five of them on duty, gathered around an impromptu campfire. They crouched around the flames, in the lee side of their war wagon, paying more attention to each other than to the road they were parked near. They wore no uniforms, but they were still of a kind. Stubble stained their necks and cheeks, and thick smudges of ash left streaks behind their ears as well as on their hands. They wore ill-fitting surplus gear, and carried a variety of weapons that looked personal rather than standard-issue. Their eyes were hard, though, and their grins had a harshness to them as they passed canteens back and forth round the blaze.

"Not that I'm complaining, Mic-Mic," one of the older men said to their squad leader, the only one to sport a thick, full beard. "But why the beef-up on road duty?"

"City's clear, Trav," Mic-Mic said, accepting a canteen that reeked of basement rotgut. He swigged, grimacing at the taste before he passed it on. "Word came down from on high, said we're gonna take back what's ours. But before we do that, though, we gotta make sure we keep what we've already got."

"Seriously, though, what are *we* going to do?" asked a younger, blonde man cradling an AR-15. Athletic tape was wrapped around the weapon's grip, and he seemed to be the only one actually watching the night. "I mean, what are we going to do that he can't? And if someone comes along that he needs to deal with personally, how are we supposed to handle that?"

The blonde trailed off when he realized the circle around him had gone quiet. His head snapped away from the road, and he found the rest of his detail staring at him in silence. Mic-Mic looked down from his busted-out camping chair, disapproval writ large in his craggy features. He looked like a grizzled warlord from another era, holding the barrel of his rifle like it was some kind of scepter.

"You want to ask that question a little louder, kid?" Mic-Mic said. "The wind is blowing the wrong way, so he might not have heard you the first time."

The blonde blanched, and his jaw worked. His eyes rolled, and he jerked his head like he thought a ghost might appear out of the night. It didn't take long before the rest of the detail was snorting, trying not to laugh. After a few moments of watching the younger man's genuine terror, none of them could hold back their guffaws. Mic-Mic didn't join in, but there was amusement in his gaze. Despite the laughter, the blonde didn't seem reassured.

"Can... can he really hear me?" he asked, with all the sincerity of a child hearing about Jesus for the first time.

"Can he? Maybe," Mic-Mic said with a shrug of his bearish shoulders. "Who knows? Better to assume he can, and be on the safe side, than to think he can't and say the wrong thing."

Mic-Mic leaned back in his chair, the plastic wicker creaking beneath his weight. A breeze blew through the night, rippling the shadows. It smelled of dry, dead things, and radiation poisoning. One of the other militiamen leaned forward, his shoulders hunched as he turned a foil-wrapped package sitting on a stone at the edge of the flames.

"Whether he can or can't doesn't really matter, though," Mic-Mic said. "We have our orders, and those orders said watch the roads. Doesn't matter if the only thing trying to get into the city are squirrels with gut tumors. We stop them, ask for their papers, and send them on their way. You get me?"

"Yes, sir!" the blonde said, raising his hand in a salute that still had some snap to it.

Mic-Mic nodded approvingly. He had his mouth open to speak when his face went slack. His jaw kept dropping, hanging open nearly to his chest. His eyes welled with tears, then with blood. It spilled from his nose, and ran over his tongue. A hideous, wet, crunching sound reverberated in his mouth as his head caved in on itself. His skull popped like a rotting melon, squirting blood and brain pulp in all directions.

A mingled cry of disgust and fear went through the squad as they leaped to their feet, scrambling for their weapons. Safeties clicked off, and they turned toward the night. Flashlight beams stabbed into the darkness, and they shouted. They shouted for whoever was out there to surrender. They shouted threats. They shouted for the bogeymen to show themselves. Without their leader, the cries devolved into a single nonsense demand; the sound of children woken in the night, screaming at shadows.

There was a cough from the roadside; a flat snap like someone stepping on a dead tree branch. Higgins's left eye burst like an infected sore, and he stumbled back. His heel caught on one of the stones lining the fire pit, and he fell into the flames. He was dead before the blaze could so much as kiss his coat.

The others broke, running for cover. Clark ducked behind the front of the armored panel truck, but he was too busy looking over his shoulder to see the shape ahead of him in the darkness. He crashed into someone, stumbling back as he tried to bring his weapon to bear. Strong hands grabbed Clark's head, and twisted. His neck snapped, and he fell on his stomach with his eyes staring at the sky. Smythe was watching where he was going, and when he ducked around the rear of the vehicle he saw the tall, black-clad figure waiting for him. Smythe opened up, firing a three-round burst. The figure held up an arm to protect itself. The bullets shredded black cloth before ricocheting off dark steel. The figure stepped forward, and drove a fist into Smythe's chest. Bones crunched as his rib cage caved in, and he dropped like a rag doll.

Jackson was the only one left, whipping his head from side to side. His greasy blonde hair fell in front of his eyes, and he twitched his head to clear his vision. Fear had welded his hands to his weapon.

"S-state your name!" Jackson said, his intended shout coming out in a strained rasp. He cleared his throat, and tried again. "I don't want to shoot you, but I will!"

"No you won't," said a calm, lightly-accented voice.

Jackson turned, nearly tripping over his own boots as he leveled his weapon at the speaker. She was slender, and wearing black battle dress uniform. She strode into the fire light, and black eyes looked out from the shade of her black cap. Her face bore the classic lines of Korean beauty, but it was hard to notice beneath the scars that crisscrossed her skull, and seamed her forehead. She stood calmly, hands at her sides, and made no effort to reach for the sidearm tilted forward on her hip.

"I will," Jackson said. He raised his weapon a little higher, lining up the iron sights in the center of the woman's face. "Do not test me!"

She smiled, revealing teeth too straight and too white to be natural. Her eyes narrowed, the scar tissue puckering at the corners. Jackson took a breath, and started to squeeze the trigger. Before he could drop the hammer, though, something yanked his weapon out of his hands. The strap jerked him off his feet, snapping across his shoulders and sprawling him in the dirt. His weapon imploded, the steel and high-impact polyurethane crumpling in on itself until it was an unrecognizable mess. It dropped in a heap, the twisted barrel sticking out like a scrap metal question mark.

Other figures stepped out of the night, convening around the fire. From the road walked a long, lean man with a clean shaved face, and a complexion more at home in the Southwest deserts than the capitol. He carried a small-caliber Bushmaster in the crook of one arm with the casual air of someone comfortable with its use. From the rear of the panel truck came another man. He was tall, and moved strangely. Every step was precise, powerful, and there was a barely audible hum that accompanied his steps. He had short, dark hair and a dark beard, but patches of his skin were bare and shiny with burn scars. From the front of the truck came a hulking figure in full armor, his face covered by a balaclava. He carried a

63

steel case under one arm. Despite the ease with how he carried it, the case sank into the ground when he put it down. There were no insignia on their uniforms, or flash on their caps. They were ghosts; black knights who wore no colors, and flew no banners.

"Well done Keun," the tall man with the burn scars said. He turned his attention to Jackson. The man blinked, and his eyes whirred as they re-adjusted. "Who are you?"

"Jackson," the blond said, getting slowly up on his hands and knees. He cut his eyes to the left, then the right, looking for somewhere to run. There was nowhere to go. He knew it, they knew it, and he knew they knew. A tremor went through him, and he tried to clamp down on it. "R-Robert Jackson."

"Do you have a rank?" the man with the mechanical eyes asked.

"N-no, sir," Jackson said, forcing himself to look into the cyborg's face. "Not anymore."

"What did it used to be?" he asked.

"Corporal, sir," Jackson said. "I... I can't remember my numbers anymore."

"At ease, Corporal Jackson," the man said. "I have questions. Answer them truthfully, and you will not end up like the rest of your squad."

Jackson looked at the sprawled bodies of the men he'd stood guard with. He sucked in a breath that smelled like blood and cordite, gagged, and spat. He got to his knees, and raised his head.

"What do you want to know?" he asked, his eyes darting from one black figure to another.

"He cannot hear you," the looming shape from the front of the truck said. His accent was thick, and unmistakably Russian. "You are more than twenty miles from his palace. Over noise of city, you are at least twice as far as his ears can reach."

Jackson stared at the man. His mouth was open to ask the questions that filled his eyes, but he shut his trap, and swiveled his gaze back to the man with the digitized eyes. "May I stand?"

"As you wish," the burned man said. Once Jackson was on his feet, he continued. "Are there any other squads within hailing distance? Are you expected to keep in radio contact?"

"No, sir," Jackson said. "Road crews are tasked with watch points, and we keep signal fires lit. Each crew has a radio, and flares, but they're rationed. We're told not to use any juice we don't need."

"Inspections?" Keun asked, idly glancing over Jackson's shoulder and into the night.

"Rare," Jackson said. "A few months ago, there was at least one a week. Now? They'd only happen if there was some kind of alarm raised."

"Are there any other checkpoints between here and downtown?" the cyborg asked. "Passwords? Documentation?"

"No," Jackson said. He jerked his head at the modified panel truck, its civilian frame sagging slightly under the weight of steel plates inexpertly welded to its hide. "Only Sunshine Units drive these rigs. Someone sees it, they either salute, or run. If you're hailed by another unit, they'll send a series of three blasts over the radio. Return four, and it means everything is steady."

"What's White House security like?" the man with the rifle over his arm asked.

"Militia walks the gates day and night," Jackson said. "Trenches and bunkers were dug around the manor. Heavy gun emplacements are installed on every side, and there's a billet of men in each wing. There's two war wagons parked at every gate, and most of them have a heavy caliber mount in the rear."

The squad members looked at each other, and they exchanged some kind of silent communication. The leader stepped forward, and looked down at Jackson with his unsettling, camera-shutter gaze. Jackson squared his shoulders, and held his head up.

"I am giving you a chance," the man said. "Take a pack, and go. With luck, you'll be into the suburbs by dawn. I would recommend you keep going. This place is about to get very hot."

Jackson nodded, moving slowly. He took his pack, and looted the canteens from the dead men. He took what grub was left, and tied his bedroll with an extra belt. He hefted the pack onto his back, and was about to leave when the squad leader spoke again.

"Take a weapon with you," he said. "It's dangerous out there."

"Sir?" Jackson said, hesitation clear in his voice.

"I don't spare a man the sword just to have him set upon by others." The cyborg's eyes narrowed, and whirred as he re-focused. "Take a weapon, and a spare clip. You'll need them out there."

Jackson did as he was bid, ensuring that he grasped the weapon by the barrel, and slung it slowly over his shoulder. He picked up two fallen magazines, and tucked them into the breast pockets of his coat. Jackson turned to the man who'd spared him, and saluted. The squad leader nodded, and Jackson turned toward the rough country. He knew as well as the team did that the roads were full of predators. Humans, and things that had once been human.

"That was a risk, Hassan," Keun said, though there was no judgment in the words.

"Maybe," the cyborg said. "Rodriguez, how is our time?"

"Minutes to spare," the rifleman said, flipping the top on his field chronometer. "Still, if we want to deliver our package on time, we'd better bounce."

Hassan nodded, and turned on his heel with a whisper of servos. "Rodriguez, Keun, strip their colors and ride up front. Kemidov, secure the package in the rear. You and I will stay out of sight until we reach our destination."

The Russian nodded, and lifted the smooth, metal case as if it weighed nothing. Hassan opened the rear doors of the panel truck, clambering into one of the jump seats. Kemidov followed, the vehicle rocking on its axles as he secured the case to the floor with a tow strap, then took a seat himself. Rodriguez picked up a black cap with the radiation symbol on it, dusted it off on his thigh, and put it on his head. He stripped the jacket from man at the rear of the truck, and slid it on. He coughed at the stink, and spat into the dust. Keun took the leader's coat, and wiped the blood from the collar. It slipped right off the windbreaker, leaving the black material glistening, but otherwise unsuspicious.

Rodriguez removed the flash suppressor from his rifle, stowed the weapon between the seats, and slid behind the wheel. Keun shut the rear doors, and got in the passenger seat just as the rig roared to life. Rodriguez dropped the clutch, shifted into gear, and they slewed onto the road. Rodriguez kicked the gear up, and the team barreled down the highway past the city limit sign.

D.C. looked like a cancer ward. Boulevards that had once been robust with traffic were anemic in the flickering whites of the few streetlamps that were still lit, and what few people who were out scuttled like roaches crossing no-man's-land. Windows that had gleamed with promise and life were cataracted with filth, where they hadn't been shattered. The green spaces so carefully trimmed by the city's minders were now ragged and dying. The leaves and shoots sagged, the sickly color of old nicotine stains. The stone towers that had gleamed white in bright sunshine were now the washed-out, no-color color of wraiths. The shade of hospital sheets a hundred people had expired on.

It was the monuments that had suffered the worst, though. The proud obelisk dedicated to General Washington was snapped in half, with its ragged stump jutting up obscenely. Lincoln's head had been removed, turning him into a forgotten king upon a marble throne. Across the Potomac, the resting place of the country's gold star troops in Arlington had been broken, the markers smashed and cracked from some colossal impact. The sacred ground itself was shattered; a jagged schism through the graveyard like hell itself had swallowed up the honored dead. A hundred other indignities had been levied on the faces of the city's history, erasing the rulers and scholars who had come before. In their places were the blooming, black petals of the nuclear flower, and the legend inscribed beneath them. The tag was everywhere, painted by the Sunshine Units that patrolled the city in their gas-mask and hazmat glory. *All Hail The Broken Arrow*, the words proclaimed in three-foot high letters.

"Didn't think it would be so fucking ugly," Rodriguez said. He shook his head, tugging the bill of his stolen cap a little lower. A pair of motorbikes roared out of a side alley, cheap methanol fumes belching from their tail pipes as the riders poured on speed. Men and machines both howled like wild animals on the prowl. "I saw the satellite shots same as everyone... but it's different, you know, actually looking at it at ground level."

"Pyongyang was worse," Keun said from the passenger seat. She was impassive, her hands in her lap, and her face forward. If talking about the fate of her home city, or the dozens of other cities that had been reduced to glass and fallout the past few years, bothered her it didn't register on her features. "But he did not mean to stay there, once he had conquered it. There, he was sending a message."

A quad-runner darted out of a side alley, sliding up beside them. The rider wore a helmet and gas mask, and he slapped his hand twice on the side of the truck. A moment later, the radio hissed, and three, sharp beeps sounded. Hassan reached up to the radio and pressed the return sequence. The rider at their side saluted, and opened his throttle. The four-wheeler snarled off down a side street. The team breathed a collective sigh. Their luck couldn't hold forever, but at least for the time being the dice seemed to be rolling in their favor.

"Curb appeal is the least of our problems," Hassan said. He turned his left arm over, pulling back the shredded sleeve. The black finish of his prosthetic arm wasn't even scratched, but he ran a full system diagnostic to be sure. His fingers, then his wrist, then his elbow all flexed, the systems coming up green in his internal heads up display. When he was sure all his systems had made it through the skirmish, he glanced over his shoulder at Kemidov. "Status on the package?"

Kemidov ran his hand over the box. A read-out blipped on for a moment, then faded. The Russian nodded.

"Ready for delivery," Kemidov said. "Plenty of time before the decision is out of our hands."

The radio crackled, and spat out a garbled set of codes. The speaker was older, male, and sounded like he was shouting through a helmet. Responses fired back, the words camouflaged by thick accents, face masks, and static. Rodriguez frowned, his lips compressing into a hard line as he tried to follow the chatter.

"Make any of that out?" Hassan asked.

"Some," Rodriguez said. "So much for no babysitters. Looks like a patrol found our mess. Troops are being put on high-alert, and it sounds like a lot of them are getting called in tight. They want a ring around the target."

"Like he needs men with guns," Hassan said. "Get us off the main roads. Head for green six if it's open, green twelve if not."

Rodriguez flicked the headlamps off, tapped the brakes, and spun the wheel. The truck stuttered, drifted, and slid down a side street. They were half a block into the darkness when a truck with a bed-mounted .50 caliber roared past their rear, followed by a mixed pack of ATVs and motorcycles. Kemidov turned his head to watch their back trail, but none of the patrol reversed course for a better look at them. No one hailed them over the radio, either.

Rodriguez zigged and zagged through side streets and back alleys, the gloom barely illuminated by the panel truck's running lights. Most of the roads were crumbling, flanked by the dead shells of scrapped cars, or the black hulks of burned buildings. Windows were almost universally dark, except where hand-cranked camp lanterns and old candles tried their best to hold back the night. They ran into two barricades, but both were old, and neither was manned. Kemidov moved them easily, sliding the half-ton concrete buttresses back in place before clambering into the truck once more.

The closer they got to their destination, the fewer of the buildings were occupied. Every now and again, though, a face peered out at them. The faces were drawn, wary, and dirty, their eyes shining with the feral light of frightened animals staring out of their burrows. When the watchers saw the tags on the sides of the panel truck, they pulled away from the windows. Most of them drew the curtains, if they had them. The truck's Geiger counter started to crackle, the noise ratcheting up as they approached ground zero. After a dozen miles of squeezing through potholes and dark lanes, Rodriguez took his foot off the gas. The truck coasted to the mouth of an alley. Ahead of them, past a few shield walls and a crowd of people, was their target.

Unlike the rest of the city, ground zero burned bright. The white mansion was pristine among the surrounding blight, its walls bathed in the light of a hundred electric lamps. The lawns were just as sickly as the rest of the city, and the bushes were charred around the edges, but the house itself still stood. If one could ignore the ragtag militiamen walking the grounds in their protective suits, the heavy weapon emplacements, and the dark banners fluttering from the building's eaves, it might have been possible to believe hope was still in residence at 1600 Pennsylvania Avenue.

The spark lights drew penitents from the city as well, summoning them like a campfire pulled ragged moths out of the night. The black iron fences were thronged with people, all of them desperate to be heard. Some shouted, waving their grimy hands, or gripping the bars with white knuckles. Others knelt and prayed, touching their heads to the pavement and prostrating themselves on the cracked sidewalks. Open sores wept pus down their cheeks, and their teeth sat loose in gray, receding gums. Blind eyes bulged from many sockets, and hair had fallen in clumps from withered skulls. The sea of atomic lepers stared at the seat of freedom, and moaned for the tyrant who sat atop it to deliver them from the misery his very presence had caused.

"Lot of bystanders," Rodriguez said. "Thought the whole point of this thing was short range? Minimize unwanted damage, and such?"

"They will run," Keun said. "As soon as they hear gunfire, they will scatter like pigeons."

Hassan leaned forward, blinking as he focused on the street. More vans and trucks were converging on the space. Some of the vehicles stayed in a holding pattern, driving round and round in slow circles. Others stopped at the front gate. Several of the units drove off again, but the gates opened for vehicles that packed heavy ordinance. After the third big gun bounced over the curb, Hassan nodded.

"Start your De-Cell, Rodriguez," Hassan said. "Keun, I want your focus on the gates. When we get close, hit them. If we get stopped there, we're dead in the water."

"Understood," Keun said.

"Kemidov," Hassan continued, raising his voice over the gargle of the Geiger counter. "Once we're inside, make some noise. Get his attention."

"Should I take out the trucks?" Kemidov asked.

"You hit the bunkers," Hassan said. "Rodriguez, you and I will neutralize the militia. Understood?"

Rodriguez tore open a Velcro pocket on his vest, and slid out a field syringe. The case was surgical steel, but a window ran the length of the injector to show how much of the contents were left. The liquid inside was clear, and looked harmless. Rodriguez pushed the sleeve of his windbreaker away from his left wrist, and turned his arm over. He unscrewed the cover, gritted his teeth, and slipped the tip of the needle into the confluence of veins in his wrist. The sweet spot was easy to find; there was a puncture scar from previous injections of lesser quality and quantity. He pushed the plunger, teeth gritted. When the needle was empty, he plucked it out, and tossed the syringe to the floor. He sucked in a breath, and his eyes shot open. The pupils were so wide his eyes were nearly black.

"Understood," Rodriguez said, dropping the truck into gear, and putting the pedal to the metal.

The truck rolled down the lane, picking up speed as it went. They drew no attention at first, but once the engine started roaring some of the irregulars glanced in their direction. They sped past the first half-wall of sandbags, bouncing a guard's head off the front bumper. His helmet smashed the right headlight, and he spun three times before falling in a heap. Men turned, peering and shouting, each of them trying to figure out what was happening, and what they were supposed to do. Rodriguez clipped an ATV, sending its rider soaring. He flew into the bystanders, which made the more sensate among them take notice. A dozen men in gas masks leaped up from where they were resting at the front gate, frantically trying to shove the bars closed. If they'd managed to close it, the barrier might have stopped them.

Keun leaned forward in her seat, her eyes narrowed. She took harsh, tearing breaths, and gritted her teeth. Veins pulsed in her temples, and the cords in her neck stood out. In front of them the iron gate slowed, as if the militia were pushing against a gale force wind. The iron crumpled like a giant hand had wrapped around the bars, and squeezed. Some of the guards let go. Those who weren't fast enough howled as their fingers were severed, or their hands crushed. The gates smashed inwards, tearing free from the supports. The wreckage pinwheeled across the lawn, gouging trenches in the earth, shattering windows, and crushing those unfortunate enough to be in its way.

The panel truck rocked over the curb, and skated through the torn gateway. Small arms fire ricocheted off the welded plate armor, and one round cracked the windscreen. Bystanders were screaming now, bolting in all directions like startled sheep. One of the fifty-calibers swiveled, and opened fire. Most of the bullets went wide, digging trenches in the dirt or whining off into the surrounding buildings, but enough of them found their mark to make the panel truck shudder. Rodriguez jerked the wheel, sending the truck into a slide. It spun, clipping one of the other weapon platforms, and rocking it onto two wheels.

"Bail out," Rodriguez said, stepping out of the panel truck as smoothly as if it was sitting still. He snatched his rifle with him, socked it to his shoulder, and started firing short, concentrated bursts. Most of them winged off the gunner's shields, but they made the shooters duck. Two of them didn't duck fast enough, and gore spurted out the backs of their heads before they could wrap their fingers around their triggers.

Hassan kicked open the rear doors, and was out on the lawn in a single, fluid movement. Heavy hammers raked the side of the truck, punching into the rear cargo compartment. Hassan gripped the rear door, and servos whined as the metal crumpled, and tore. He ripped it off the hinges, cocked his hips, and hurled the door at the machine gunner like an ungainly discus. It wavered, but when it hit the door ripped the gun right off its mounts. What was left of the gunner hit the ground with a sound like wet laundry on a concrete floor.

"Any time now, big guy," Rodriguez called, ducking down behind the front of the truck and dumping his empty clip. He slid a second one in smoothly enough it looked like a magic trick, and tilted his head a quarter inch to his left just as a bullet tore through the air where it had been. It was like he was playing dodge ball, instead of being shot at.

Kemidov stepped out of the truck, setting the package on the ground. He rounded the rear of the truck, and turned to face one of the entrenched bunkers on the lawn. He started walking, arms swinging at his sides, head up, and chest out. Rifles cracked, the rounds hammering the Kevlar weave and the plates beneath. They didn't shatter, like traditional ceramic plates would. Instead, they deformed, bending inward like butter under the impacts. If he noticed the bullets' impact, he gave no sign. Kemidov leaned forward, pumped his arms, and ran headlong into the hail of fire. He lowered his shoulder, and when he hit the wall the concrete shattered like it had been made of sugar glass.

Panic held the field. Grenades bounced across the lawn, but they did more damage to the militia and the grounds than to the assault team. Hassan and Rodriguez destroyed what armor was left standing, leaving behind blood-drenched, bullet-ridden hulks. Keun picked off stragglers, using the truck for cover and firing across the hood. The second emplacement on the front lawn exploded, and Kemidov walked out of the fire. He batted at a flame on his shoulder, and pulled at the melted section of his armor. The lead-lined patch fell away, revealing undamaged, maggot-white flesh through the ragged hole.

"Think we got his attention?" Rodriguez asked, plucking a fresh clip from the small of his back and hammering it home.

The question was no sooner out of his mouth when the front doors of the mansion boomed open, and a figure emerged. He was tall, broad-shouldered, and he had the square-cut good looks made famous by a thousand recruitment posters. Sergeant Jason Quinn, former army ranger, had been the only survivor of the nuclear accident, but rather than being left as a withered mummy rotten with cancer, he'd become something else. A walking force of mutually assured destruction that the American military had renamed Liberty's Arrow. For a time he had maintained the status quo, keeping the world on the brink of uneasy peace. Then something changed. Whether the accident had long-term effects on his mind, he'd gone mad with power, or he just realized there was no real authority over him anymore, he'd decided to alter the balance of the world to his own liking. Here, with his white hair spilling down his back in a thick, tangled mane, naked but for a tattered American flag, he didn't look like a soldier. He didn't even look like the champion he'd once pretended to be. He looked like some old testament prophet who'd been too long up the mountain. As he surveyed the battlefield with his cold, disinterested gaze, the Geiger counter in the panel truck coughed like an old man with the flu.

"Fire at will!" Hassan bellowed. He ran out from behind the truck, lifting his left arm. The black metal of his palm irised open, and a barrage of fire erupted. The caseless, depleted uranium shells smashed into the man in the flag, ripping through the faded glory he wore, and tearing through the wall behind him. Rodriguez flicked his rifle to full-auto, and opened up with everything he had, aiming at the target's face. The grouping was tight enough there was barely enough room for a hair between the impacts. Keun shrieked, blood running from her nose and eyes as she hit him with every ounce of force her mind could muster. The porch crumbled beneath the onslaught. A dust cloud puffed up, obscuring the front of the building. The echoes of the gunshots faded, and the team stared into the wreckage.

The Geiger counter screamed, the needle burying itself in the danger zone. The dust blew outward, and the man the world now called the Broken Arrow rose into the air from the smoldering pit. He clutched his tattered flag, and looked down at them. Angry bruises mottled his flesh where the specialized ordinance had impacted. His flag was even more ragged than it had been, and blood ran from a cut on his lip. The injuries metabolized in moments as his body knitted itself back together.

"So who is it this time?" he asked. His voice was surprisingly soft, the edges raspy as if he'd either screamed himself hoarse, or nearly forgotten how to speak. "What's left of the NSA? A CIA sleeper? The New World Order?"

"Would you believe us if we told you?" Hassan shouted back.

The little god appeared to consider the proposition. Then he shook his head slowly.

"No."

The Broken Arrow turned his head, and his blue eyes flared with impossible brightness. Rodriguez moved a fraction of a second faster, shoving Keun out of the way. A wave of focused power with the intensity of a star's dying heart melted the front of the truck to slag. In a fraction of a second the liquid metal melted a crater in the ground. Rodriguez screamed as the beam erased his foot, and the lower half of his leg. There was no blood; the limb had been atomized so thoroughly there was nothing but a blank face of cauterized flesh. Hassan raised his arm to fire again, but the Broken Arrow sped toward him faster than a bullet. He snatched the cyborg's arm and pushing it skyward as a dozen rounds fired from his palm.

The blond godling frowned, staring into Hassan's face. A crease appeared between his brows.

"I know you," he said. "Where have we met before?"

Hassan spit in the atomic dictator's face. Rather than fury, a smile split the Broken Arrow's lips. It was a white, toothy grin utterly devoid of humor, or pleasure. A mechanical expression that shone a light into the bright emptiness of the man who wore it.

"Now I remember," he said, wiping the spittle off his face with his free hand. "My unpopular solution to the Palestinian problem."

The Broken Arrow squeezed. Steel squealed as the supports in Hassan's arm began to buckle. The fingers twitched spasmodically, and he tried to pull free. The mechanism whined, then groaned as it was crushed in the inhuman grasp.

"You people had years to resolve it yourself. When I came, I warned you. Make peace by the third day, or I would make it for you. When I arrived to ask if you had made peace, you shot me in the chest. I don't know what with, but it was big enough to hurt." His smile grew wider, and he stared into Hassan's face. "How much of you survived that day, I wonder?"

The Broken Arrow twisted, and Hassan's arm tore away at the shoulder. Wires and cyberfiber trailed like mechanized gore, and sparks snapped from live wires. Hassan wrenched himself back, breathing hard. He went down to one knee, half-turning away from the white-haired figure who'd crippled him again. The Broken Arrow had one foot in the air to step closer, when a truck hammered him from behind. He cried out, stumbled, and spun with the impact. The three-ton hulk of steel went flying, and he turned back to Keun. She was on her knees, blood filling one eye and breath tearing in and out of her throat.

"Quite the trick," he said, walking slowly toward her. "And, as my daddy always said, one good trick deserves another."

The Broken Arrow cocked his arm back, but before he could do anything Kemidov grabbed his wrist. The white-haired man turned, and stared at the imposing figure in black. He seemed more confused than angry that anyone would dare to touch him. His expression shifted to surprise, then horror when he tried to pull away from the Russian's grip, but nothing happened. That was when Kemidov drove a fist into his stomach, knocking the wind out of him.

Fire flared in the Broken Arrow's eyes, and he poured it onto Kemidov. The blue blast tore away the big man's armor, the lead plates and ballistic weave evaporating as if they'd never been. Kemidov remained, pale as death. His limbs were swollen with muscle, his torso thick and deformed. His face was worse, though. One eye bulged sightlessly from its socket, and his nose was nothing more than a bulbous mass of cancerous flesh. His teeth were crowded together in a heavy, malformed jaw, and a single, impossibly blue eye glared at the Broken Arrow from beneath the heavy shelf of his brow. The Russian forced his arm up through the beam, and covered the dictator's left eye with his palm. Jason Quinn shrieked, and there was a wet, rupturing noise as blood jetted from his face.

"What are you?!" Quinn shrieked.

"I was supposed to be you," Kemidov said, bringing his fist down again. Quinn's head rocked, and his lip split, spilling blood. "I, and a thousand others. No one else survived Darkened Mirror."

Quinn returned a blow of his own, sinking a fist into Kemidov's shoulder, weakening the Russian's grip. Quinn jerked back, his flag falling away. He could have fled, but half-blind and enraged, he made no attempt to.

"Come on then," Quinn howled, his fists flying as he stepped in close.

They fought like something out of myth, each blow landing like a small clap of thunder. Quinn jackhammered Kemidov's chest, and the malformed clone drove an elbow into the American's neck. Kemidov wrapped a hand around Quinn's throat, but Quinn twisted free, and slammed his heel into the bigger man's knee, almost knocking him sprawling. Blood spattered the dying grass, and tooth fragments flew. Bones cracked as they grappled and gouged, butted and wrestled. They grunted and snarled, heels gouging the earth as each sought to bring the other down. The Geiger counter in the truck rose to a fever pitch, screaming its warning as the atoms in the two creatures who had once been men heated up, spilling power through their veins.

Kemidov was strong, but in the end he was no match for the man he was a mere copy of. The Russian fell beneath Quinn's assault, his broken chin slumping into the dirt. Naked, his knuckles bloody, face swollen, and holding his ribs, the Broken Arrow parted his lips. Steam escaped his mouth on every exhale, as if there was a fire burning in his belly.

"I knew about the experiments," he spat, kicking Kemidov in the head. "Seems the Kremlin's best wasn't good enough."

The Broken Arrow turned his remaining eye on Hassan. He smiled, parting his ruined lips as he turned away from his beaten, broken foe.

"You better have another trick up your sleeve," Quinn said, taking a step closer to where Hassan crouched at the rear of the truck. "Because it looks like your big gun is out of bullets."

Hassan met Quinn's gaze. The package was at his feet, the black shell removed. Inside was a sleek, chrome device. A single, red plunger rose from the top, and Hassan's remaining hand grasped it. He smiled, offering a scarred, death's head grin to the man who had styled himself as a god among men.

"I do," Hassan said, priming the weapon.

Quinn rushed forward to stop him, but Keun locked her mind around him, holding him back. Kemidov lunged from the ground, wrapping his shattered, bloody arms around the tyrant's waist. Rodriguez panted, leaning against the truck. With his senses heightened, and his experience of time slowed to a crawl by his De-Cell, he watched the end of the world in agonizing slow motion. The plunger fell, and there was a soft click as the Hind was released.

He'd seen videos of the weapon in testing, and read the reports of the aftermath. If you needed something to kill a god, this was what you'd use. But recordings could not convey the bright, golden light of the initial reaction. The blinding, almost heavenly brilliance of it. Then, like a setting sun, the Hind dulled to a burnished bronze, then a deep ocher. Rodriguez watched as a black filaments wove through the light, swallowing it until only darkness remained.

The void erupted from its prison, reaching into the world with dark fingers. It spilled across the air like ink, roaring as the void sucked at all the light and life it could reach. Quinn tried to retreat, but he couldn't get away fast enough. The liquid emptiness engulfed him, devouring him. He pulsed in the void, screaming as his nuclear fire flared, and went out. Rodriguez started to smile, but the message hadn't fully reached his lips before the Hind's emptiness was upon him.

So the darkness shall be the light, he thought. *And the stillness the dancing.*

Then he, like his team and the man who might have murdered the world, was gone.

Mark of the Legion

Gaius had fought many enemies. He'd slain Haparat tribesmen with their necklaces of fingers and shields of stretched hide. He'd held the line against Korrish cavalry, who were as swift and vicious as the dust devils of their native deserts. He'd battled Saranish pirates along the black coast, and stalked the heady mists of Ronarin jungles where the fangs of a serpent were deadlier than any blade. Even after all those campaigns, the legionnaire had never fought a foe like a Chadrian winter. It held no grudges, and gave no ground. It stole light from the day, warmth from the night, and breath from every living thing. It understood attrition, and it knew patience, but it celebrated no victories, and mourned no losses. It was a perfect soldier; Gaius respected that. Still, orders were orders, which was why he sat and kept watch. His blade was no use against the frigid cold, and his armor did nothing to stop the raking wind. Despite that, he endured with a torn cloth wrapped around his face and the warmth of a dead man's candle cupped in his lap keeping his blood from freezing solid beneath his cloak. Only his eyes, the same coal black as his skin, moved as he observed the empty field.

The sun was a finger's breadth above the horizon when a patch of snow shifted. A piece of the white carpet shuddered, and a single, gauntleted hand broke the surface. A figure hauled itself from the ground, shivering and shaking like it was newly born. It bent down, tugged the taught oil cloth back over the hole, and smoothed snow over the break to camouflage the narrow grave. It trudged toward Gaius's scant refuge beneath a wind-twisted pine, hunched over and favoring its left side.

"Belloc's black balls, why is it so cold?," Calix grunted, sitting with her left side against Gaius's right.

"Because the gods despise us, and wish to see us suffer," Gaius said, his smile cracking the frost coating his impromptu mask. He slid a hand beneath his tunic, and pulled out his brass-bottomed water skin. He blindly added tea leaves with half-numb fingers, and held it over the candle flame.

"I should think they'd have had enough by now," she said, her full lips twisting, pulling at a narrow scar bisecting her chin. The corners of her mouth were crusted with ice flakes, making her olive skin look like frost-bitten fruit. "How do you stand it? Didn't that hell you were born in to the south thin your blood?"

"Mostly I sit, and make sure to keep a candle lit. You didn't sleep well?"

"No," Calix said. She wiped her face and shifted, gritting her teeth to stop them chattering as she pulled her hood even lower. "My godsdamn hand froze solid. The shit-shod thing got wet digging my hole, and I didn't feel it till it was too late. I had to take it off."

Gaius nodded, and weighed his bag of tea. It was warm, near to hot. It would be perfect in a way only the first brew of blackroot could be. He sighed, opened his cloak, and pressed the bag into Calix's remaining hand. She stiffened, then cupped the water skin carefully. She closed her eyes, and her jaw relaxed. The expression changed her completely, and Gaius saw that beneath the sharp tongue and old wounds was a countenance only fine breeding brought. She handed the tea bag back a few minutes later, lukewarm and edging toward cold. Gauis took it, and drank. Calix bent her head, grunting as she strapped her iron fist over her wrist stump.

"How long have you been saving that lump of wax?" Calix asked.

"It's not mine," Gaius said, trying to work at least a little heat back into the bag.

Calix paused. "Who?"

"Brutus," he said. "He was hoarding it, hoping to make it one more day before he had to light it."

"Stupid bastard," Calix said, though not unkindly. "We're going to miss him tonight."

Gaius nodded, but didn't say anything else. Calix fumbled at her throat, pulling up her own scarf guard against the cold. Light fled the field, and as it went the others began to rise. Hands and heads slipped from shallow holes, and the legionnaires pulled themselves back above ground. They shuddered and shivered, flocking to cover and forming small groups to share what heat the earth hadn't stolen from them. A cohort went into the earth, and at least a century of them remained there.

"It's an ill omen when graves are filled before the battle even starts," Tiberia said, ducking her head and sitting down with her legs crossed. Her cheeks were stung red as her greasy curls, and she was enthusiastically chewing something that smelled fresh and sweet.

"You don't believe in omens," Gaius said.

"Truth," she said. Tiberia sniffed, and grinned as she pointed at Gaius's tea. "Make you a trade for a slug of that?"

Gaius handed over his bag, and Tiberia offered him a chunk of something amber. Gaius raised an eyebrow at her.

"Just put it between your cheek and gum," Tiberia said, drinking deep and wiping her chin. "When it warms, you can chew it."

"It smells like a tree," Gaius said.

"It tastes like one for a while too," Tiberia agreed, handing him back the bottle. "But it wears off, and what's beneath is sweet."

Gaius stared at the lump of sap, then shrugged, lifted his cloth, and put it in his mouth. He moved it around, grunting before pushing it into his cheek. Tiberia grinned, cracked lips pulling back over strong, square teeth.

"So, did anything happen while I was down?"

"The sun set," Calix said.

"I saw a bird fly over the hill," Gaius added.

Tiberia waited, her gaze level on Gaius. Calix turned, regarding him as well. Gaius made a thoughtful sound, and started chewing.

"Well?" Tiberia asked.

"It seems I made a good trade," Gaius said, swigging the last of his tea before tucking the empty flask away. "No, nothing of note happened."

"The prisoners didn't say anything new?" Tiberia prodded.

"No," Gaius said. "It seems they already told Varus everything they knew."

"Does Varus even speak the hog-swallow they talk up here?" Calix asked.

"Every tongue speaks fear," Gaius said.

"Speak for yourself," Tiberia said. "I fear no man."

A twig cracked, and hands shifted to hilts. As if the name had summoned the man, Varus stood just outside the pine's branches. Pale as moon shadow, and nearly as thin, wisps of his corn silk hair hung lank and still around his face. He wore no hood, but thick lines of blue paint streaked across his face. If he noticed the cold, he gave no sign it troubled him. Gaius glanced at the snow, just to make sure the scout had truly left tracks in it.

"Varus," Tiberia said, her hand still wrapped tightly around the horn hilt of her knife. "I see you crawled out of your hole."

Varus smiled a wide, saurian smile, revealing a double row of bone daggers filed to bloody points. Tiberia flinched, and Varus sheathed his teeth with the wet, shucking sound of a blade being pulled from a child's back. His eyes tightened at the corners, and a ragged, dusty sound came from somewhere in his bony chest.

"It's time?" Gaius asked.

Varus nodded, his amusement gone as quickly as it had come. Gaius sighed, and got to his feet, stamping to try to bring back some life back into them. When he looked up, Varus was gone again.

"You were saying?" Calix asked Tiberia, her brows winging up above her face cloth.

"I fear no man," Tiberia said, shuddering as she stood. "I don't know what Varus is, but he isn't a man."

"Whatever he is, be pleased he fights for us," Gaius said, blowing out his candle and carefully wrapping it in a strip of hide.

Calix stood, her face turned toward the clearing where the others were beginning to form up. She didn't say anything.

"Gather the others and take formation," Gaius said. He clapped Calix on the right shoulder, and then Tiberia. "What is dead."

"Can never die," they finished, returning the clasp before tugging their hoods low and ducking into the night.

They marched like silent ghosts beneath a dead man's moon. Exposed skin and burnished metal alike had been covered with strips of cloth, and the possessions of the dead had been stripped and shared among those who yet lived. With every step the legionnaires faded into each other, until their feet fell in unison, and their eyes roamed as one. They came in rows stretched wide, like the very hand of the empire ready to ball into a fist to crush its enemies.

The first farmhouse they found was dark; abandoned for weeks by the look and smell of it. The second was little better, with signs of hasty packing the only trace left behind. There were others as well. Some had crops left piled in the frost, and others had animals that had been left behind, shivering and hungry in their paddocks. Wandering eyes made note of the dark windows, the empty yards, and then of the provisions left behind. No order was given to stop, so they marched on into the teeth of the north wind.

Beyond the frozen farmsteads and seemingly endless pine barrens, the city of Chadrian crouched at the edge of the world. Little more than a collection of docks, taverns, and craft houses, a crescent-shaped wall arced out through the trees. Unlike the ramshackle homes and leaning docks, the wall was built of strong stone whose masonry left no cracks for eager hands to grab. Twice the height of a man, with barred gates of hardwood imported from far to the south, the walls were a testament to the improvements the empire had brought. Heads hung from the wall, the distended jaws and leathery flesh rendering them unrecognizable, and all but inhuman. The dead still wore the helmets and crimson tatters of the thirteenth auxiliary legion though, which made it clear who they'd once been.

Men stood guard on the wall, but their burnished helms and secondhand armor looked about as sturdy as a beggar's jawbone. They stood in clumps, huddled around braziers and cupping torches against the night's chill. In their thick cloaks and hand-dyed woolens, with numb fingers wrapped around relics once wielded by fathers or grandfathers in forgotten battles and skirmishes, they looked like what they were; feral dogs who'd turned and bitten the hands that fed them.

It had been months since the town shuttered its gates to hide the blood it had spilled. Weeks as the cold blew in off the sea and down from the hills, leaving frost and misery in its wake. Weeks as the fear of the empire's wrath ebbed, and the immediate tedium of standing watch took its toll on their vigilance. Time enough for the watchers to decide the escaped members of the auxiliary had died in winter weather, or succumbed to the beasts that roamed beyond their borders. Time enough for arguments about whether they should have taken up arms at all to spark, and to smolder behind closed doors. The defenders, such as they were, seemed less concerned with centurions in the trees, and more concerned with staying out of the wind and around their fires. The empire was far away, beyond the ice and the snow, past the trees and the endless miles. It was an idea, and ideas are easily forgotten in the face of such immediate concerns.

The scouts' first volley cleared most of the wall. Some of the defenders fell with arrows in their throats, or buried in their guts. Others cried out, shooting to their feet as pilfered skullcaps and stolen armor turned the vicious points away from their flesh, but left the wearers panicked. Fire-blinded eyes stared out into the night, and those left standing drew swords and daggers, snatched axes and readied spears. They shouted to one another in their garbled, barking language of the northlands, beating their hilts on their shields and on the brass warning bells installed on the wall, but there was no sense of order in the chaos. The second volley thinned what was left of the ranks, and those who remained ducked out of sight.

The advanced line rushed forward, a full century of conturbernales in their ten-man units. The legionnaires pelted to the wall, two men boosting up the others. They vaulted the barrier with blades ready, standing back to back in forms rehearsed until they became graceful as memory. The invaders closed ranks, reinforced by more of their fellow soldiers as they swarmed over the wall. Steel rang on steel, and blood spilled hot and steaming in the night air; imperial or Chadrian, it all ran the same color in the darkness. The gates boomed open, and a short, shrill horn sounded from the frozen forest.

The second line came at a run, with their shields up and spears ready. A few shafts flew toward them, and one or two stones were flung from the wall, but the missiles found no chink in the shield wall. The line collapsed through the gates and spread out inside the city, cutting off what was left of the defenders from the rest of the town. Some leaped over the wall and limped for the woods. Others threw down their weapons and babbled in terror with chapped hands raised to the skies. The rest went down with steel in their fists, and death bubbling on their lips.

Chadria was a kicked anthill. Men and women boiled out of every structure, clutching staves and swords, knives and bows. They stared in horror at the ghost legion, with its flapping rags and bloody blades. Many of the townsfolk goggled, disbelieving. Some came forward, bellowing as they spit their defiance in the faces of the invaders. They fought bravely, but every legionnaire they killed was replaced by another. Every Chadrian who fell did so alone.

They broke. A woman fled, arms pumping. Two boys followed, one with a wet patch of piss soaking his pants. An older man with age spots on his balding pate hobbled down a side street, wheezing as he tried to go unnoticed. The trickle became a stream, and the stream grew into a torrent. The legion followed the rout, dispatching those who resisted and grinding the town's blood and mud beneath their tread. They pushed until there was nowhere else to go, and held their ground. With the frozen sea at their backs, and a ring of bloody spears at their throats, the Chadrians knelt. They did not kneel as one, but with their comrades' blood dripping and drying on the invaders' steel, every one of them surrendered.

The town was secured by sunrise. Small groups of prisoners were taken from the docks, searched, and marched to the parade ground just inside the city's wall. Those who'd escaped into the woods were brought back, caught by the reserves who waited just out of sight of the walls for the runners. Patrols went from house to house, bringing those who were hiding or lurking to join the others. Men, women, children, they were led past the carnage and made to stand shoulder to shoulder under guard. Fires were lit, and the stripped bodies of the dead were piled along the outside wall like kindling.

Gaius stood with the remains of his unit, surveying what was left of those who had turned traitor on the empire. Calix stood on his right, and Tiberia on her other side. Horatius leaned on a spear, his thick beard caked in frost and blood. On Gaius's left, swarthy, tattooed hands held out to the fire, stood Augustus. Behind him stood Camilla, her pert lips pulled into a frown and her almond eyes narrowed as she took in the crowd. Varus stood apart from them, beneath the battlements near the main gate. Gaius's left arm throbbed from a gash he'd taken in the initial skirmish, and frozen blood crackled along the right side of his ragged cloak. His weapons were sheathed, but he kept his hand near his knife.

"You look nervous for someone on the winning side," Calix said out of the corner of her mouth.

"It isn't over yet," Gaius said.

Augustus had his mouth open to speak, lips curled for one of his cutting jibes, when the horn blew; three, sharp blasts sounded, and they were accompanied by the sounds of hooves. Almost as one the legionnaires straightened their backs and adjusted their grips on their weapons. Eyes roamed the crowd, the walls, or stared into bonfires. No one looked toward the gate; the Legatus was there to be seen by the prisoners, not his troops. Anyone caught neglecting to fulfill the responsibilities of a legionnaire would be flogged. Augustus closed his mouth and snapped his head around to face the remains of the fallen town.

Five horses galloped through the gates. Four of the riders wore rich, purple cloaks and were sheathed in black armor. The man in the front and rear each bore the gilded skulls of the legion's standards. The four Praetorians dismounted, hands on hilts as they formed a cordon around the fifth beast. The last rider surveyed the crowd, his sparse, white hair blowing in the wind. The Legatus dismounted, climbing onto the battlements with his honor guard in tow. He positioned himself above the gates; a vulture in black weighing the butcher's bill before him. The eyes of the city rose, but the legionnaires maintained their vigilance. Every one of them had seen what was about to happen for themselves.

"My name is Legatus Scorpius," he called in a leather-lunged rasp which Varus repeated in the guttural growl of the northern tongue. "I am the commander of the Foresworn Legion."

The crowd sighed, a sound that told a hundred stories without a single word. Some wept, wincing as the morning chill quenched their hot tears. Others slumped, falling against their neighbors if they had them, and to the ground if they didn't. A select few clenched their fists, staring up at the Legatus as if their fury could strike him dead. The Legatus drew another breath, unhindered by the suffering at his feet.

"Chadria has been a part of the empire for many years," Scorpius continued, his voice cutting through the human noise. "She came unwillingly the first time as well, but there was peace afterward. We set aside our swords and spears. We kept you safe, and we allowed you to continue your lives with no further harm. We trusted you, and you betrayed that trust."

There were grumbles from those assembled, and one or two shouted at the Legatus. As the noise died, two men crossed beneath the battlements. One was tall and thin, his cheekbones honed and his skin discolored with old, ugly scars in the shape of crude letters. The second was wide, his pudgy hands always busy as he took deep, sucking gasps of air. The former carried a quiver full of iron rods, a bag of charcoal, and a folded brazier. The latter carried a great tome under one arm, and a bookkeeper's satchel over the other shoulder. They began assembling the tools of their trade.

"Every one of you has a choice," Scorpius continued, shouting down the last coals of protest. He threw back his cloak and pulled up his tunic's voluminous sleeve. "Die here with your fellow traitors, or join us and repent your crimes."

The commander's arm was a map of branded scar flesh. The black blade of a murderer held prominence on his wrist, below the crossed bones of a convicted pirate. The broken manacles of an escaped slave wrapped around his bicep, just above the bloody sword of an attempted assassin. Atop them all, prominent on his shoulder, was the ascendant, winged skull of a legionnaire who had served his sentence, and chosen to remain. The scars were as old and worn as the man who bore them. Scorpius shook the cloth back down over the vellum of his skin, and rested his hands on the splintered railing.

"Look around you. Every soldier here has stood at the foot of the same gallows where you now stand. They fought with the same fervor you did, and they bled the same blood on the battlefields of a hundred different lands. In the end it was all for naught." Scorpius paused, and pushed back from the railing. "In the end you must choose. Do you fall today, forgotten in the mud? Or will you rise up, and take your place among us?"

The two Praetorians who weren't carrying the funerary standards descended and crossed between the ranks of guards. They pulled a man from the crowd, his beard ragged and his heavy, work calloused hands red with the cold. He didn't resist, stumbling between the two men as he was led to the staging area just before the gates. The pungent scent of smoke and heated steel wafted on the breeze, and Gaius braced himself for the stink that would follow.

"Did you raise arms against the legionnaires assigned to this outpost?" the fat man asked.

"Yes," the Chandrian said, raising his head slightly. "I killed two of them myself."

"Your crimes then are murder, and treason against the empire. The sentence is twenty years, or fifty successful missions. Do you declare loyalty to the empire as a member of the Foresworn Legion?" The record keeper wheezed, holding his bottle of ink beneath his arm to keep it warm.

The man stood silent for a long time, frowning in concentration. He licked his split lips, but no words came. Finally he nodded his head once.

"Excellent," the fat man said without emotion, scribbling the man's details into the book. "Bare your right arm."

The man's eyes went wide. He took a step back, and the Praetorians each drew three inches of steel. The prisoner froze. With numb fingers he shrugged out of his coat, and pulled up his shirt sleeve. With the grace of the artist he'd been before convicted of sedition, the brander pressed the hot iron against the presented flesh. The skin sizzled, and the prisoner cried out. The first scream hadn't ended, when the second brand found its mark. They were clear, precise, and unmistakable. The brander knew his task, and had practiced it on a thousand canvases. Perhaps more.

"Your name is now Barca," the fat man said, sprinkling sand onto the ink and removing the leaf from his booklet. "Praetorians, escort him to the choosing ground."

The Praetorians stepped forward, their movements precise as clock cogs. The first clapped snow over the wounds, and the second caught the man as his knees gave out. A ragged red cloak was put over his shoulders, and he was led out through the gates. The Praetorians returned a moment later, taking another from the remaining prisoners.

The day dragged on, and the stench of burning flesh settled like a smokehouse over the square. Murderers, traitors, conspirators, defectors, and deserters all passed before the record keeper. Most accepted the terms, their new names, and their brands. Those who didn't were cut down before they could say another word, dragged off and stacked alongside the rest of the dead.

Calix frowned, watching a mother and her unbranded baby stumble through the gates.

"Is she the one?" Gaius asked.

Calix shook her head slowly. "No. Not her."

Gaius shrugged, but said nothing. Calix's mouth narrowed into a hard line, but the words behind her eyes never parted her lips. A girl approached the name takers; a waifish, dark-haired thing with the hands of a farmer's daughter and the big, red eyes of a doe who had been weeping. Calix stiffened. Gaius followed her gaze.

"Did you raise arms against the garrison in this city?" the fat man asked her.

The girl said nothing. She yanked up her sleeve and stood defiant, her right hand balled into a fist. The fat man repeated himself, and Varus translated. She didn't say yes or no, and didn't shake or nod her head. She clenched her teeth, and held her arm out a little further. She shifted, offering her flank to the brander. The thin, scarred man turned to his brands, and withdrew an unused iron from an oil skin. He added it to the fire, carefully burying the head in the coals.

"The penalty for an Unconfessed is forty years, or a full century of successful missions," the fat man said. "Do you accept this and declare loyalty to the empire as a member of the Foresworn Legion?"

The girl nodded, her nostrils flaring as she took deep, ragged breaths.

"Your name is now Cassandra," the record keeper said, scribbling in his black book. The brander gently cupped her elbow, holding her gaze. He worked his mangled jaw, but made no sound. He drew the new brand from the fire, and pressed it to the girl's arm. The cords on her neck stood out, and blood trickled from her bit lip. The brander held a handful of snow over the wound, gently patted her shoulder with his free hand, and stepped back. The Praetorians led the newly-minted Cassandra through the gates.

"Her," Calix said.

Gaius nodded. He and Calix headed for the gates, and the others fell in step behind them. There were no smiles now. No laughter. They had business to attend, and it was as serious as the grave.

The recent recruits were lined up along the outer wall like goods at a market. They stood in rows, but there was no sense of order beyond that. Men and women, boys and girls, mothers and fathers, all of them reduced to what they were now; fodder. Several of them shook, from fear, from the cold, or just from the gazes of the Centurions as they passed among the ranks. The legion's officers examined prisoners' teeth and hair, gauged their muscles, and felt their palms. They asked pointed questions, offering insults and threats to test the branded's reactions. Those who made the grade were pulled out of the line, and when one century was replenished, the next commander stepped forward to pick recruits from what was left. A tall woman with burnished black eyes and skin the color of fresh ashes stood before Cassandra. Cassandra looked at the woman, refusing to blink.

"Are you stupid girl, or just trying my patience hoping I will end you?" the Centurion asked, her voice a harsh snarl. "I will not. I will work you till your bones creak and your limbs snap. I will break you, do you understand me?"

Cassandra said nothing. She didn't turn her head, or give any indication she heard the Centurion at all. The others raw recruits looked away, trying to escape notice. The clerk, an older woman with the near-sighted squint of one who'd worked for years by candlelight, stood by impassively.

"I will take this one," the dark-skinned Centurion said. "She is hard like iron, and I want to see if she is as brittle as well."

"Centurion Helena," Gauis said, clapping his fist to his chest in salute.

"Decanus Gaius," Helena said, inclining her head slightly to acknowledge his presence. "At ease. What news do you bring?"

"Apologies, Centurion," Gaius said, shifting his stance as ordered. "My second is invoking the right of Cacula."

The Centurion tucked a thumb behind her weapons belt, shifting her gaze to Calix. When she spoke, it was to the clerk. "Is this truly her hundredth mission?"

The clerk frowned and flipped through her records, running her finger along the lines until she found what she was looking for. "It is, Centurion."

"Pray, tell me why her?" Helena asked Calix. "Do you hate your Decanus so much you would saddle him with breaking and training another Unconfessed as your replacement?"

Calix said nothing, standing at attention and staring at the middle distance. Helena nodded once, a satisfied smirk twisting her mouth. "That's how it is then. The right of Cacula is recognized. The girl is yours, and I wish you great fortune with her."

The Centurion continued on down the line, dragging the clerk in her wake. The remains of the unit relaxed, no longer under the scrutiny of a commanding officer. Cassandra stood, suddenly adrift in the sea of conscripts. Gaius lowered his face cloth and stood before her. Calix did the same.

"Cassandra," Gaius said. "That is your name now, yes?"

She nodded, the muscles in her jaw tightly clenched. Her lips were beginning to turn blue where they weren't bloody, and she shook where she stood. Gaius shrugged off his outer cloak and handed it to her.

"Put this on," he said. "You are no good to me if you end up frozen in a snowbank."

Cassandra hesitated, but she took the cloak and slung it around her shoulders. Calix nodded approvingly, but said nothing.

"Do you know what Cacula is, Cassandra?" Gaius asked.

Cassandra shook her head.

"Every member of the legion has a price to pay for what they've done. Once that price is met, in years served or blood spilled, the legionnaire is released from service. The soldier is given a full pardon, as well as a payment for time served. After a legionnaire has completed the term required they have the option to choose a replacement." Gaius gestured with his head toward Calix. "My second just chose you."

"I didn't do anything wrong," Cassandra said, spitting the words out like dirty pebbles.

"No, you probably did not," Gaius said, shrugging his shoulders. "It

87

doesn't matter. You're here now."

"I am not a soldier," Cassandra said.

"Do not worry," Gaius said. "You will be."

One by one the walking wounded found their places. They left their home with hollow eyes and empty hearts. They were assigned to dig graves, tend fires, gather wood, and to carry and haul. They filled the gaps in the ranks, and took the places of those who had fallen before them. Chadrians joined Haparats and Korrish, Ronarin and Saranish, as well as those whose lands had no names on the empire's maps. It did not matter who they were, or what they had done before this. What mattered was every one of them now bore the mark of the legion.

Hero's Wake

Gwen stood, and listened to silence of the pine barrens. She knew academically that she was only a few miles from the Garden State Parkway, and that if she flew up above the treetops she'd see the afterglow of New York City against the skyline. But here, surrounded by the endless ranks of quiet, patient pine, was like being in another world. A place out of time, where people hadn't forgotten their reverence of nature, or lost sight of where they stood in the bigger, grander scheme of things.

"Sun's getting low," Abe said. He stopped a few feet from his sister, waiting for her to acknowledge him. "Want to give everything a last look before the train pulls in?"

Gwen smiled, and wiped at her eyes. It was funny, how she'd never really noticed how many of their father's sayings her older brother had latched onto. Except for his hair, just starting to turn gray and braided into neat rows, Abe even looked like old photos of their dad. Before the sickness had eaten into him, and the experimental treatment that had turned him into far more than just a man. And now, hearing her dad's words come out of Abe's mouth was enough to kick a few embers up from the ashes of her grief. She folded into him, and Abe put his arms around her. She let him hug her, since she didn't trust herself enough to return the gesture safely right then.

"Sure," she said. "Come on, slowpoke. If we leave Uncle Jimmy down there on his own, he'll set the whole place on fire."

They walked around the side of the cabin, an old, wooden affair that had been in their family since the days of the Underground Railroad, and looked down the hill. Three rows of folding chairs were set up, facing the mound of black dirt where they'd buried their father that morning. The lectern still stood just to the side of the mound. Their family and friends, the ones who didn't know what went on behind the curtain, had paid their respects while the sun had been high. Now, as it began to set, those who'd been privy to the old man's truths were coming to mourn his passing.

Jimmy "Surf" Kapule was lighting the last of the torches ringing the three rows of folding chairs when Abe and Gwen came down the hill. He had a smile ready for her, and seeing that smile almost broke her. Gwen wrapped her arms around the gray-haired Samoan, and squeezed him tight.

"Hey, hey, easy girlie," Jimmy gasped, putting his arms around her. "I'm not as invincible as I used to be."

"Sorry, Jimmy," Gwen said, loosening her hold. When she tried to pull away, he squeezed her tighter.

"The hard part of the day is over," he said, patting her on the back before holding her at arm's length. He glanced over his shoulder at the sound of an engine, and nodded. "Looks like the party's getting started. Want me to grab you a drink?"

"Sure," Gwen said. "Something fruity, with a kick."

Jimmy threw her a mocking salute, and walked to the side tables he'd set up for snacks and drinks. He set a glass on the tabletop, and lifted one of the kegs he'd brought with him. He poured a dash of rum from it, before re-corking it and setting the 25-gallon drum back in its place. He mixed a half dozen ingredients into the glass, his thick hands swift and sure. He sliced a lime, squeezed the juice, and left the peel floating in the glass. Gwen took it gingerly, and sipped.

"No one makes these like you," she said.

"That's because I invented them."

The first car to arrive was a bright red Jeep. The doors had been stripped out, and the top was down, but the eye-catching blue fireman's bubble was still affixed to the roll bar. Stacy Gomez stepped out of the passenger side, wrapped in an uncharacteristic black dress, with a pair of high wedges on her feet. Richard Stone pulled himself out of the driver's side, tucking his keys into his pocket. A big guy, Richard's slightly-too-small sports jacket and crooked tie made him look like a kid grown to unusual proportions. Still, there was genuine affection when he pulled Abe into a one-armed hug; the universal symbol of uncomfortable male solidarity. Stacy shook her head at the boys, pushed her sunglasses up onto her close-cropped hair, and smiled at Gwen.

"How are you holding up, sky child?" Stacy asked, pressing one cheek, then the other to Gwen's.

"Weight of the world," Gwen said, taking another sip of her drink. "And why are you wearing those ridiculous shoes?"

"They slow me down," Stacy said. "And they make my legs look great."

"Hey, kid, how you been?" Jimmy said, holding up a hand for Richard to slap. "Want a beer?"

"Really shouldn't," Richard said, tapping the side of his head. "Last thing we need is a wildfire out here."

Jimmy shrugged, and handed him a bottle of water. "Saw you with the new war paint. Good look. Real fear of god stuff."

"Jimmy," Gwen said, and Jimmy raised his hands in surrender.

"Right, right, rule zero, I remember," he said.

"Rule zero?" Stacy asked.

"No cape talk out here," Abe said, popping the top on a bottle of beer.

"It was dad's ironclad rule, so to speak."

Richard and Stacy had been the first, but they were far from the last to arrive. Laura and Katie arrived in Katie's beat-up rust bucket, the two of them dressed in jeans and blouses that would have been identical if Laura didn't tower a good foot over Katie. Martin arrived on the purring, WWII-issue BMW that was only a little older than he was, though both of them still looked like snapshots out of time; pictures of vigor and strength, time capsules of yesteryear. He left his goggles and helmet hanging from the handlebars, but kept his jacket on. At least it was black. Sparke and Raymond arrived in a rental, since neither of them really had a need for a car, and Daisy parked her mom's Suburban at the end of the line. Of everyone who'd showed up so far, it was the skinny girl just out of her teens who was visibly the biggest wreck.

"H-hi," Daisy said, sticking her hand out to Gwen. "I'm Daisy Marshall. We... umm... we talked on the phone?"

"It's a pleasure to see you in casuals, Daisy," Gwen said, taking the proffered hand.

The girl flushed to the roots of her golden hair. "I didn't... I mean, I didn't think I should have worn my-"

"You're just fine, Daisy," Abe cut in, giving the girl his calming, counselor's voice. "Dad always said this place was a sanctuary. It was where we could go to be ourselves, and to remember we still had faces under our masks."

Daisy beamed, tossing her golden hair behind her shoulder. "You're Abraham?"

Abe smiled, and nodded. "No one calls me that unless I'm in trouble, though. Abe will do fine."

Daisy offered her unsure grip again. "It's a pleasure to meet you, Abe. I just wish it was under better circumstances."

Abe shook her proffered hand, and smiled. "Better late than never, as we say at times like this."

Daisy laughed, and her eyes filled up with tears. She tried to wipe at them, but they just came harder. Around her feet, the grass started growing unseasonably lush, and flowers bloomed, tilting back to look at her. Abraham put an arm around her. He didn't say anything, but the storm was over in a few minutes. Daisy took a handkerchief from the small purse she was carrying, and blew her nose. Then she looked down at where she'd been standing, and flushed again.

"Sorry," she said. "It just... it happens sometimes."

"Don't worry about it," Gwen said, putting a hand on Daisy's shoulder. "Later on, when half of us are drunk, you'll get to hear all the bed wetting stories from when we were just starting out."

It took an hour or so for everyone who said they'd be there to show up. Some drove, but most didn't. Jarod burst out of thin air in the small clearing behind the house, his shirt on backward. His grin was sheepish, and his eyes were a little red around the rims. Rena stepped out from behind a tree that was nowhere near big enough to hide her, but whose shadow was more than deep enough for the elegant Filipina to step through. By the time everyone arrived, exchanged greetings, and taken a seat, the sun was truly gone from the sky. Gwen stood, and stepped to the lectern. Those gathered turned their attention to her, each of them waiting for the heir apparent to begin the healing process.

Gwen had her mouth open to speak, when something caught her eye. Headlights were rolling through the trees, peering through the ground fog that had formed between the evergreens. The purring of a high-toned engine thrummed in the air, and a silver ghost slid out of the mist. The car, with the smooth lines of a bygone era and the spirit of ecstasy on the hood, rolled to the edge of the gathering, dimming its lights as it approached. It idled for a moment, and the engine went silent. Everyone stared at it, instincts ready for the slightest hint of trouble. Gwen glanced to Jimmy, who shrugged from where he stood with his arms folded across his wide chest. The door opened slowly, and a man emerged.

He was tall, broad, and carried himself with the kind of confidence only conferred by experience. He was dressed in uniform black, with a row of silver buttons down his formal shirt. The driver pushed back his thick, brown hair, and settled his cap on his head, before opening the rear door. A second man emerged, levering himself out of the rear seat with the aid of a silver-handled ebony cane. The second man was old, with wispy white hair, and the kind of thin build that only comes when someone had truly reached their twilight years. His suit was black, his shirt and tie were black, and he even wore black gloves, and a black pocket square. In the flickering light of the torches, he almost looked like a pale, disembodied head.

The driver offered a hand, but the old man waved it away. He walked toward the gathering, his head high despite his shuffling steps. The driver stayed a step behind, matching his pace, his gaze sweeping the seats. No one moved, but everyone glanced at each other, wondering what to do. Gwen looked to Abraham, who walked slowly to meet the old man.

"Excuse me, sir," Abe said, keeping his voice down. "Is there something I can help you with?"

The old man stopped, and leaned on his cane. He looked at Abe, and offered a small smile that showed no teeth. "You'd be Abraham, then?"

"Yes, sir," Abe said, but before he could say anything else, the old man continued.

"My apologies for not reserving a place, but I wasn't sure I should come," he said, clearing his throat. "But, in the end, I thought it best. I know that, were our positions reversed, David would have done the same for me."

"That's probably true, Mr...?" Abe asked, letting his voice trail off.

"White. Alfred White," the old man said, giving Abe another of his small, tight smiles. "I do hope we didn't interrupt?"

"No, we were just getting started," Abe said, half turning to look back at Gwen. She nodded, and Mr. White continued his approach down the center aisle, toward the grave mound. His driver followed like a shadow, and the two of them sat quietly, taking the two far seats in the front row. Gwen licked her lips, and took a sip from the bottle of water she'd brought with her. She swallowed, and when she didn't choke, let out a long, slow breath.

"When I was a little girl, my father said something to me that I've never forgotten," Gwen said, her voice loud among the quiet mourners, and silent trees. "He said it isn't what you can do, but how you use your power to help people. He also told me that no matter how strong I was, or how hard I worked, or how fast I ran, there would always people I couldn't get to. And that, rather than focusing on all the things I *didn't* do, that I should look at all the people I did help. That if I remembered my actions mattered, that the scales would always tip my way."

There were nods from a few of the assembled. There were also one or two lowered heads, and blown noses. Gwen paused, giving them time to find their equilibrium again. She looked down at the grave, and swallowed.

"I could stand up here all night, and tell you all the things my dad did when no one was looking. The little things that the camera crews never saw, and that didn't go out on social media pages. The way he responded when people came at him with hate on their faces, or how he endured the scorn that came with being a black man that bullets couldn't hurt. The sort of stuff that showed me what heroes are really made of, when there's no one around for them to impress." Gwen's voice cracked on the last word, and she closed her eyes. She took two, slow breaths. "But, this isn't just for me. So, before some of us drink too much to make sense, I want to open up the floor to anyone who has a story they want to tell."

Heads turned, but no one stood for a moment. Then Martin got to his feet, and walked down the center aisle. Gwen stepped aside, yielding the lectern. Martin took a swig from his beer bottle, then unwrapped a heavy-concentrate granola bar, taking a bite of it.

"Apologies," he said as he chewed and swallowed. "Metabolism issues. Beer's got the calories, but it's not enough to feed the beast."

There were a few, quiet laughs. Stacy, in particular, thought it was funny. Martin took one more swallow of his beer, and took a deep breath. He dusted off his hands, like a man getting ready to do a difficult job.

"Dave was a guy who had greatness thrust upon him," Martin said. "Before the accident with his treatment, he was a good man. He was a teacher, and he cared about people. He was also a family man trying to do his best. He tried to help everyone in little ways. When he got sick, he thought that was the end. Then he got better, and he realized he could help more people. That he could do things he never imagined he could."

Martin swallowed, and licked his lips. He looked away from the crowd, and down at the lectern as if what he wanted to say was hidden in the wood grain somewhere. When he spoke again, his voice was raw. As if the words wounded him on their way out.

"Dave never wanted what happened to him. He didn't want the strength, the power, or the responsibility. I did, though. When I saw him on the news, or read about him in the paper, I wanted it so bad I could taste it. During the protests and riots, with all the people scared of the war in the jungle, and the wars in the streets, I felt powerless. I was scared. That was why I signed my name on the line, and joined the biggest gang in the world." He paused for a moment, running his tongue over his teeth. "I was less scared, dressed in fatigues and with a gun in my hand, but it wasn't enough. That was why I volunteered for special projects, and it was why I agreed to the experiments, no matter how low my chances of success were. No matter how much the drugs hurt, or what side effects there were, I didn't want to be normal in a world where anything was possible."

When he looked up, he was blinking away tears. "It worked. Bigger, faster, stronger; a warrior of the new world. I wasn't bulletproof, maybe, but it would take a lot of them to put me down. I wasn't afraid anymore, and I was never prouder than when I put on that new uniform for the first time. But I didn't think about what those colors really meant. What other people who saw me in red, white, and blue were going to think."

Martin smiled. It was a wolfish expression, but there was no humor in it. It was the sort of smile you saw on junkies at meetings, remembering what happened before they went straight. A hollow expression, with a half shot of shame pooled in the bottom.

"I wasn't doing it for them; I was doing it for me. Every time I brought somebody down, or ended some crisis, it was because I needed to feel that rush. I needed to be a big man. And pretty soon, I got out of hand." Martin swallowed, and the sound of his throat clicking was like a hammer cocking on a gun. "I made some bad calls, and every time I tried to make it right, I just dug myself deeper. When I didn't have anyone in my corner, Dave was there for me. He could have put me down hard, and everyone would have said it was the right thing to do. He didn't, though. Instead, he walked through a hail of bullets, and kept talking until I listened to him. He let me lean on him, and showed me I could still make things right. I didn't get it right every time, but when I fell, he was there to pick me back up."

Martin turned to the mound of dirt, and raised his mostly empty bottle in salute. "Here's hoping that, one day, I'll be half the man you were, buddy."

There was a smattering of applause, and more than a few raised glasses. Jimmy downed the contents of his mug in a single go. Martin returned to his seat, color riding high in his face. Raymond laid a hand on his shoulder, and Martin squeezed it gently. The ripples calmed, and when they had, Gwen asked if anyone else wanted to throw a stone into the water.

It seemed like everyone had a rock to toss, though some were bigger than others. Richard talked about how he'd been using his gift on the sly, trying to help fight fires with his mind, but that Dave had talked him into finally putting on his warpaint and getting out in the streets. Celia talked about how her unique gift for reading minds had led to her first divorce, and how it took someone with a skull as dense as Dave's to get her to relax, and trust people again. Sparke joked about how it seemed no one took him seriously, until Dave pointed out that, with a little creativity, he could be so much more than the one, glittery gimmick he'd come up with for his powers. Even Jimmy took the stand, telling a rambling story about when he and Dave had been young, and the world of heroes had been a very different place. About how America, and the world, had reacted to men with dark skin being some of the first Dawnbreakers. About how, sometimes, it wasn't about how you won, but how you got back up after you lost that made you who you were.

Gwen was about to step up to the lectern, and say a few final words, when Mr. White struggled to his feet. He took a dozen, halting steps to the front of the group, and with each step the gathering grew quieter. When he leaned his cane against the lectern, the soft knock of the wood sounded like the proverbial pin drop.

"I would like to begin with a small list of apologies," the old man said in his reedy voice. "To those who are gathered, I feel like the specter at the feast. You've come here to be together, to draw strength in this time of need, and here I am taking up a seat at the table."

Mr. White's driver stood, and made his way to the drinks table. He poured two glasses of wine with the same efficiency he'd done everything else. A few eyes followed him, their owners keeping the stranger on their radars. The driver held one of the glasses out to his employer, who took it carefully by the stem. The uniformed man returned to his seat, and Mr. White raised his glass toward Gwen and Abe.

"I wish to apologize, and offer my condolences, to the both of you. David was a remarkable man, and despite the challenges I'm sure you both faced as his children, there is nothing more difficult than losing your father."

Everyone in the audience nodded that time. Even Mr. White's driver, who had sat still and silent through every other speech offered that night. Mr. White carefully set his glass on the lectern, before he returned his gaze to the other guests. He swallowed, and licked his thin, dry lips.

"I first met David in the early days of the Dawn, as the papers like to call it. Our paths crossed just after the Phantom Robberies in Manhattan." Mr. White smiled, a fond smile that wrinkled the corners of his eyes and for a moment made him look kindly. "I would like to say we met on amiable terms, or that we became friends that day, but both of us were younger men, full of power and self-righteousness. We each thought we were doing what was right, and that the other was just getting in the way. In time, I found out who David really was behind the cape. He did the same, though I like to believe I found him before he found me."

Mr. White paused, putting a hand to his mouth to stifle a cough. It was a dry, hacking sound that rattled in his thin chest. His driver leaned forward, a concerned look on his face. Mr. White shook his head, flapping his free hand at the big man. Jimmy was frowning, the corners of his wide mouth turned down as his thick eyebrows drew together. He poured himself another beer, lips pursed as he stood and listened.

"There were letters and calls first. Anonymous things that let the other know they'd been found out. It was, in a way, like we were lovers. Each trying to test the waters to avoid putting too much of ourselves at risk." Mr. White chuckled at that, shaking his head. A shock of his white hair floated loose, and he pushed it back into place. "In time, we agreed to meet. A small park near the East Village, where they left out chess pieces during the day. It was bulldozed six years ago, written off after someone threw a gas truck into the fountain during a rather extreme disagreement."

The old man frowned at nothing, staring off into the middle distance. He clenched his jaw, rubbing his right hand with his left. His gloves shushed and creaked as he flexed the bony fingers beneath. He took a slow, shuddering breath, and blinked the crowd back into focus.

"And I'd like to apologize for my wandering mind. I promise you, my mental faculties are running on all cylinders. Though they could probably do with an oil change." That got laughs out of a few listeners. Mr. White showed them his teeth, and there was a touch of real charm in the grin. A ghost of the man he must have been, when newsreels were shown in technicolor for the first time. "Again, I'd like to say that David and I put aside our differences that day. But we didn't. Words were said, threats were made, and we each walked away with our fingers on our mutual triggers. A small voice said I should just do it, tell the whole world who the man called Iron really was, and get it over with. But I didn't. I wasn't going to be the one who started that fight. So I waited for him to make the first move. A week later, I got an envelope with a white king in it, and an invitation to a chess game the next Saturday."

Mr. White coughed again, and took a sip of his wine. His left hand rubbed his right again, like a nervous tic. Jimmy slugged back his beer, and set his mug on the table when he'd finished. He folded his arms, the heavy muscles of his biceps and forearms flexing.

"David was a better chess player than I gave him credit for. He won the first three games, though none of them handily," Mr. White continued. "And as we played, we talked. It was like there was a second match going on in the background of all the games we played. Philosophies of right and wrong, each trying to find weaknesses in the other's guards, and to defend against ripostes. He didn't change my mind that day, nor did I change his, but that was the day I think we began to respect each other.

"It wasn't the last time we played, either. We had a standing game every third Saturday, rain or shine. But sometimes he'd call me, or I'd call him, and ask for another. Whenever we had something we needed to get off our chests, we knew we could trust the other to keep it quiet, and to help work through it."

Mr. White turned, and fixed his gaze on Gwen. There was an intensity in his eyes that hadn't been there when he'd arrived. A driving will that, despite the years that hung on him, hadn't dimmed. If anything, it burned brighter inside the old man's papery skin.

"When he wasn't sure if he and Marion should risk having another child after he developed his powers, we talked about it. We sat in that park all day, snow up to our ankles. When he wanted someone who wouldn't hold his track record up as an excuse for his mistakes, he came to me. And when he told me I had a son I didn't know about, he did it just before he checkmated me."

Mr. White raised his glass, and his driver did the same. Several of the others answered the toast. Mr. White turned to the mound of grave dirt, as so many others had before him.

"You gave so much, David. Now it's your turn to rest," he said, his voice starting to crack.

Mr. White's hand twitched. The wineglass fell, the plastic bouncing on the grass. The wine sprayed out, pouring into the ground. His black, leather glove was still wrapped around it. The old man fell against the lectern, breath hissing through his teeth. His left hand was clamped around his right forearm. His right hand, though, was little more than a wisp of smoke; a ghostly appendage that passed through the wood of his cane, leaving it untouched when he reached for it.

"No," he whispered, sweat beading on his brow. "No, no, no. Pull yourself together, Al."

The driver moved fast. He stood, and was around the lectern in two steps. He pulled a device from his belt, and pressed it into Mr. White's arm. The sharp snap of electricity crackled, and the old man cried out. The wisps of smoke pulled themselves together, and his hand was just a hand again; age spots and all. Ozone, and the smell of burned skin, filled the air like a night flower's perfume. Mr. White crumpled into his driver's arms, panting.

"Deep breaths, pop," the driver said. His left arm was under the old man's shoulders, and he gently cupped Mr. White's wrist in his other hand. "Don't fade out on me."

"No," the old man said with a tired, wheezing laugh. "Not for a while yet."

The attendees weren't sure what to do. Martin was on his feet, his eyes wide. Sparke's forehead was furrowed, like a man staring at a restaurant bill he knows is wrong, but he can't put his finger on why. Faerie fire danced around his head in a halo. Katie was half out of her seat, and Laura was leaning forward in her chair, her weight balanced on the balls of her feet. Muscles rippled below their skin, like predators ready to pounce. Richard had his left hand curled at his side, flickering flames dancing around his fingertips. Stacey had stepped out of her wedges. Jimmy unfolded his arms, and walked up the center aisle. The driver stood, his feet spread apart and dug in as he gently pushed his father behind him. The chauffeur flexed his fists, and he sank into the ground a few inches. As if he'd suddenly become a man made of stone. Jimmy stood in front of the driver, looking up at him.

"I remember you, now," Jimmy said. "First National Bank of California. You wasn't so tall then. You had acne on your neck, and a gut."

"That was the old me," the man in the black uniform said.

"Before you got prison fit, eh?" Jimmy said.

"Before my dad helped me grow up," the driver replied.

Comprehension was dawning on a few faces in the crowd. Even

those who didn't get what was going on, though, recognized a fight was making noise on the horizon. Tumblers clicked in Gwen's head, and her jaw dropped open.

"You're the Specter," she said, blurting out the name of one of the most infamous white collar thieves since the Dawn. The amount of money he'd stolen was second only to the corruption he'd exposed in the hidden backrooms of big business, and bigger government. The invisible man who had literally disappeared off the radar around the time she'd been born. Her eyes shifted to the man who was his bodyguard, his chauffeur, and his son. He was younger than she'd thought at first, and he looked more like his father now that he'd grown into his frame and face. But she remembered a newspaper clipping of a pudgy teenager, walking through a hail of gunfire. His one moment in the spotlight that had lasted less than a week. "The Heavy is your son?"

"We've got a rule around here," Jimmy said, speaking loud enough that everyone gathered could hear him. "Dave called it rule zero. When you're here, in this place, you leave your capes and masks at home. Here, you're just you, whoever that happens to be. He once told me he thought of it like the green room. A place people could go to get out of the spotlight, and just take a few."

Jimmy held out his hand. The Heavy looked at it for a long moment, saying nothing.

"Jimmy Kapule," Jimmy said. "Nice to meet ya."

The driver looked around at the crowd. He nodded to them, then took Jimmy's hand, and shook with him. "Christopher White. Call me Chris."

"Hell of a grip you got, Chris," Jimmy said. "Care to ease up on an old man?"

Christopher smiled. It was a charming, disarming smile. He let out a breath, relaxed, and stepped out of the divots he'd made with his suddenly-increased density. "I don't think I could hurt you if I tried."

"Maybe you could," Jimmy said. "Nothing in this world lasts forever. Get you a drink, big man?"

"Beer, if you have it," Christopher said.

A collective sigh went through the mourners. Fists relaxed, flames snuffed out, and the gathering tension of kinetic forces dissipated. Chairs creaked as everyone took their seats again, though most stayed on the edge. Jimmy gestured toward the makeshift bar, and Christopher looked to his father. The corner of Alfred White's mouth quirked.

"Go on, Chris," he said.

Christopher went, following in Jimmy's wake like an ocean liner behind a tug boat. Alfred took his cane in his left hand, but before he could bend down for his glove, Gwen was at his side. She offered it, and he accepted, with a little bow of his head.

"Thank you, young lady," he said, carefully tugging the glove back on.

"Mr. White-"

"Alfred, please," he said, leaning both hands on the head of his cane. "I think we're past formality now, don't you?"

"Alfred," Gwen said. "Do you need anything?"

"I have the very best doctors money can hire, Gwen," he said, his mouth a wry twist. "Sadly, what I have is a terminal case of old, compounded by a misspent youth, and an unfortunate condition that causes me to discorporate. I used to have a firmer grip on it. As long as I don't sneeze, though, I think I'll be fine."

Alfred sat, and Christopher joined him a moment later. Gwen stepped back to the lectern, and took a deep breath. She wasn't sure what she said, but it was good enough to get some applause. It also started tears flowing. And then, just like that, the dam was broken. People congregated, talking, laughing, drinking, and telling stories. Stories Gwen had heard her whole life, floating to her in bits and pieces. When Alfred stood, and turned to go, Gwen brushed his shoulder with her fingertips.

"Mr... Alfred," she said. "How well did you really know my father?"

"Intimately," he said. "More intimately than anyone but your mother. You have a question. Ask it."

"You said dad talked to you, about whether he should have another kid. After he put on the cape." Gwen swallowed. "What did you tell him?"

"David wasn't sure he should risk Marion, after the changes he'd undergone." Alfred pursed his lips. "I asked him if he, and she, wanted another child. He said yes. I told him that they should, then."

"Why?" Gwen asked, the question out before she could stop it.

Alfred smiled at her. It was a naked, heart-wrenching expression. "Because the world needs more heroes, big and small alike. And heroes need people who love them, but who see them for who they really are."

Gwen tried to say something else, but when she opened her mouth she found there were too many tears in her throat. Alfred nodded, and held out an arm. "There isn't much of me left to give, but if you need it, you're welcome to it."

Gwen leaned into the old man, unsure whether she was laughing or crying. He stroked her back gently, his fingers a bare whisper against her. The world faded into a dull roar, and came back to her slowly. When she looked up, Alfred handed her his pocket square. She took it, and wiped her eyes. She knew if she blew her nose with it, the fabric would shred like she'd held it over a shotgun barrel.

"Is there more?" Gwen asked.

Alfred nodded, his face composed. "There's always more."

"Will you tell me?"

Alfred rubbed his chin. This time his smile was small, and sly. "If you'd pour an old man a drink, I think I could be persuaded to tell a secret or two."

Heart and Soul
A Caulbearer Case

I was playing solitaire with tarot cards, and losing badly, when she came into my office. Long and lean, she had the kind of beauty you tended to admire from the other side of the bar. The kind with teeth cold enough to leave frostbite on your ego. She was all in white, washed out and shining from the tips of her shoes to the corona of wispy blond hair that trailed her like she was the queen of the North Sea. I didn't bother glancing at my calendar. I already knew it was Wednesday, and it looked like my shot of woe had just walked in ready to tell me her story.

"Can I help you, miss?" I asked, once I'd picked my jaw out of my lap and swept up my cards. She looked down at me with crushed ice eyes, and her smooth lips pursed like she was contemplating buying me.

"You're Gerald Caul?" I nodded and thumbed the worn edge of my deck. Her eyes flicked to my just-too-long haircut, and lingered on the pale, crescent moon scar that curved around my right eye. I watched as she discarded half a dozen conversational gambits before she said, "You are not what I expected."

"I didn't expect you at all." I gave her a smile, and tried to make it warm enough to melt some of her frost. "You're still one up on me."

"My name is Ilyena Petrova." Her accent pirouetted on the name before it slipped back underneath her tongue. "I was told that if something is lost, or if something was taken, that you can find it, Mr. Caul."

"My reputation precedes me." I shuffled the cards, a nervous habit that gave my idle hands something to do. "What is it you need me to find?"

"My heart, Mr. Caul." She swallowed, and the first genuine emotion I'd seen yet crossed her face. Fear. "I gave it away, and I can't get it back."

I took a long, slow breath through my nose. I smelled sandalwood and furniture polish, along with a hint of the sharp, fruity scent of the woman herself. It made me think of bitter grapes and winter wine. I box shuffled the cards, and the deck made a machine gun rattle as faces and paintings slid one over the other in rapid-fire succession. I set the deck down, and gestured to one of my client chairs.

"Start with, 'Once upon a time,' Ms. Petrova," I said. "Once you get to the point where you walked into my office, I should be able to tell you whether or not I'll be able to help."

Her lips quirked, an automatic gesture with as much meaning as a call girl's cries. She slid her coat from her shoulders and sat, crossing one smooth leg over the other. She didn't bother to tug down her skirt, and her eyes never wandered from that middle distance between my face and hers. A white gold band winked in a shaft of late morning sunlight on the third finger of her left hand.

"Years ago I fell in love with a man named Peter. He was a charming boy from a good family, and my parents had known his since they were both children. His family came to America, and mine stayed in Ukraine. We wrote letters, then as we got older and our parents trusted us with technology we would send email and chat nearly every day. When I began attending University he came to visit me as a surprise. A surprise that, though he would never admit it, I believe our parents financed."

Again she smiled; an empty cookie jar with the lingering scent of warmth and sweetness that held nothing but a memory. She turned the ring round her finger like she was trying to wind back time.

"He spent a week in the city. He'd stay with me until curfew when I had to show him out, though he'd always try to persuade me to let him hide and stay the night. When that failed, he'd beg me to come and spend the night with him. I always told him no, but the night before he returned home I relented. I stayed with him, and we each laid claim to the other. Our first time giving or receiving.

"The next day he went home, and I went back to class. We kept on as we had, but we planned more visits. By the time I graduated we had made our plans, and I came to America. We were to be married two years ago. In September."

"I see," I said, just to show her I was keeping up. She nodded.

"Peter was killed by a drunk in an accident. So was the other man," Ilyena said. "I was left behind to try and cope with what had happened. I had no one to blame, and none of it made any sense."

She told her story the same way she would have ordered a salad with the dressing on the side. Her eyes never wavered, and her voice never faltered. It sounded like she was talking about a completely different person, and what had happened to that woman's life. She fetched a sigh that was more habit than heartfelt.

"I was inconsolable. I sat in bed all hours, I barely ate, and I cried till my lips chapped because I was so dehydrated. I couldn't even stand at the funeral, which was closed casket because of what had been done to Peter. Six months ago I woke up, looked at myself in the mirror, and knew that if I didn't do something that night I was going to kill myself."

She blinked her eyes twice, a Polaroid shutter snap. She looked at me, really looked, for perhaps the first time. A worry line creased her forehead and she re-crossed her legs. I looked back at her, half reclined in my busted out chair with one arm that sat higher than the other. I realized what it was about her that bothered me, and once I realized that, I saw where her story went.

"Where do you live, Ms. Petrova?"

"On West Haddon Avenue," she said, and gave me the street address. I pursed my lips, and nodded for her to go on. "I got dressed and went out. I didn't lock my door, and I barely remembered to grab my purse, but I went all the same. I walked for hours in the rain, but I finally found who I was looking for."

"The witch," I said. Ilyena jumped a bit, and her eyes went wide. I shrugged one shoulder. "That's what she is, so you might as well say it."

"How did you-" Ilyena cut herself off and narrowed her eyes. I waited. After a long pause she started again. "I was cold, shivering and I'd started crying again at some point. I probably looked half crazy by then, and there she was sitting up on a stoop with a little kettle next to her under the awning. I didn't have enough space left inside to be scared, so I walked right up and asked for what I wanted."

"You asked her to take the hurt away." I tried to keep my voice level. If I failed, Ilyena didn't give me any sign.

"She asked me if my heart was full of pain, and I told her it was. She asked if I gave it to her of my own free will. I said yes, as long as the hurt would go away. She poured me a cup of tea, and I drank it. I know I sat there for a long time, and I know she said a lot of things to me, but I don't remember what she said or what it was about. She gave me a kerchief, dark blue with small red dots on it. I remember thinking they looked like little drops of blood. I dried my eyes before I gave it back to her."

"And then it was sunup, and you were alone on the stoop?"

"Yes." Ilyena twisted the ring again, and looked down at her hands. "I'd gotten turned around somehow, because when the sun came up I was sitting right outside my building. I went inside and passed out. When I woke up, I didn't feel anything."

"Anything at all?" I asked. She frowned slightly, a child trying to remember which letters came next in the spelling words she'd gone over again and again at home.

"I didn't feel sad, but I wasn't happy. I felt empty, like there was a big, black hole inside of me somewhere. I ate and drank, but it was still there. I took lovers of all shapes and sizes. No matter how many or how often, it was still there. I waited, but it didn't scar over and go away."

"And then?" She shrugged.

"I tried to find her again, but when I asked people if they knew where she was they walked away and wouldn't talk to me. I looked night after night, but I didn't find her. When I ran out of ideas I went to Holy

Trinity and prayed. On the fourth day the priest, a man named Ivanovich, asked me what I was praying for. I told him what I'd done, and asked him to help me. He told me that there was nothing he could do, but that he knew a man that might help me. He gave me an address, and that led me here."

I leaned back in my chair and closed my eyes. I focused, frowning as my scar puckered. I could feel the hole in her, like a draft along the skirting boards of her soul. The sensation made my guts clench, and my skin crawl. I opened my eyes, but it didn't help. I couldn't unsee what was right in front of me. Ivanovich had sent her though, and I owed the clergyman a favor. Looked like it was time for me to make good on it.

"He called you something. A dowser." Ilyena uncrossed her legs and leaned forward, her hands in her lap. "What does that mean?"

"It means I can find anything that's been buried. Especially if it doesn't want to be found." I stood, and came around my desk as I started collecting the tools of my trade. I pawed through lacquered hinge-top boxes and wicker baskets, fired clay jars and wrought iron cages, all of them neatly and carefully arranged and labeled in my own shorthand. "Do you have anything else pressing to do with your day, Ms. Petrova?"

"No." Her gaze followed me, a pressure between my shoulder blades. "I didn't know what to expect after I came here."

"Give me your phone number." I slid a set of plain silver rings onto the first and last fingers of my left hand. I put a silver dime with the stamp practically worn off in my boot, and a pure copper penny turning green at the gills in my right hand pocket. I carefully hung a lodestone in a golden cage around my neck on an unblemished chain. I slipped an iron nail taken from a threshold frame of a church through my top buttonhole like an ugly, scabby flower that had lost all its petals. I stuffed a butcher paper packet of salt into my left hand pocket. I settled my lucky hat on my head, and ran a fingertip along the fraying gray corduroy of the trilby's brim. "I don't know how long this is going to take. I might have something for you today, I might not."

"What are you going to do?"

I shrugged into my herringbone overcoat, then turned the top three cards off my deck. The Three of Swords, The Devil, and the World. I shuffled the deck and pushed it into my breast pocket.

"I'm going to see if I can get your heart back."

***

The day had lost its freshness, and cut its teeth, by the time I crossed

Chicago Street into the southern border of the Ukrainian Village. Dirty snow choked alley mouths like gum cancer, and icy melt dribbled into open drains like old man's drool. People walked with their hats jerked down and hands in their pockets. It was Spring on somebody's calendar, but the neighborhood all around me seemed to have missed the memo.

When people heard the name Ukrainian Village, they expected a little piece of the Old Country in the New World; a skin graft still raw and rough around the edges. It wasn't. To the casual eye it was just another middle class Chicago suburb, with its smooth facades and clean curbs. Except for the rounded domes of the Orthodox Churches, anyway. Stores sold sandwiches and magazines, coffee and clothes just like anywhere else in the city. The only differences were the accents you heard, and the languages the residents spoke to each other when there weren't any outsiders in the conversation. Some women covered their hair, and some men grew thick beards, but that was all the average passerby was likely to notice.

Beneath that though, running under the surface like a subterranean river, was the magic that grew wild in the neighborhood. Magic flavored by old people and old ways, and not to be trifled with if it could be avoided. Most people didn't notice it, but the magic pressed against the soles of my feet and echoed in my bones. It was a thrum I felt more than I heard. It was a thing that, once you had the knack of seeing it, you couldn't ignore it. Being born with a caul over your face helped, but I didn't need any of my parlor tricks to find the witch. I knew exactly where she'd be on a day like today.

I smelled the place before I saw it; the crispy, greasy smell of fried chicken that slid up your nostrils and into your belly. There were hints of garlic, along with a splash of lemon and half a dozen other herbal cues my palate wasn't worldly enough to separate, too. The source of the aroma was a swinging door set in a simple brick front with big, open windows on either side as wide and innocent as fairy tale panes in a candy cottage. I stepped inside just as the low-slung sky puckered up and started spitting sleet.

The restaurant managed to be warm and inviting, even with cheap linoleum floors and faux leather booths lining both walls. Huge chalkboards were set in sliding tracks above and behind the counter, and the sounds of sizzling fat and spitting grease wafted through the concrete cut out below the hand drawn menu. It was a mom and pop set up inside the cast off rib cage of a corporate chain that had long since moved on, and it created a pleasant vertigo between what it had been and what it was now.

The witch sat in the corner, hunched over a plate of broken bones sucked dry of everything but the meanest strands of gristle. She was bad luck in Sunday black; a stringy-haired scarecrow with a pock-marked face like a crescent moon. Her long nose reached toward her chin, and her bony fingers flashed with gaudy rings that hung loose behind every swollen knuckle. When she raised her head, her eyes flashed beneath heavy brows; the gimlet gaze of a vulture with blood dripping from its beak. She smiled at me, and revealed two rows of perfect, porcelain teeth shiny with oil and speckled with flecks of burned skin.

"Well, well, what have we here?" She ran her tongue over her teeth, slurping the flesh she'd left behind. Her voice made me think of a bear trap after it had been slicked up and oiled down. It was throaty, whispery; a young woman's voice in her old throat.

"Baba Black." I touched the brim of my hat deferentially. "May I join you?"

"Sit yourself." She dipped one claw into a cardboard bucket and withdrew a drumstick. Juices sprayed when she bit into it, and her white teeth sheared away thigh muscle. She chewed with relish. "Could I offer you something, dearie?"

"No thank you, miss." I sat, and folded my hands on the table in front of me. She laughed, swallowing between her chuckles. Her thin shoulders shook, and she took another bite. Her eyes narrowed and her gaze crawled over my skin like an ant colony that smelled sugar.

"Flattery will get you nowhere with me, dowser." She swallowed, then smacked her lips before any of the flavor could escape. She pointed the leg at me, the knobby, gnawed joint gouged and bare. "Speak plain, and make it fast. Foul weather makes my joints hurt, and my patience is worn thin."

"You have something I'm looking for." She swallowed, and her thin throat bulged as the meat slid down her gullet like a migrating goiter. She smelled of the street, and of the secret things that lurked in hidden corners, and peeked up through sewer grates. She felt worse; a polluted river where fish with bulging, blind eyes swam. "Something my client gave to you that she'd like back."

Baba Black chewed thoughtfully. She nodded, thick, dirty strands of her gray hair bobbing like strings of soiled clouds. She snapped her teeth, and the bone crunched with a hollow, splintery sound. Her jaw flexed, and she ground the bone to nearly nothing before she swallowed. It was like watching a meat grinder go to work.

"If your chippie gave me something, then the something is mine to keep." She slurped the rest of the meat off the drumstick, and dropped it to rest in the pile with the others. "If that's all you came for then you've wasted your time, and mine as well."

"I'd be willing to work for the item in question."

"Would you now?" Her voice was sly. I nodded.

"If it's reasonable."

The witch leaned across the table, and breathed deep. The hairs in her nostrils waved like anemones at the bottom of the ocean. Baba Black grinned, a perverse parody of a kindly old woman as she drew back from me again, and settled herself.

"All those charms just for little old me?" She cackled, throwing her head back and howling. The woman behind the counter looked down and crossed herself. My left hand twitched, but I made it lay still. It was one thing to sneak into a bear's cave while it was hibernating. It was another to kick it in the balls and hope you could outrun it. So I returned her smile, kept my teeth behind my lips and my eyes on her face.

"Stupid rabbits get put in the pot, isn't that how the saying goes?" I asked. She laughed again, more quietly, a teacher amused at a pupil using one of her favored phrases.

"Close enough." She wiped her hands on a soft towel stained dark from her leavings. "You're not afraid of me are you?"

"No," I said. She snorted, and blew her nose into the towel before tossing it aside.

"And are you a good man?" She asked.

"I like to think so."

"You are, and an honest one as well. You stink of it. That and the sea, like all caulbearers do." She stood, her ragged layers swishing as she pulled on her coat. I stood as well. She was taller than me, or at least gave the impression she was. "I've no use for an honest man, dowser. Run along home and tell your sweet taste you can't help her. Or maybe you could try a lie on for size, and tell her you couldn't find me."

Baba Black passed me like a cold front. She had one hand wrapped around the door handle when she turned her head and glared. The eye inside her eye opened, and something twisted and dark looked out at me. The filthy, blasphemous thing that lived inside her skin reached out and ran a tendril over me like an invisible tongue. My charms sizzled and popped, biting into my skin as the force of the witch's evil eye raked over me. I clenched my teeth, and held her gaze. The terrible touch of her magic lingered a moment more, then curled back inside. She flashed that putrid smile again, and stepped outside into the wet misery like she was taking a walk in a flower garden.

As soon as she was out of sight I swore and dropped into a chair. I snatched at my laces and yanked my boot off. The silver dime had curled up at the edges and bitten twin tracks through my sock and into my heel. It wasn't deep, but it still hurt. I tossed the bent coin onto the table and reached into my pocket. My penny was seamed with cracks, and when I set it on the table it crumbled to dust like a relic from a pharaoh's tomb. I brushed my hands off and kept the curse behind my teeth. It wouldn't do me any good.

I took a quick inventory. My hair hadn't turned white, I wasn't blind, and when I opened my mouth the words I wanted to say came out properly. That was more than a lot of people who had run afoul of the Bone Lady could claim. On the other hand I felt like I'd been dipped mouth first into a sewer, and dragged along the bottom to the other side. My bowels churned, and my head ached like a mad bastard. As I took inventory, the coins seemed to be all that had been really damaged though.

"That went well," I said to no one in particular. I smelled a hint of burning sage, and glanced up. It seemed the cashier had decided to duck into the backroom, and was doing what she could to cleanse the place. Simple herb rub probably wouldn't do that much good, but it was worth a try. I took a deep breath, and let it out slowly while I carefully worked my foot back into my boot and laced it up tight.

I sat there for a moment and considered my options. I'd stuck my nose in the dragon's cave, and gotten it singed. I could limp away, go home, put on some smooth jazz, draw a bath and call the day a wash. Write it all off as a fool's errand, and say that I'd given it an honest try. The idea appealed, and I was giving it real consideration when the church bells rang the hour. The ringing was deep and sonorous, and as it rolled over me I felt like I was waking up from a bad dream. I shook my head. Going home wasn't an option. If I crawled under the covers, the monsters won.

I took out my deck and shuffled. The cards were old, hand-painted, and covered in clear coat to keep what was inside on the inside. The trumps chattered, and I made them dance. Images flashed by too quick to be seen, but I closed my eyes anyway. I listened for that little whisper that told me when to stop. When I heard it, my hands went still. I pulled the top card and opened my eyes. The Magus. I smiled.

"Of course." I put my deck away, buttoned my coat and took one last breath of the warm, delicious place. Then I started walking. I was off to see the Wizard.

***

Stony Island Avenue ran through a lot of the city, cutting across neighborhoods good and bad. The part of the street I was looking for was one that most people avoided if they could. It was a stretch where the shop windows bared their iron teeth at passersby, and the concrete zigzagged with cracks like fractures on a no-talent boxer's nose. Streetlights buzzed like swamp mosquitoes, and the cars sped up as the sun went down. It was a part of the city where if the bricks weren't covered in old smoke and new stains, then they'd be tagged with garish, eye-searing colors to let you know whose borders you were crossing.

The witch's hex clung to me like toilet paper on the bottom of my shoe, and it drug a trail of misery in my wake. A cab had splashed me about two blocks up from the restaurant, and my feet squished numbly as I walked. A bus had eaten my last two dollar bills, and refused me my change. A cold was trying to work its way into my throat, and the button on my slacks had snapped off. If I still had more ill fortune on the wheel, I didn't want it sneaking up on me. So I walked as fast as I could, with my head up and my eyes open. I managed to make it to where I was going without any more trouble, though that was probably because the bad weather was keeping the streets clear of everyone but the desperate and the stupid. At that particular moment, I wasn't sure which category I fit in. Both seemed likely.

The alley in question didn't look that much different from any others in the neighborhood. Dumpsters overflowed like stinking cornucopias, chunks of the wall had fallen and sat in one place so long the stone underneath was a lighter color, and a rusty chain link fence barred any through traffic. A sign that was surprisingly clean given the state of everything else, hung on the fence. I didn't read it; I already knew what it said. I stepped carefully through the few clean spots I could see in the street lamp spillover, and rapped on a steel door recessed in the shadows. Two short knocks, and one long one.

"What is it?" An intercom crackled. The voice was indistinct, the accent all but impossible to determine through the electric buzz.

"I'm here to see the wizard."

"No one sees the wizard," the voice grunted. I banged on the door with my fist.

"Open the door Hector!" I blew hot breath into my hands. "It's freezing out here, and I need your help."

For a minute I thought he was going to leave me out in the cold. Then locks snapped and clacked as they opened. Bars drew back, and chains rattled. The door swung open, and behind it stood a man in loose pants, a sleeveless crew neck shirt, and a ragged bathrobe with the belt hanging out of the last loop. A mane of straight, black hair hung to his shoulders, and his thin face looked like a sculpture of some ancient Incan priest; severe, with dark eyes full of things man wasn't meant to know. By the light of a black candle, with the whorls of tattoos peering out from beneath his shirt and peeking from the sleeves, he would have been a frightening sight. If he wasn't wearing lopsided bunny slippers, that was. He lifted the candle regarding me closely. Once he was sure I was who I said I was, his lips split in a thin smile.

"That is a horse of a different color," he said.

"You really need a new code phrase, Hector."

Hector Garcia stepped aside. I took one step over the threshold, and I could feel the bad luck that had been clinging slink away. It felt like I'd been spiritually squeegeed, or like I'd been unclean for so long I didn't notice until the bathwater turned gray and I was toweling off. I had no idea what protections he'd laid on his entrances, but they were nothing to fool about with. Hector eyed the door frame, then slammed the iron portal behind me. He flicked the light switch, blew out the Soothesayer's Tallow he'd been carrying, and started re-locking the door.

The place was a cavern of knowledge. A balcony barely wide enough to walk on ran around the ground floor level like an interior widow's walk. Beyond the railing, like a below-ground atrium, was a sea of bookshelves. Meticulously cataloged, the shelves held books of every size, shape and description. There was so much literature that the hardwood sagged and groaned beneath the load like Atlas getting a cramp. The collection swarmed up the walls, until the shelves had to be built at angles to contain the weight. Free-standing cases filled with the unusual and the bizarre dotted the collection like refugees from the museum macabre. I'd learned not to look too closely at Hector's curiosities, and under no circumstances to try and open anything he'd locked up. Chandeliers hung from the ceiling, and spark lanterns dangled all around the upper walk. A fire burned in a brick hearth against the far wall, and the fireplace was big enough that one end of the room looked like a diorama of Dante's Inferno.

"Aren't those things sort of valuable to burn just because visitors show up of an evening?" I asked, nodding at the candle. I knew how rare the fat to make them was, and how coveted the candles that could reveal the true nature of things were among those in the trade.

"Not this close to sunset." Hector snapped the last bolt home, then turned to me. When I looked at him under the purely mortal lights, I could see the gray streaking through his hair, and the salt scattered through his stubble. His face was lined, where a moment ago in the light of the candle he'd been smooth and ageless. His eyes, though, were the same.

"You want to tell me what you've done this time, or am I going to have to drag it out of you?" he asked.

111

"Whatever do you mean, Hector?" I widened my eyes, trying for innocent. His jaw hardened, and I stopped. "All right, all right. It seems I jumped into the deep end of something, and I need a little direction to know which way I should be swimming."

"How deep?"

"I've got a case," I started. Hector waved a hand like I'd blown cheap cigar smoke in his face.

"How deep?" He repeated. My shoulders sagged and I took my weight off my bad foot.

"I need you to tell me about Baba Black."

Hector looked at me as if I'd started speaking in tongues. Then he closed his eyes, and shook his head slowly back and forth. It made him look like a disapproving parent faced with the latest in a series of schoolyard screw ups.

"Is your client someone who lost something to the witch?"

"She is."

"And she acted rashly, and you want to help her mitigate the mistake she made?"

"I do."

"And she is also a very beautiful woman, whom you deeply desire to take to bed."

"Well, I wouldn't say deeply." Hector folded his arms and met my gaze. I shrugged one shoulder and tried my charming smile. "I've known her less than a day."

The facade cracked into laughter that stole the years from Hector's face. He whooped a war cry full of mirth as his shoulders shook and his belly clenched. It was an infectious laugh, but my foot throbbed, and I winced instead of joining in. Hector dried his eyes on the sleeve of his robe and put his hands in his pockets.

"Dowsers." The one word held so many feelings packed into it that the tinctures couldn't be separated. He led me down the stairs, and through the stacks to the scattered workplace where he tended to end his days reading by the fire. I slid out of my coat, and collapsed into the dusty, wing back chair Hector kept for company. He picked up a bound stack of junk mail and tossed it into the flames. They roared higher, blues and greens dancing as the tongues of fire lapped ink from the cheap circulars.

"Tell me everything." Hector sat across from me, elbows on his knees and head forward. He looked like an eagle, sharp and ready. "Leave nothing out."

I gave him the tale, so far as I had it, from start to finish. He barely moved, and if not for the way the firelight danced in his eyes he could have been mistaken for a man who'd been stuffed and mounted. When I finished he relaxed into his cushions like he'd just eaten a large, if not exactly fine, meal. The hint of a smile lingered on his lips, and he chuckled dryly as he turned over what had happened.

"You are not a man that does things by half measures, Caul."

"No sense screwing a thing up halfway, is there?"

I held my hands out to the fire. Hector stood, and walked off toward one of the massive cabinets that dotted the walls. I added another Marshall's book to the fire, and stretched my feet a little bit closer. The pins and needles were just starting to turn back into real feeling when he returned with a small sack over his arm. He set a stool in front of my chair, and settled onto it. "Take off your boots. Leave them by the fire."

I didn't argue. I gently tugged at the rugged leather and set my run-down boots at the foot of the hearth stones. I peeled off my damp socks and laid them out like shed snake skins still wet from molting. Hector cupped my ankle and rubbed a cool cream across the swollen cut on my heel.

"Ancient herbal remedy to cleanse evil spirits?" I asked.

"Neosporin," Hector said. "Probably about the same thing when you get down to it."

Hector finished with the minute wound, and applied a bandage. He nodded, then set a sack on the floor between his feet. He laid out the contents on the ground in a semi-circle, and started talking.

"No one's really sure where Baba Black or her magic comes from. Some people claim it's a title handed down from one old witch to another, and some people say it's the same witch who changes herself every generation or so. Some people say she's older than Chicago, and that she only came across the ocean because there wasn't room left in the hinterlands for her anymore."

"Who are these people?" I asked. Hector cut the air with his hand, snipping off the question.

"Whisper mongers, storytellers, old women, young men, and more. They're people I trust, and that's all you need to know. All the trustworthy records I have about the big, bad Baba go back at least a hundred years. Before that time things get sketchy. Now shut it and let me talk." I held my hands up, palms out. Hector nodded and went back to his story. "This woman is bad medicine, and she'll ail the things that cure you. Curdled milk, busted luck, and broken homes follow her like bad weather does the storm crow. People who approach her, especially people who promise her something, take their lives in their hands."

"What does she take from people?" I asked. "And why? She shouldn't need to, should she?"

"Who knows?" Hector shrugged. "The witch has never turned down anything that might be of value. At the same time, she's done favors for people just for the asking. She's a hurricane with the mind of a pack rat. She's accepted tokens from scorned lovers, she's taken the guilt of murderers, and a lot of other potent types of pain from people trying to unburden themselves of a thing that's of no use to them."

"Powerful stuff, mixed together with the proper intent," I said. Hector nodded, his face grave.

"Breakouts of urban blight, the sudden deaths of men and women both great and small, along with half a dozen other crafts have been laid at her feet over the years. She haunts the Ukrainian Village and the surrounding neighborhoods, but she doesn't seem tied to any one place in particular. She goes where she wants, and whoever runs that part of town closes his shutters and goes home for the day. Cleaning up the mess that Baba Black leaves behind is usually preferable to being a part of the mess because you got in her way."

"You're preaching to the choir," I said, fishing the bent dime out of my pocket and handing it over to Hector. He took it like it might bite him, then looked at me with a raised eyebrow. I licked my bottom lip, and realized that somewhere along the line it had split open Just my luck. "Pure silver. She also dusted my Indian head like it wasn't even there."

"Too bad. It was a pretty penny." Hector set the dime down in front of the fire. "You must have annoyed her."

"I'm glad I brought a few extra precautions. Otherwise I think I might have gotten hit by a car on my way over here."

"Shot. It's more likely, and the bad medicine fever wouldn't have to work so hard to make it happen." Hector paused and ran his tongue over his teeth. "This girl you're working for. She gave up her heart to the witch?"

"Yeah." I shook my head sharply, like a dog trying to get water out of its ears. "I thought maybe the witch would barter with me. No luck."

"There is a way... but it will be like finding water in the desert." I grinned, but Hector's frown wiped the smile off my face. "You'd be taking a serious risk, Caul. More serious by far than what you did earlier today."

"All right," I said, and pushed my hat back on my head. "Lay it on me."

***

At a quarter of nine the next morning I sat in the food court of the mall on Block 37, and sipped instant coffee gone muddy with fake creamer and artificial sweetener. The place was about as well-populated as a graveyard at dawn. Empty store fronts sat like boarded up plague houses, and behind their welcoming smiles the cashiers and managers kept sneaking glances at those ugly gaps. All the clapping, singing, and other sales rigmarole was just so much superstition in the face of economic mortality, and deep down they all knew nothing would stop them from being next. The mall had moved the tombstones from the old tinker shops and peep shows that had been left on that block decades ago, but they hadn't moved the bodies. Block 37 was haunted, and there wasn't enough money in the world to sanctify the empty halls of that chapel of commerce.

Ilyena walked through the street doors, and a blast of morning chill nipped at her heels like a yappy dog. She wore mourning white again, her coat a woolen shroud and her shoes barely more than leather slippers. In the gray light she looked like a wraith, hungry for whatever it was that had been taken from her. I shivered, and drank down the rest of my coffee fast enough to burn my tongue. I stood and met her in the middle of the vast, empty cafeteria.

"There you are." I tilted my hat back on my head, and ran the pad of my index finger across the spines of the black crow's feather stuck jauntily in the band. One of several gifts Hector had given me last night. "I was worried you wouldn't make it in time."

"You told me to be here by nine, so here I am." Ilyena peeled off her gloves, slipping them into her pockets. "What would have happened if I'd been late?"

"Bad luck." I glanced at the clock on the wall, an ostentatious thing that had just four hash marks like a minimalist compass. I plucked my pocket watch from my vest and clicked it open. It didn't tell me anything the wall clock hadn't, except for the date and the moon phase. "And I think we've had more than enough of that to last us a while. Did you bring what I asked?"

"I did." Ilyena slid her fingers down her blouse and brought out a small Saint Christopher's medal. It was old, tarnished around the edges and rubbed smooth in places. The chain was silver. So were the clasps woven through her hair, masterfully crafted into the shapes of pale roses. The former had been worn across the ocean by her grandfather, and the latter had been the last present given her by her fiancee. Powerful amulets, and just as good as anything I could have given her.

I led Ilyena through empty halls where Muzak played like bird song in tracts of primordial forest. Our footsteps were flat, muffled by the oppressive weight of all the polished tile and brooding concrete around us. Cheery advertisements looked on from the walls, and colorful lights beckoned from open shops, trying to entice us to come in, stay awhile, and maybe buy something. I ignored them. I angled right, and walked past a stunted column map lit up from the inside. It looked like an abandoned crossroads sign; You Are Here, Turn Back Now. I started down the stairs, and felt a draft. We were at the edge of it now; that nowhere place where the dark things of the world always made their homes.

"Where are we going?" Ilyena asked.

"Have you ever heard of the Pedway, Ilyena?" She shook her head. "I'm not surprised. Short version is that it's an underground pedestrian walkway so people can ignore busy streets, bad weather and the other inconveniences of city life. Problem is that, like everything else in this town, it's been carved out with corruption and seeded with lies. The thing is a miles long concrete maze, and if you manage to get through it without getting lost you should probably pat yourself on the back and buy a drink for a job well done. The chances of finding any one, specific place without a guide aren't good. Things change down there when people aren't looking."

A revolving door led out of the garish mausoleum of the mall, and into the underground. Beyond the glass doors, bare rock and steel sat stark and cold as the grave. One step through that door would mark something significant, and it would set things in motion I couldn't stop. It was the first line of a formula, and the beginning of a ritual. I knew some of it at the top of my mind, but the rest came from somewhere else. Intuition, maybe. I had a feeling of pressure on my shoulders, and a sense of the gears of the universe getting ready to move in a way my conscious mind couldn't explain. I checked my watch again. We had two minutes.

"There's no correct map of this place, despite what the city will tell you, and no one's entirely sure what lives down there," I said. "The burrows go all over, and there's subway tunnels where the trains have never run. Somewhere down there is a pocket where the witch keeps her loot. It's guarded of course, and there's every chance that she might be there if and when we do find it."

I glanced at Ilyena. She seemed mildly worried about the prospect of coming face-to-face with Baba Black again, but if I had to guess I'd say that fear had gone into that kerchief along with love. I tucked my watch back in my vest pocket, feeling it tick against my fingertips.

"I don't know what's waiting in the tunnels. If something happens I'm going to need to act fast, and I'm going to need you to trust me. So if I ask you to do something, even if it seems like the worst idea in the world, don't hesitate. I'm doing it for a reason."

"All right," Ilyena said, adding a nod for emphasis. "I can do that."

I tried to think of any other cautions I needed to give. I thought about asking her if she was sure she wanted to go through with this, but decided not to. I checked my watch again, then put it away. Together we stepped out of the world above, and entered the world below. It was precisely nine in the morning; a sacred hour full of potential and promise. I tried to avoid it as a rule, because there's no guarantee the day's potential is always the potential for good.

At first, the Pedway didn't seem all that bad. It was just plain concrete, but it was roomy enough that it might have been an access tunnel for unloading goods, or for handling serious foot traffic. What began as a wide path beneath the urban sprawl quickly turned into a rat warren of passages, though. Doors along the walls led to businesses whose names I knew, but from down below the glassed-in entrances peering into well-lit shops looked wrong. It gave me a sense of looking at a familiar place through the back side of a mirror; a voyeuristic vertigo that slid through me like I'd had one drink too many. We passed the subway station originally built to service Block 37. The metal gleamed dully, and the turnstiles looked eager as the toys left behind on the day after Christmas. I smelled something dank behind those gates, and caught a hint of swamp gas bleeding up through the floor. Something watched us, and I walked on. I never let go of Ilyena's arm, in case whatever it was decided to do more than look.

The path shifted subtly, and the four coats of industrial paint changed colors as the storefronts took on different faces. On our right, fitness nuts and morning swimmers did laps in a health club behind glass panes thick enough to stop bullets. Across the way, small convenience stores the size of walk-in closets sold cigarettes, lottery tickets, microwave lunches, and energy drinks. Heavy grilles protected LED lamps along the walls, but despite the brightness, shadows still lurked around the edges. Little puddles of darkness just waiting for the power to go out. I fingered the rabbit's foot hanging from my wrist on a leather cord, and kept up our pace.

The halls spread and narrowed, went up and down, and detritus collected in corners like forgotten meals in some great beast's digestive track. Half smoked cigarette butts sat next to empty paper bags filled with broken bottles. Tattered magazines that had been out of date for months sat with their pages open and spines broken. Some of them had pages torn out of them, probably used as insulation to keep out the wind. Dry, dead leaves shifted in the errant breezes that came from vents. It sounded like they were whispering as we passed.

I took note of everything we passed, including the people. While the ones behind the glass and in the bright lights were off in their own little world, the residents who shared the tunnels with us were just as tattered as the other things driven below by the cold. Some of them nodded, and some looked away, but none of them tried to stop us. I dropped a few quarters into a Styrofoam cup in front of a man playing a harmonica. It felt like the right thing to do.

We came to a fork in the path; one road went right and one left. Against the wall was a map, the glass streaked by the passage of hundreds of fingers trying to follow the routes laid out on it. I spit on the glass and wiped it clean with a kerchief, trying to get a better look at where we were supposed to be.

"I thought you said there weren't any maps?" Ilyena wasn't out of wind yet, but she had to take a deep breath in the middle of her question.

"There aren't any correct maps. This one's four years out-of-date. Mostly it's useless, but it will do." I slipped the lodestone from around my neck and carefully ran the chain around the first and third fingers of my left hand. I drew the links tight, until the natural magnet swayed under my middle finger. I looked around. We were alone. I turned my left hand over so the natural magnet rested in my palm. I turned to Ilyena. "Take a deep breath, clench your teeth and don't cry out."

I saw the question in her face, but she did just as I asked. Her chest swelled as she breathed in, and deflated as she breathed out. As her lungs bottomed out, I slapped her. My right palm cracked against the fleshy part of her cheek, hard enough to turn her head like something out of a black and white movie. Before the shock wore off I caught the one, surprised tear in my left palm. It splashed through the gilded cage, and turned the lodestone a damp, storm cloud black.

I inhaled and unfocused my eyes. The world drifted, sharp edges dissolving until all that was left was the essence of color and shape. I raised my left hand, and blew breath over my knuckles in a slow moving current. The lodestone dangled, and stilled. I felt it start to sway, tugging at the chain. I let my hand follow that magnetic tug until I heard the stone clink against the glass. I blinked rapidly, and reminded myself how to see properly.

"We need to go West," I said.

I carefully unwrapped the chain and hung the stone back around my neck. It rolled to my left and pressed against the cage wall like an animal that scented food. Ilyena touched her cheek, then looked at her fingertips. They were damp. She stroked her flushed skin, forehead furrowed. She looked like she was trying to remember something she'd nearly forgotten. Like she'd heard a snatch of music she knew, but for the life of her she couldn't summon the words to. I touched her shoulder, and she turned her far away gaze on me. She focused, and her hand fell back to her side.

"I'm sorry. We need to go, Ilyena." I held her eyes making sure she was with me. "The trail won't last long. Come on"

"What did you do?"

"I'll explain when it's over." I took her hand and drew her down the left fork. "Right now, we don't have time."

For a moment it looked like she was going to dig in her heels, and argue with me. Then she followed, not saying anything, but saying it loud enough it made my ears ring. I tuned her out, and concentrated on my talisman. I wanted to get this right the first time.

We headed west at something faster than a walk that wasn't quite a run. Signs pointed this way and that, trying to distract us with food, with trinkets, and with other destinations, but the lodestone drew me steadily down the left hand path. We turned down corridors without signs, and slipped into doorways no one would notice if they weren't looking for them. First into access tunnels, and then into smaller holes hidden behind steel doors and maintenance panels. The new tunnels constricted, and as we went deeper the cinder block gave way to fired brick and crumbling masonry. The floor sloped and angled, and old grates whispered like toothless serpents as we passed. Water dripped down the walls and ran in clotted, yellow streams like a dying man's piss into rusted grates. The tunnels smelled acrid. The trail led through the bones of the city, riddled with age and cancer under the healthy, robust skin.

I ran my fingers along the wall, feeling for the flow of the city's magic. We were treading close to one of the many secret hearts of the city, and the pulse got stronger with every step closer. Power thrummed through my silver rings as if my fingers were a set of old rabbit ear antennae. It wasn't light or dark, good or evil; it simply was. Like lightning, this was power that could strike down the wicked or the just, and it wouldn't pause for reflection before it moved on. We rounded a corner, and stood face to face with an old, wooden door. It looked like a palette banded together with strips of iron, symbols carved deep into the wood. I didn't try to read them, but even at a glance I could tell they hadn't been made with a knife. Gas lanterns burned on either side of the strange door, making the tiny hallway reek of scorched methane.

I glanced over my shoulder at Ilyena. A few strands of hair had come loose from her clips, and her white clothes bore streaks of dust and dirt. Her face was flushed, though, and the firelight burned in her eyes. She looked more real, more alive, than I'd ever seen her. Her heart was very close. She smiled, and it held a glimmer of the woman she must have been before all this happened to her. I returned it in kind.

"Get ready," I told her.

I knocked three times. My knuckles rang hollow on the door, like an inquisitive tapping from the wrong side of a coffin. Neither of us so much as breathed. I half expected to feel the witch's nails on the back of my neck, or to hear that horrible, stolen voice of hers in my ear. Instead, the door opened into darkness, and the musty smell of a basement left neglected for a generation or more wafted over me. My fingers vibrated from the sheer potential energy built up in that room. I clenched my hand into a fist, and gave Ilyena what I hoped was a reassuring smile. She didn't look like she needed it. I stepped into the blackness.

As my eyes adjusted to the mean, yellow light of thick candles that burned in dripping stands around the room, my mouth went dry. Mahogany book cases as tall as a man lined the walls, each one of them a unique work of art covered in leering grotesques and delicate forms re-enacting timeless myths. Tables sat in front of the shelves, groaning with the weight of the things they held. Hands floated in pickle jars next to bottles of clipped toenails, and envelopes of balled up hair were clearly labeled in short, scratchy writing. Dusty wedding rings gleamed on dirty velvet next to torn veils, and baby shoes too pristine to have ever been worn. Tear-stained Dear John letters lay cheek and jowl with rejection slips and form letters. It was a gallery of pain; an entire vault of human suffering going through a blue period. Jars of misery congealed in the cast-off mementos, filling the room with the salty smell of sorrow and suffering. It felt like standing in the bottom of a dam, with all that weight crushing down on me.

"My god." Ilyena's mouth worked, but she couldn't seem to find more words to describe what she was looking at.

"Let's just find your kerchief and get out of here." No sooner had I whispered the words than the door shut behind us, and the latch squeaked into place. "Oh hell."

"Who are you?" A voice rumbled, echoing off the blind vault of the ceiling and bouncing back from the stones until it became a chorus. Ilyena whipped her head around, her eyes darting and seeking.

"Look for the cloth," I whispered, gently pushing her behind me. She nodded, a bare dip of her head. I turned slowly until I faced the shadows between the two stacks at the far end of the room. A collection of graveyard bouquets filled one of the tall sets of shelves, and stripped bones covered the shelves of the other. I had the sensation you get during a black out when you're in standing in a room, and you know there's an open door in front of you even though the darkness doesn't look any different. That open, empty sensation like a low-pressure system rubbing against your skin. I showed my teeth and stepped forward. "My name is Caul. I'm looking for something."

A man stepped out of a patch of shadows that was far too small to have hidden him. He was black as secrets, his arms hung nearly to his knees, and his neck stretched high, leaving his face mostly draped in gloom. His eyes glimmered in the candlelight, along with a mouthful of square, straight teeth displayed in a ghastly grin. His clothes were the gray linen of hospital sickrooms, and he leaned down, putting his hands on either end of a table lined with other people's miseries. Even bowed, I had to look up at him. His breath reeked of spoiling meat, and his gaze was a pair of hungry pits that took in everything, but gave back nothing. I had known his name even before I went to Hector. Baba Black was a holy terror, but the Deathless Man who ran her errands, and watched her horde, was almost as bad.

"The dowser," he said, his voice quieted to a dull, grumbling roar in place of thunder he'd first addressed us with. "You roll weighted bones, caulbearer. You shouldn't have come to this place."

"I shouldn't have been able to find this place either," I said. I stepped closer to the Deathless Man, though everything in me said to do the opposite of that, and added a dash of insolence to my grin. "But here I am."

"Here you are." The giant's nostrils flared, and he looked over my shoulder at Ilyena. He licked his lips, but Ilyena kept her mind on why we were here. He looked at me again, deciding whether or not to step on the bug that has crossed his path. "And why are you here, Caul?"

"I'm looking for the lady's broken heart." I shrugged and slid my hands into my pockets. "She wants it back."

"We never know what we have until it's in someone else's hands," he said, a note of bitterness in his voice. He straightened, looking like a tree falling in reverse. He fished inside his shift and removed a cloth. It was dark midnight blue, with bright red dots that shone like fresh blood. Ilyena cried out, and the hairs on the back of my neck stood up.

"Did you think you would just walk in here and take it?" The Deathless Man asked. He raised the cloth to his nose, and breathed in deep. Ilyena shivered. "It's still fresh, as trinkets go. The witch would be very upset if it went missing."

"I didn't expect you to just give it to me for the asking," I said. I took another step closer, until the table was the only thing between me and the giant. "I have something to trade for it."

"Do you?" Though his face remained impassive, I felt the shadow of the raised boot recede slightly. I nodded.

"Rumor has it the witch has your soul." I took my hands out of my pockets, and held them out. "I can find it for you."

The Deathless Man stood still as a cemetery angel, a frown cutting deep lines through his heavy jaw. I waited, and tried not to count the grains of sand running out in my head. The longer we stood there, the shorter our chances got of walking out without being noticed by Baba Black. After a condensed eternity, the Deathless Man fixed his gaze on me, and leaned close.

"Why should I trust you, dowser?" His teeth ground like millstones; powerful and heavy as he chewed the words. His knuckles cracked as he gripped the kerchief we'd come for. I shrugged. The giant smiled, and laughed. It sounded like continents coming apart. "Very well. Find it, and I'll give the girl back her heart. Be quick."

He didn't have to tell me twice. Hector had said that the soul of the Deathless Man had been placed into a silver needle, which had been put into an egg. As long as it stayed safe and protected in the needle, he was invincible. But if someone had the egg, he was their servant as surely as a djinn bound in a lamp. The egg was somewhere in the witch's storeroom, hidden cleverly enough that the giant hadn't found it in all his years upon years of service. All I had to do was uncover that one secret among a thousand others in the witch's lair, and we'd be on our way. Piece of cake.

I took a silver needle out of my pocket and pricked him. If the Deathless Man noticed, he gave no sign. I threaded the eye of the needle with a string from a Romani funeral shroud, and let the needle dangle. I walked the aisles, and waited for the tell-tale tug. It didn't come. I waded through the palpable despair wafting off the collected objects of power, but the needle didn't twitch to left or right. I waved it over the tables, and along the shelves, but it hung limp and lifeless. Heat flushed along my neck, and my scar began to throb. My temples pricked, and pain started worming its nails under my skin.

I circled the room once with no results. Ilyena worried her lip, and shifted her weight from one foot to the other. She wasn't sure whether to wait and hope, or to take her chances and run. I smiled like this was all part of the ritual, and began a second sweep. I was most of the way around the room, investigating one of the stacks of shelves, when the string snapped. The needle tinkled on the ground, leaving small spots of dark blood on the stones. I swore and crouched. I was down on one knee scrabbling at the floor, when the door crashed open and a cold chill went up my spine.

"You," Baba Black hissed. From under the table I watched her walk across the room, thrusting a heavy cane into the floor like a gondolier pushing herself over the water. "And what are you doing here, little pretty?"

Ilyena stood very still. Her eyes darted around the room trying to find somewhere, anywhere to look except at the witch, or at me. Baba Black snarled, a wordless sound of malice and grabbed Ilyena by the hair. Ilyena didn't cry out, but it was a near thing.

"I came for what you took," Ilyena said. She panted with pain, but refused to let it into her voice. "Give me back my heart!"

"And I suppose you made it here all by your onesome, did you?" Baba Black laughed. Ilyena tried to say something, but the witch shook her. Baba Black's voice rose to a raptor's screech. "Where is the dowser? You didn't find this place on your own, *where is he!?*"

I ran through every trick I knew, and discarded them all out of hand. Everything I had on me would have been about as useful as shooting a pistol at a tank; it was more likely to bring the barrel swiveling around toward me than to do anything helpful. I turned my head, and the crow feather in my hat band brushed against something hidden on the inner lip of the table. My hand shot out on instinct, and a dull, brown egg fell into my palm. It was warm, and there was a pinhole in the bottom. As if something had been pushed into it. I stood up.

"Looking for me?" I asked.

Baba Black whirled, and her evil eye lashed out like a crackling whip. I thrust out my left hand, first and last fingers forked out in the ancient warding sign. My hand went numb as the cold, reptilian magic slid down my fingers and slammed through my rings. Her power doubled up and folded over, reversing on her like a feedback scream. The witch howled and clutched her face, stumbling and snarling. Ilyena kicked the old woman's stick from under her, and narrowly ducked a swipe of her clawed hand. I hefted the egg aloft, and looked at the Deathless Man. He offered the cloth to Ilyena, who grabbed it and bolted for the door. I tossed the egg, and did the same.

I didn't see what happened, but I heard it. It was the roar of a bursting levy, the howl of a forest fire, and the bellow of a beast as it broke open its cage. The walls shook as we ran, the lights shuddered in their sockets, and brick dust fell all around us. The halls lurched and buckled, undulating like lungs trying to cough us out. Doors slammed open and closed like the mouths of half-mad street preachers, metal squealing and smashing in busted, breaking frames. Bulbs flared and dimmed, then burst as electricity arced like captured lightning set free from a bottle. We ran until we'd left the secret paths behind; until we found familiar concrete, steel, fluorescent lamps, and helpful signs entreating us to spend money we didn't have to buy things we probably didn't need.

Ilyena collapsed onto a wrought iron bench that was both decorative and uncomfortable at the same time. I sat down next to her, panting and wiping beads of sweat from my cheeks. Ilyena wiped her face with the kerchief, then stopped and stared at it. Her expression was that of a woman who'd reached into her closet for a scarf, and instead come out with a cobra wrapped around her arm. I laughed. I couldn't help myself, and when Ilyena turned her wide-eyed gaze on me, I laughed even harder. Ilyena's lips twitched, and she tried to say something, but all that came out was a breathless giggle. I smiled at her, she smiled at me, and then we were gone.

Our laughter bounced from the curved walls. People who saw us walked faster, but that just pushed it up another notch. We rolled like drunks, clutching each other so we didn't spill onto the floor. Ilyena wiped her eyes, and looked up at me. She was close enough to taste, and all it took was a single breath of her heady, sharp scent to smother my humor. I licked my dry lips, and color bloomed in Ilyena's cheeks.

"Thank you," she said. Those two words, barely a whisper set my heart hammering in my chest. I made myself lean back. I stood up, and made a show of adjusting my hat and looking around. The feather was brittle and limp, now, the rabbit's foot around my wrist patchy and shedding. Whatever good luck had been in them had gone bust when I uncovered the egg, which I was pretty sure couldn't have been found in the absence of the witch. I slipped them both into my pockets. I didn't know if Hector would want them back, but he might still have a use for them.

"Don't thank me yet." I cleared my throat. "We've still got to undo that little trap you've got there. Can you walk?"

"If I must." Ilyena stood and stretched. She didn't look like a woman who'd spent hours crawling through the seedy underbelly of Chicago's Strange. She seemed vibrant, excited, and full of anticipation.

"Unless we want to wait for trains that don't come in," I said. No sooner were the words out of my mouth when I shivered. I'd heard stories about the things that sometimes ran on the tracks late at night, when no one was supposed to be there. I offered Ilyena my arm. She took it, her prize twined between her fingers, and we headed back the way we'd come.

The sun was going down outside. It didn't feel like we'd been gone that long, but time was a funny thing in the city's thing places. I glanced at the clock in the mall, and waited until the hands pointed down where the six should be until I opened the door. Nine hours, from start to finish. We stepped into what was left of the day, and I sighed with relief. Standing on the sidewalk, buffeted by the wind and the shoulders of people trying to get out of it, the full weight of what I'd done settled on me. I shuddered, a full body convulsion that shook me from the top of my head to the soles of my feet. I hailed a taxi. I'd had more than enough walking for one day, and I wanted to see an end to this business before another sun rose. I settled into the back seat, and Ilyena climbed in with me. I told the driver where to go, took off my hat, and leaned my head back against the seat. I took slow, measured breaths, and tried to clear my head. I could feel Ilyena next to me, but she just sat quietly. There were questions coming, though. There always were.

The cab made it to my building just as true darkness was really settling in. I tipped her well, then headed through the lobby and up the stairs. There was an elevator, but it was slow and I didn't trust it. Ilyena followed, practically pressed against my back until I unlocked the door with my name across the pebbled glass. No sooner had I shut the door, then she asked the same question everyone that came crawling back to my office asked when it was over. I could set my watch by it.

"How did you do that?"

I hung up my coat and hat, and ran a hand through my hair. "Do you want Reader's Digest or War and Peace?" I asked.

Ilyena shrugged. "Just tell me the truth."

I smiled. It took fewer muscles than frowning, but it was still exhausting.

"All right, the truth." I unlocked my desk, took a key from a hidden section of the drawer and pulled aside a drape on the right wall. I unlocked the covered door, turned on the lights and held the curtain back for Ilyena. "That's going to take some time. Might as well get comfortable."

The room was small but serviceable. A futon filled the far wall, and two shelves above it held most of my worldly possessions. A few changes of clothes, a spare set of shoes or two, and a few books I hadn't finished reading yet. A microwave and a hot plate shared space atop a re-purposed chest of drawers that held most of my food. Next to it was a sink that hadn't been part of the original construction of the building, but which had been installed after. A comfortable chair sat against one wall, along with a dreamcatcher that had been given to me by an Ojibwe spirit worker. Ilyena turned around twice, her eyes roaming over what the building's previous owner had no doubt billed as a large, walk-in closet.

"Is this where you live?" she asked.

I shrugged, took my kettle off the hot plate, and started filling it at the tap.

"I don't need much," I said, putting the kettle in place, and flicking the switch on the plate. The few droplets of water that had run down the side hissed as they evaporated. "Besides, the water closet has a claw-foot tub. Any time I start feeling too down, I just remember that."

Ilyena stepped out of her shoes, sat in my chair, and tucked her feet up under herself. I got out a coffee cup with a chip over the handle, and waggled it at her. She shook her head, and I hunted for a tea bag. Blueberry tea was awful stuff, but the connection I got this particular blend from put an extra something in it that cleansed the spirit. The silence trembled between us, waiting to be filled.

"I think it was Aleister Crowley who said magic was the ability to force changes on the world using nothing more than your will. That's a lot like saying Lake Michigan is wet; accurate, but misleading." I folded my arms and sighed, trying to find the right words to part the mists for someone who'd only had a single glimpse behind the veil. "What we call magic is nothing more than ideas and desires made manifest. But you can't just say a few words in Latin and wave your hands over a fire with bat guano smeared all over your face. You have to have the juice to make it happen."

"Juice?" she asked. The kettle squealed and I poured the hot water into my cup.

"Mojo, medicine, power." I shrugged. "There has to be a driving force behind magic. It doesn't matter how much you want to change the channel, if you don't get up and flip the dial, nothing's going to happen. Do you follow me?"

"I think so." Ilyena frowned and gently stroked her cheek where I'd slapped her. The skin was a little red, but otherwise unblemished. "But I don't see how slapping me helped."

"A single tear caused by sudden pain and betrayal," I said, dunking the tea bag and letting it steep. "It wasn't very strong as far as energy goes, because you barely knew me. But the feeling in it, the idea of it, was similar enough to what you'd lost that it provided the current. Sort of like striking a tuning fork to try to find a similar vibration."

Ilyena licked her lips and frowned down at the kerchief. I sipped, and grimaced as the steaming beverage boiled my tongue. It was better to drink it hot, though. Cold it was muddy, and harder to get down. She ran her fingers along the cloth, and I winced. I didn't hear the magic jangle, exactly, but the heartstrings buried in the weave thrummed like a poorly played instrument.

"So my tears did this?" she asked. "They... what? Trapped my heart in this piece of cloth?"

I sipped more tea and sea-sawed my free hand.

"Your tears, and your promise." I licked my lips and set my cup aside. "That was all Baba Black needed. When you gave her a part of yourself, cried out all that pain, she created a little object of power. She bottled your grief, wove it into those strands and kept it tied down. It was hers to do with as she pleased. She could have kept it in that hole and let it rot, or if she'd wanted to she could have used it for her magic. Pure emotions like that are like spraying lighter fluid on an open fire."

"Object of power?" Ilyena asked. I blew out a breath, and rubbed the back of my neck.

"People can't do much in the way of magic. It doesn't matter what words they chant or what they believe, the human spirit is a drop in the bucket when it comes to power. If you try to use what little juice you've got inside you, you'll be a dried up husk without any real change happening in the world around you. So what people do is they find stuff that soaks up the ambient power of events. These things are like sponges, sucking up spilled energy and holding it until the object is broken. Usually it's just released harmlessly as the memories fade. When it's done as part of a ritual, whatever is inside that object pours out into the spell." I counted off on my fingers, starting with my index. "Hangman's rope, whether it was used to kill the wicked or the innocent, is a powerful thing. The badge of a lawman killed in the line of duty. The tongue of a man that died telling a lie. A crow's feather that fell into hallowed ground nib-tip first at night. All of these things have power in them, and that's power that anything could use to make magic happen."

"Anything?" she asked. I waved a hand at that one.

"You're better off not knowing." I took another drink and sighed. My tea had thickened up. I slurped it down, trying not to grit my teeth, and for the hundredth time reminded myself to get a mug that would actually hold onto heat for longer than a few minutes. "Trust me, on this one."

I could practically see the rest of her questions running across her forehead. What else was out there? How did I know what I knew? Why didn't more people know about all of *this*? They ran one after the other like a curious stampede, but they bottle-necked behind her eyes. Ilyena smoothed the kerchief over her lap and stared down at it.

"So now what do I do?" she asked.

"That depends on you." I unfolded my arms and crouched down in front of my client. "Do you want to do this slow and steady, or do you want to tear the band aid off all at once?"

"I just want this to be over with," she said.

"You're sure?" She nodded. "All right. Grab the corners, and hold it up in front of you."

Ilyena did as I asked. I slid the small, silvered knife I kept in the small of my back out of its sheathe, and found the center of the kerchief. I pushed, and the threads tore apart as if they'd barely been held together at all. As the cloth parted, what had been woven between them washed over Ilyena. For a moment, she just sat rigid in her chair, her eyes going wide.

Then she crumpled, leaning forward in the chair. I caught her, and held tight while the maelstrom rode through her.

She cried into my chest, clawed at my back and shoulders, and wept like heaven itself had gone dry. She struggled and struck out, but I'd been ready for it and I held her tight. In time the worst of it passed, and she clung to me like she'd drown if she let go. I soothed her as best I could, and slipped my knife back into its sheathe. We stayed like that for a long time. Eventually she pulled away, hiding her face and wiping at her eyes. I let her go, and she stood.

"Do you feel all right?" I asked.

She nodded, then shook her head and laughed. "I'm sorry."

I shook my head and took a seat on the futon. "Don't worry. That's pretty much how these things go. Everything you gave her was in there. Now you have it back, but it's like a starving person getting turned loose on a buffet. You'll adjust, just give it time."

"Are you sure?" she asked.

"I am," I said. "Go home. Rest. Give yourself some time. Get used to being you again."

Ilyena nodded, and turned to go. I bent down, fighting with my laces. My heel was aching like a mad bastard, and I couldn't tell if it had started bleeding again. Ilyena's slippers walked back across the boards, and when I looked up she ran her fingers through my hair and kissed me. It was a hard kiss, full of fire and hunger. The volume dropped out of the world around me, both the seen and the unseen, and my head spun. She broke the kiss, pulling back just enough to take a breath. She tasted like roses set aflame.

"Thank you," she said. Then, before I could say anything, she turned on her heel, and headed out the door. Her footsteps receded, heading for the stairs. I blinked a few times, and smiled a little.

"Save the girl from the witch, and get rewarded with a kiss," I grunted, pulling my boot off and tossing it aside. "Who says fairy tales don't come true?"

Suffer the Children

Hollywood looks different in the rain. The false-fronted glamour washes off like a starlet's makeup, revealing the pitted scars and cracked foundations just beneath the surface. The hand and footprints of the old kings and queens of tinsel town fill up with dirty water, and their names are drowned as if they'd never been. Pacific thunder rumbles through the alleys in nameless, wordless sermons, and lightning streaks between the clouds in bright flashes like the whole city was a crime scene being photographed. The place would never be clean, but beneath the weeping sky it had the good grace to be honest.

A faded sedan turned off the boulevard, heading downstream toward the oceanfront. It drove three blocks, then four, slowing a little more at each intersection the way people do when they're trying to find a place they've never been to in the dark. The car stopped halfway up the block, and pulled to the curb. A man got out, tugging at his windbreaker's zipper while trying his damnedest to get to the sidewalk without soaking his shoes. He wrestled open the back door, and struggled with something. He lifted out a bundle, and over the rain and thunder I heard a baby cry. The driver froze, then quickly looked left and right. For a moment I figured he'd get back into the car and drive away. Instead he patted his swaddling package, turned, and pushed his way through a revolving door. The door shushed past three, empty slots and went still.

I gazed up at the building. It was a statuesque black thing, all glass and steel that stood tall above its two neighbors. There were no red warning lights on the roof, and no security lamps out front. There were no doormen, and no matter how hard I looked I couldn't find an address plaque. The place was set back from the street, and it would have been easy to miss in full daylight. On a night like tonight it was all but invisible. I puffed on my stogie and waited. A taxi drove by, then reversed back the way it had come. A sodden newspaper gave up the good fight, and sank into the gutter. The sedan's automatic headlights shut off. The rain fell. No one came out of the building. I blew out a lungful of smoke, then tossed my cigar into the deluge.

"Thus you may walk in the way of good men, and keep to the paths of the just," I said, reaching under my arm and checking my weapon before turning up the collar of my olive drab. "For the upright will dwell in the land, and the honest will remain in it. But the wicked will be cut off from the land, and the faithless will be rooted out of it."

I ducked into the rain, and splashed over to the sedan. The keys were gone, the doors were locked, and except for an old car seat in the rear and a thin manila folder in the passenger foot well the interior was empty. I shook my head, jammed my hands into my pockets, and shouldered my way through the tower's front door.

I stepped into another world. Acres of marble floors the color of fresh cream rolled away from me, the stone shot through with veins of gold. Gilded lamps held softly glowing half-moons, and sumptuous leather chairs the color of fine chocolate clustered atop carpets that cost more than most people's condos. Hand blown glass bowls held refreshments, and fountains along the walls filled the room with a liquid music that was fine as any instrument. Caryatids supported the roof, but every structural statue had the face of a beautiful woman and the body of some intricately carved beast of burden. Hanging plants and potted fronds breathed out their clean, fresh scents, and provided privacy by turning every sitting area into a tiny oasis. In a town that had made wealth its religion, this place was a temple. I shook the rain off my coat, and headed up the center aisle.

The rear wall was blank, except for seven narrow, identical hallways. Each was dimly lit, like the mouth of a cave where some devil lay sleeping. Between the halls and the rest of the sumptuous suite was a desk the size of an ancient altar. It was carved from the same stone as everything else, and inlaid with the heads of stylized animals in a fashion that would have been more at home in a museum than an office building. Taloned feet big enough to clutch a child were carved into the corners. It was imposing, and beautiful in its own way. The same could be said of the woman who sat behind it.

She was dark-haired and long limbed, with a straight back and sharp collarbones. Her eyes were smoky, and her too-long nails were a garish red. She dressed in ragged-edged silk, and when she smiled her teeth were very strong and very white. She was too old to be young, and too young to be old. Most people wouldn't notice that her grin was a little too sharp, or that between her teeth were graying morsels that perfumed her breath with the scent of a carrion feast. Her nostrils flared as I got closer, and she writhed like an excited cat scenting prey.

"Well, well, well," she purred. "Look who's come in from the rain."

"Better look fast, I ain't gonna be here long."

"When are you ever, Malachi?" She laughed, and it was a raw, unbridled sound that echoed in the empty halls. "I take it you don't have an appointment?"

"Is your boss busy?"

"Too busy for messengers who don't have the common courtesy to call ahead," she said, flashing me her serrated smile again. "There's a lot of people in this town. A lot of fools, and a lot of gold. He can't make time for all of you."

"He'll make time for me."

"Oh?" she asked, leaning her elbows on the slab. "And why is that?"

"A man came through here about ten minutes ago," I said. "Average height, bad haircut, wearing a sopping Raiders jacket and carrying a baby who wasn't happy about it."

"Mmm... yes," she said with the same understated moan you'd use to talk about a piece of chocolate cake you remembered fondly. "They were here. Just in time for their appointment, too."

I said nothing. Her smile faded, and she narrowed her eyes. "The child isn't his to give, is it?"

"He's one of mine."

"Oh." She shook her head slowly, tangled tresses dancing like half-charmed serpents. "That won't do. That won't do at all."

"No, it won't," I said, biting the end off each word.

"Do you want me to go get them?"

"No," I said. "The kid's my responsibility, I'm the one who's got to do it."

"You're so handsome when you're righteous."

"Where are they?"

"Seventh corridor," she said, gesturing to her left with a flick of her wrist. "Take it all the way to the top."

I followed her finger, my shoulders little more than a hair's breadth from the stone as I walked down the narrow hallway. Maybe a dozen steps in there was a panel with a single button, and a set of intricately cast brass doors. Tiny figures cavorted through the sky-scraping spires, and dust devils of some ancient desert danced between the horizons. Men flew in the clouds, and beasts standing on their hind ends pranced around fires. I pushed the button, and the doors opened as if they'd been waiting for me. Four harp notes sounded, expectant and welcoming. I grunted, stepped inside, and pressed the only button on the wall. The doors slid closed, and I began rising.

I stood with my feet apart, staring at the vague outline reflected in the matte finish in front of me. A big bruiser with too much hair and too much stomach watched me with a blank, smeared countenance. A minute went by. Then another.

"The fuck are you staring at?" I grunted. The reflection jerked, and faded like mist on a bathroom mirror. It wasn't used to being spotted, much less recognized when someone caught it playing magic mirror, which meant the Watcher was running off to tell the master of the house who his unexpected guest was. That was good; I didn't want him to be surprised. It took seven minutes to reach the top floor. The lights dimmed to a candle glimmer, and the doors slid back with little more than a whisper. I was out and moving before they'd finished yawning.

The sky parlor was a huge, open place with a tinted glass roof, and floors of burnished black stone that shone like obsidian. A crowd blocked the center of the room; a ring of black suits and expensive coiffures that stood three or four deep all looking toward the center. Above their heads loomed a massive, golden throne set on a concrete pillar half the size of a train car. A figure leaned forward in the chair, with one huge hand resting on the carved arm and its great, bovine head tilted down to look at the scene before it. I smelled smoke, and heard crackling flames. A child's wail, scared and plaintive, rose and was silenced.

I hit the crowd and started pushing. I shoved a tall woman with a model's hips and a queen's icy glare to the floor, and elbowed a fat man with enough jewelry to shame a merchant king out of my way. A young man with the build of an action hero and a face I almost recognized stumbled when I bulled him under the arm, and an older lady with the severe bun and disapproving gaze of a nun teaching school half-fell trying to back out of my way. There were grunts and curses, but I didn't look back to see who they were from.

The driver from downstairs, a two-time loser named Manny Flores, stood above a roaring fire pit. His hair was plastered to his head, and water dripped from the hem of his jacket. He was holding the baby out in his arms. The kid had managed to get one, pudgy arm free, and he was struggling and screaming his little head off. It didn't seem to be doing him any good, but that didn't stop him from trying.

"I offer this child, the seventh sacrifice I have made in Your service," Flores said, his voice quavering like a kid at his first championship spelling bee. "With this offering I prove my loyalty, and ask that You shower Your blessings upon me."

"You'll do no such goddamned thing," I shouted at him.

If he'd been focused on what he was doing, Flores might have made the sacrifice in time. All he had to do was let go, and the kid would have tumbled into the hungry flames and been eaten up in seconds. But Flores was nervous, scared, and that little part of him that didn't want to do what he'd been doing hadn't been held under water long enough to drown completely. So he turned, and when he turned I sank a fist in the side of his neck. His eyes rolled up, and he made a gagging, sputtering sound as blood flow to his brain stuttered. I snatched the child as Flores went down, and held him close. The kid stopped crying, but the look he gave me said he had the howling on a hair trigger, and wasn't afraid to start again.

A sound like a stone rolling back from a tomb echoed in the vast chamber. The Ensi all around me fell to their knees, uncaring about how prostration would treat their designer shoes or bespoke suits. A shiver went through them, and for all their piety, all their devotion, in that moment the corporate priests remembered what it was to be frightened animals in the face of some vast, unknowing creature. They shrank down, keeping silent, squeezing their eyes shut tight and hoping not to be noticed. The baby glanced up, his little face tight with worry at the loud, unexpected sound. I turned to the idol, and inclined my head.

"A thousand pardons, Ba'al Molech," I said, taking care to pronounce the title correctly. Ancient Sumerian's tricky if you don't practice it once in a while, and I hadn't had the need. "I mean you no disrespect, but I had to act in haste."

The golden god stared at me, it's cavernous eyes filled with fires no man could ever conjure. It leaned forward, and blew hot breath over my face. It smelled like burning metal, and charred flesh. When the god spoke its voice came from everywhere, and nowhere.

Malachi of the Thrones it demanded, calling me by name. *Explain yourself.*

I bowed again, going a little lower than I had before. I didn't take my eyes off the thing, I wasn't stupid, but I tried for humble. I had not been made with an overabundance of that quality, but I put in the effort. "There's an understanding in this city; an agreement reached long ago. Flores here almost started a war because he didn't abide by that agreement."

I held up the child, careful not to bring him so much as one inch closer to the bull-headed giant. "This boy's name is Ibrahim Goldstein. His father died before he was born, but his mother lived long enough to have her rabbi perform a bris over the boy before he was taken to child services. He is under my protection, as per the arrangement."

I looked around at the men and women getting to their feet. Executive producers and money men, pharmacy tycoons and silicon valley pirates. They had each done terrible things to claw their way up in the service of such a harsh master, and I could see the stains across their skin when I looked with the Eyes of God. A blonde woman in the front row with bee stung lips had blood on her hands that she hadn't confessed. A fat man wheezing over a puddle of puke had the ghostly, too-wide eyes of one who coveted everything he saw. A young man, one of the crowned princes of the movie monarchy had green-tainted cheeks to go with his hands, stained black by theft. All of them bore phantom smears of greasy, gray ashes across their foreheads to show they had left burnt offerings to the ancient king they bowed before. Flores moaned, and stirred. I looked at him, and saw everything I needed to see. I shut my eyes, and relaxed the sight.

I warned him the gilded god said. I nodded, and tried not to let it show that my mental ears were ringing.

"I'm sure you did," I said. Ibrahim turned toward me, and I held him against my chest. I ran one scarred hand down his back, and he quieted. "He didn't listen closely enough, it seems."

The colossal king leaned back on its throne with the sound of a slow-motion train wreck. It waved one hand. Ba'al Molech didn't speak; it didn't have to. We had an understanding that went way back.

"You." I pointed at a man in a pink shirt whose spectacles were askew after his face's impromptu introduction to the floor. "Hold this child. You keep his face turned away, do you understand me?"

He tried to speak, but nothing came out. I raised an eyebrow, and he came forward in short, jerky steps. I placed Ibrahim in his arms, and the man held the boy like he was made of glass. I caught his arm.

"The boy sees none of this," I repeated. I looked at the others. They stared with bared teeth and dead eyes that gleamed in the fires like desert jackals. I let the man go, and he retreated back to the ranks.

Flores was returning to the land of the living. He rolled to his knees, and found his feet with the weaving grace possessed only by the punch drunk. He tried to focus on me, but was having difficulty.

"Who the fuck are you..." he asked, words slurred as he tried to remember how to use his tongue.

"It doesn't matter," I said. "I'd say a prayer if I were you. It probably won't help, but it can't hurt. Not where you're going."

I was sure Flores was going to run, but he surprised me. Instead of heading for the door, or trying to hook around the assembled witnesses to buy time, he came straight at me. Flores had his fists up, and he bellowed a wordless cry as he swung. The blow never landed.

Flores struggled in my grip. He spit, he swore, and he strained. In moments his battle cry turned to shrieks, and not long after that his shrieks faded to choked, wet sobs. Bones broke, muscles tore, and blood pattered the floor like spilled sacrament. I took my time, and did what I had been made to do when the world was young, and god had been in a particularly bad mood. The watchers went white. Some of them spewed, leaving steaming puddles of muck that had probably cost three figures when they'd first eaten the meal. Not one man or woman looked away, and when I was finished I dropped the breathing, moaning meat that had once been a down-on-his-luck social worker named Manny Flores to the floor.

I raised my gaze to the congregation of child killers. They flinched. I smiled, and held out my bloody hands. The babysitter came forward. I took Ibrahim back. He shifted, and waved his pudgy arm around. I tucked it back inside his wrap. He closed his eyes, and passed into sleep. I stepped forward, and the Ensi parted before me like the Red Sea.

No one got in my way as I left. Nothing followed me either. I stepped out into the rain, and tucked Ibrahim under my coat to keep him dry. The heavens scoured the blood from my hands, and washed it into the gutter where it wouldn't be missed. There was no amount of rain that could wash me clean, though. I'd made peace with that. I opened up the car still parked at the curb, and got Ibrahim situated in the car seat again. He sneezed quietly, but it wasn't enough to wake him up all the way.

I got behind the steering wheel and started up the engine with the keys I'd taken out of Manny's pocket. I plucked the folder out of the passenger foot well and opened it. Ibrahim was there, along with six other names. Melissa Black, born to a rape victim of no particular religious persuasion who'd given her up. John Baker, whose mother had died and whose father was nowhere to be found. Nikki Watts, whose mother had given a fake name and who, as far as they could tell, had just vanished out into the night. Brandon Cooper, who had made it home from the hospital just in time for his parents to be killed by a home invasion. Jarod Fletcher, who'd somehow survived the car wreck that had killed his guardians. The last was Jessica Butcher. Her parents hadn't thought they'd be shot dead on the way home from the movies, but that was the way things went in L.A. One by one they'd been abandoned, lost, then forgotten.

I looked at those names and read their files over and over again. I knew more than the pieces of paper did. I'd watched as one by one they'd been taken and traded in for favors. For money to pay off gambling debts, or for help making a few accusations disappear off Flores' legal records. I had sat in the shadows, and done nothing because that was the agreement. Not one of them had been blessed, baptized, or otherwise protected, so it had been open season for anyone who wanted to take them. Too young to be believers themselves, they couldn't ask me for help, and there was nothing I could do if nobody asked.

I glanced in the rear view mirror at Ibrahim. He fussed, and blew a spit bubble, but other than that he didn't move. I tossed the folder back in the foot well, and pointed the car's nose east toward the bright lights of Hollywood Boulevard, and the orphanage Ibrahim had been taken from in the first place. I drove through the rain, and smiled a little bit. I'd gotten one, and I would have to be content with that for now.

"Suffer the children to come unto me," I said, quoting my least favorite of the two testaments. "For the kingdom of heaven belongs to such as these."

Eyes, Hands, and Heart

"Well, that's the last of them," Isinglass said as he dropped into the armchair near the window. The fire crackled in the hearth, competing with the quiet music of the gramophone. The tall, thin man rubbed his face, and sighed. "Maybe now that the Christiansons are on their way, I'll be able to get a decent night's sleep again."

"Not a moment too late, either," Elkins said from the sofa. He had his rifle disassembled on an oil-stained canvas pad atop the coffee table, and he was going over every piece of the high-caliber Primitive with the air of a child assembling a much-loved jigsaw puzzle. "While I appreciate the energy and dedication of newlyweds, it was going to be difficult to bag any game with the two of them consummating all over the trails."

"You could always have moved to the other side of the mountain," Isinglass offered.

"True," Elkins said, holding up the firing pin and blowing some grit off of it. Elkins grinned at Isinglass, his strong, white teeth a contrast to his black skin, and dark mustache. "But if I were over there, where would you be?"

"Right here in this chair," Isinglass said. His smile was more subdued than his friends, but something flashed in Isinglass's sharp, blue eyes. He meaningfully tapped the pair of capped field glasses sitting on the side table next to him. "I can watch more than birds with these, you know."

"You're a dog, Isinglass," Elkins said, shaking his head and chuckling as he returned his attention to his rifle.

"Looking hurts no one," Isinglass protested. "And if they valued privacy that strongly, they would have stayed in their quarters."

"Our recent guests' proclivities aside, gentlemen, we could use more business like them," Mueller said from the writing desk where he'd been going over their accounts all morning. He took off his glasses, and ran a hand back through his thick, blonde hair. "With that said, as of this particular moment, we find ourselves firmly in the black. Even accounting for upkeep and repairs, as well as for Elsa's salary, we should be able to reach springtime without the need to either dip into our pensions, or into previous years' proceeds."

Isinglass smiled, and crossed one leg over another. Elkins nodded, and reassembled his weapon. He slid the magazine in place, and stood. He checked the action, then drew on his old hunting jacket.

"I found some tracks early yesterday," Elkins said, slinging his rifle over his shoulder. "A doe or two, and perhaps a buck. I'll be back in a few hours with dinner, and we can celebrate properly."

Elkins gave the other two a mocking salute, grinning at them before he turned and shouldered open the front door of the lodge. The gramophone reached the end of the record, and the needle arm automatically rose to its resting position. A knot popped in the fireplace, and Isinglass cleared his throat.

"Do we have it in the budget to keep Elsa on for the off-season?" Isinglass asked. "Just out of curiosity."

"In theory. Assuming it's just us living here, and that food expenses remain around their average costs, it wouldn't be too much of a burden." Mueller looked at Isinglass, his face carefully neutral. "Has she asked if we would keep her on past this season?"

"Not as such, no," Isinglass said, coughing as he got to his feet. He opened a small, wooden box, took out his pipe, and began filling it. "Though if the grouses are anything to judge by, we should be looking at a more mild winter. I thought it might attract more guests than we typically have."

"That would be a blessing," Mueller said, closing the heavy leather-bound book where he kept the lodge's tallies. "I would ask that she accept a minor dock in her wages, assuming we have no guests for her to care for, but other than that I see no reason she couldn't stay on if she was of a mind to."

Isinglass took a twig from the fire, and lit his pipe. Once he had it puffing the way he liked, he turned back toward Mueller. "Should we wait until she returns from her errands in town, or should we wait to ask Elkins for his blessing?"

"You know him as well as I do," Mueller said, slipping the log book back into his writing desk. "As long as he has enough money for a glass or two of whiskey once a week, and he can shoot to his heart's content, he cares for little else."

There was a rumble from outside the lodge; the familiar, roaring purr of the all-terrain's diesel engine. Isinglass coughed on his pipe smoke, and thumped himself in the chest. Mueller allowed himself a smile, pushing past the swinging door into the kitchen. Isinglass tapped out his pipe, and set it on the mantle as the motor outside died. He threw on his threadbare officer's greatcoat, opened the front door, and stepped out into the early winter chill.

Elsa had the rear door of the half-track open, lifting out canvas shopping bags filled with the week's allotments of foodstuffs and necessities. She had on a heavy sweater, and a pair of fingerless wool gloves. Golden hair spilled down her shoulders, and the cold had kissed a blush into her cheeks. She smiled at Isinglass, who returned the expression.

"Let me help you with those," Isinglass said, bending down to take two of the heavy bags.

"We may have to make two trips," Elsa said, opening the passenger side door. As she did, a man slowly got out of the cab. He was broad shouldered, and lean in a way that looked more sickly than strong. His hair was disheveled, and he sported a thick, dark beard. He had on an army-green surplus coat, a scarf round his neck, and a pair of dark glasses. He also wore a pair of black leather gloves that fit him like a second skin. He turned somewhat awkwardly, shrugging on a rucksack, and retrieving a gnarled, wooden walking stick from between the seats.

"This is Mr. Johann Kerner," Elsa said, smiling. "He was told about the lodge by a friend, and was making his way here when I met him at the Cransock Market. I thought it would be in keeping with our hospitality to offer him a ride."

"As well it is," Isinglass said, putting down the shopping bags and dusting off his hands. He held out his right hand, and offered the man a smile. "A pleasure to meet you, Mr. Kerner. I'm Josef Isinglass, one of the three owners of the Surgeons' Lodge."

Kerner made no effort to take the proffered hand. He didn't even glance at it. Isinglass's smile faded, and his brow furrowed. A breeze blew, ruffling Kerner's hair, and that was when Isinglass noticed the runnels of scar tissue around the edges of the dark glasses he wore. He sucked in a breath, and Kerner smiled. It was a small smile that didn't part his lips.

"You just held out your hand for me to take, didn't you?" Kerner asked.

"I did," Isinglass said. "My apologies. I didn't realize you were not sighted."

"Then my disguise is working," he said, his smile retreating back beneath his beard.

Elsa shut the rear gate of the half track, making Isinglass start. She took Kerner by the arm, guiding him gently toward the front door of the lodge. "There's loose dirt here, but it's fairly smooth. There are two, shallow stone steps just ahead of you. Let me get the door, and three strides in front of you is a desk. If you'll wait there a moment, Josef will get you taken care of."

Elsa returned a moment later, and she and Isinglass carted the groceries inside. Kerner stood at the front desk, resting one hand on the wood and waiting patiently. Isinglass shucked his coat, and blew warm breath into his hands.

"Now then, Mr. Kerner," Isinglass said, sitting behind the desk and unlocking the drawers. "How long are you looking to stay with us?"

"A week, if you have the room?" Kerner said, turning the statement into a question.

"Oh, I think we could find space for you," Isinglass said, quoting a price as he took out the guest log book. "Do you think that's fair?"

"It will do fine," Kerner said, unsnapping his breast pocket and pulling out a worn, leather billfold. He opened it, frowning as he awkwardly slipped two bills from the rear sleeve, and three from the nearer one. Isinglass took the bills, and nodded.

"Do you have your identification?" Isinglass asked. "I hate to bother over it, but you know how things are these days."

"It's no trouble," the man said, replacing his wallet and taking out a slimmer folder of brown leather. He held it out, and Isinglass flipped it open.

"Johann Kerner," Isinglass said, noting his particulars before offering the identification back. Then he remembered, and pressed the folder into the man's hand. Kerner's index finger and thumb responded, but the other fingers stayed crooked and motionless. Isinglass realized the man was missing more than his sight, and cleared his throat. "A pleasure to have you with us, Mr. Kerner."

"A pleasure to be here," Kerner said, carefully tucking the identification back into his jacket.

"You'll be in room one, here on the ground floor," Isinglass said, standing and coming round the desk. "If you'll permit me, I can lead the way."

"That would be appreciated," Kerner said, reaching out until he found the wall. "Are there any framed pictures or hangings here?"

"No, no, just bare boards," Isinglass said, walking down the hall. He put some emphasis in his steps, making sure they were loud enough for Kerner to hear. "It's about halfway down the hall here... about ten steps or so."

Kerner approached slowly, measuring his steps and occasionally sweeping the ground before him with his walking stick. Isinglass slid the key into the lock, and opened the door for his guest. "There's a bed in the center of the room, and a washroom off to your right once you enter. There's a small table right next to the door with a telephone on it, and a chair on the other side of the room. There's also a window, and the light switch is..."

Isinglass trailed off, but Kerner kept walking as if he hadn't noticed. He found the door frame, and stepped inside. He found the table, and leaned his walking stick against it before shrugging off his rucksack and setting it on the floor.

"My friend mentioned you serve meals for guests as well?" Kerner said, ignoring Isinglass's awkward silence.

"Ah, yes, yes we do," Isinglass said, nodding before he realized Kerner couldn't see the gesture. "Dinner is typically at six or so."

"What time is it now?" Kerner asked.

Isinglass checked his wristwatch, pushing back his sleeve. "It's around two-thirty."

"That's good," Kerner said, shuffling back until he found the door. "I will likely be resting. If I'm not there when the meal begins, please come wake me."

"Certainly," Isinglass said, holding out the key. After a beat, he set the key down on the side table, making sure the metal rang loudly enough that Kerner knew where it was. "If you need anything, feel free to let us know."

"Thank you," Kerner said, closing the door. There was a fumbling sound, and a moment later the bolt slid home. Isinglass frowned, and walked back down the hallway toward the main room. He found Elsa emptying the sacks in the kitchen, and Mueller chopping up vegetables.

"How is the new guest?" Mueller asked, pushing a small pile of sliced onions aside with his knife blade.

"Settling," Isinglass remarked, picking up an apple and shining it on his sleeve.

"Good to hear," Mueller asked, washing his hands before rubbing them with a stainless steel ball. Isinglass took a bite of the apple, chewing thoughtfully.

"Poor man," Isinglass said after he'd swallowed. "After what he's been through, I hope his stay here is comfortable."

A shot rang out over the mountainside. Mueller plucked an apple out of the basket, and started peeling it. "If nothing else, at least he'll enjoy a fine meal."

It was over an hour after the rifle's report that Elkins returned. There was fresh blood under his nails, and he had a stack of steaks he'd wrapped in butcher's paper. He had the satisfied expression of a man who had done a good day's work. Mueller prepped the meat, adding spices and sauces before he tossed it in a pair of skillets. Elsa set the table, and Isinglass got out of his seat to help her. Elkins watched through the kitchen doors, speaking softly to Mueller.

"Does he really think she'll tell him yes?" Elkins asked.

"We live in an age of miracles," Mueller said, shrugging as he cut into the meat to check it. "She hasn't told him no. Whether that's because she's flattered, I couldn't say. But we will see what we see."

Just as Elsa poured water into the last cup, Kerner stepped into the room. His hair was damp, and he had on a high-collared black sweater, whose frayed cuffs nearly fell to his knuckles. He still wore his gloves, as well as his glasses. He was in stocking feet, and he'd moved so quietly that his sudden appearance startled Isinglass, who dropped the knife and fork he was holding with a clatter. Kerner tilted his head, frowning as he stepped away from the wall, tapping his stick in front of him.

"I can tell dinner is almost ready," he said, scenting the air. "And by the sound of silverware, the table is that way."

"Mr. Kerner," Elsa said, turning toward him. "If you'd like I could-"

"No, no, it's fine," Kerner said, holding up his free hand. "I remember places better if I walk them myself."

Kerner slid his steps forward, lips pursed in concentration as he felt the boards beneath his feet. His stick tapped against a side table, and he paused for a moment to re-orient himself. He ran his hand along the back of the sofa, brushing along a lampshade before he turned, and made his way into the dining room. His toe tapped against the slight rise, and he stepped over it without tripping. Kerner put his hand on the back of a chair, and smiled his small, enigmatic smiled.

"While I appreciate the quiet, I have navigated unfamiliar places before," Kerner said, sitting down and laying his stick on the floor beneath the table. "What's for dinner? It smells divine."

"Venison steaks, taken from a doe this afternoon," Elkins said, sitting down at Kerner's left side with a glass of wine. "As a side dish, artichokes that have been buttered and grilled. Along with some kind of small, dark potato whose name I don't know, but which I can say is quite delicious. You aren't a vegetarian, I hope, sir?"

"The furthest thing from," Kerner said, cautiously feeling around his plate. He found the napkin, and spread it over his lap. "Though if I could request my meat be cut for me? Seems childish, I know, but it makes life a great deal easier."

"Not a problem, Mr. Kerner," Elsa said, touching him on the shoulder as she headed toward the kitchen. "Would you care for a drink?"

"Wine, if it's dark," Kerner said over his shoulder. "Funny thing, ever since this all happened, I just can't stand pale wines anymore. Too sweet."

"It's a common enough phenomenon," Isinglass said, sitting on Kerner's right. "With the input from one sense going dark, the brain adjusts to gain more awareness from the remaining senses. As if there wasn't enough to adjust to with no longer being able to see."

"Do you know much about it?" Kerner asked.

"I do, since you ask," Isinglass said, scooting out slightly as Elsa and Mueller brought out the meal. "During the war I was a surgeon, specializing in battlefield medicine."

"Then I suppose you've seen a fair number of cases like mine," Kerner said, gesturing toward his face with one hand.

"We all did," Elkins said, nodding toward Elsa as he began to cut into his meat. "Mueller and I were there right alongside Isinglass, here. Up to our elbows, some days. When peace rolled in, we decided we'd had our fill of the butcher's trade."

"And who are you, sir?" Kerner asked.

"Hah, my apologies," Elkins said around a bite of venison before he swallowed. "Major Alphonse Elkins, retired, at your service."

"Hopefully I won't have any need of your services during my stay," Kerner said as Elsa set his plate before him, and guided his hand to the stem of a wine glass. "I don't think I'd survive another incident that requires a doctor."

Elkins laughed at that, taking a deeper drink of his wine. Isinglass frowned, his expression thoughtful as he chewed one of the artichokes. Mueller sat at the head of the table, and Elsa slid into the chair on Isinglass's right. She squeezed his forearm once, before she began to eat.

"If you don't mind my asking, Mr. Kerner," Isinglass said, choosing his words carefully. "It sounds like you lost more than your sight."

"I did," Kerner said, swallowing a bite of the venison. "My sergeant had his eyes on the sky during an airship raid. If he'd looked where he was going, he would have seen the mine under his boots. I was a dozen yards from him, and it was one of the last things I saw."

"Terrible business," Elkins said, sipping his wine.

"Quite," Isinglass said, pursing his lips slightly. "Again, I don't mean to pry, but could you not be fitted with a set of optic implants? Or a set of graspers? There have been amazing strides made for those who were wounded, and-"

"Johann, leave the poor man alone," Elsa said. "Mr. Kerner is our guest, not a conversation piece like that moose head above the mantle."

"There's a moose above the fireplace?" Kerner asked, carefully spearing a chunk of steak on his fork. "Not sure how I missed that."

Elkins roared with laughter, banging his fist on the arm of his chair. Mueller choked on his water, coughing chuckles into his napkin. Elsa covered her mouth. Isinglass smiled, saluted Kerner with the remains of his artichoke, and then popped the rest into his mouth.

The meal continued on familiar grounds from that point forward. Elkins shared what he'd seen during his trek further up the mountain, telling Isinglass where he could find promising caches of his precious birds. Mueller asked about the foot trails, and when Elkins mentioned they were still in good condition after the rain, Mueller said he'd hoped to get a few more good runs in before the snow finally came. Kerner listened more than he talked, but would interject from time to time to ask a question. Elsa cleared the dishes away, and brought out dessert. Mueller took a small portion, Elkins a second helping when he'd finished his first. Isinglass and Kerner both declined. When Elkins lit a cigar, Kerner stood and excused himself.

"It's been a pleasure to meet you all," he said, picking up his stick. "But after that meal, I feel I shall call it an early night."

"Don't worry, we won't be too far behind," Elkins said, puffing on his smoke.

"There aren't many late nights here," Isinglass added.

"Not for us, anyway," Mueller said.

Kerner nodded, and clicked his stockinged heels in salute. Then he turned, and walked back toward his room. His steps were surer this time, and he reached his room without incident. His lock turned quietly.

"Peculiar fellow," Elkins said, tapping ash from his cigar.

"I suspect you would be, too, if you'd sustained the injuries he bears," Mueller said.

"Point taken," Elkins said, plugging the cheap roll back between his lips. "I'm for bed, gentlemen. Might be able to take a few more skins before the cold really settles in, but I'll need to rise early for that."

Elkins padded to the lower bedroom, on the opposite side of the lodge from Kerner's. Not long after, Mueller climbed the spiral stairs to his loft. Isinglass brought the dessert dishes into the kitchen, and then slunk away to the converted sunroom where he slept. Elsa stood at the sink, washing the dishes, and humming a soft tune under her breath.

"Three little roosters, all in hand," she sang, placing the clean dishes in a drying rack. "Strut while you may, and crow while you can..."

Mueller woke to the sun streaming in through his windows. For years after his service he'd awoken at dawn, but time had finally begun to reset his circadian rhythms. He rolled from beneath the covers, stood, and stretched. He followed the same calisthenics routine he did every morning. When he'd finished, he checked his pulse. His heart was steady and strong, used to the demands he placed on it. He armed sweat from his brow, pulled on an old sweater, and descended the stairs to make himself some tea. Once he'd dipped the bag, he stepped onto the back porch, leaned on the rail, and took a deep breath of the crisp, cold air. It prickled his nose, and ran raw down his throat like fine whiskey.

As he sipped his tea, a movement caught his eye. Someone was coming up the Lover's Hike, the lower of the two trails that led from the rear of the lodge up the mountain's slope. The figure emerged from the treeline, and Mueller was surprised to see Elsa. Her hair was loose beneath a brown jeep cap, and she had her coat buttoned to her throat. One hand was jammed into her coat pocket, and from the other swung an insulated lunch pail. Her head was down, and there was rigid tension in the set of her shoulders. Mueller pursed his lips, and sighed.

"Good morning, Elsa," he said, as she drew near. "You're up early."

She started, and stared up at him. She tried to fix a smile onto her face, but Mueller saw the scowl that twisted her lips. "Yes. It seems I am."

Mueller gestured back toward the lodge. "There's tea, if you wish some?"

"No, thank you," Elsa said, coming up the stairs. Before she could dart past, Mueller put a hand on her shoulder.

"Did Johann do something?" Mueller asked.

Elsa made a sound in her throat that was the bastard child of a laugh and a sob. Tears started in her eyes, but she shook her head. "No. He... he just..."

"It's all right," Mueller said, keeping his voice soft and soothing. "You don't have to tell me, if you don't want to."

Elsa nodded, and swallowed. There was a click in her throat. Mueller patted her back gently, and gave her a small smile.

"Go inside, Elsa, it's cold out here," he said.

Elsa nodded again. She just stepped inside the lodge, and quietly closed the door behind her. Mueller sighed, and turned back to his quiet view of the mountain slopes. Isinglass was a fool. No matter how sharp his eyes were, he never saw that politeness was not an invitation to intimacy. Mueller could imagine him, sulking in one of his bird blinds, nursing a thermos of cooling coffee and a sore cheek. He shook his head, and climbed back to his room to put on his trail clothes. Once outside, Mueller tugged up his hood, and headed for the Lover's Hike.

His blood was still warm from his morning routine, and he set a brisk pace. The Hike was only a handful of miles long, if one took none of the branching paths, and most of Isinglass's favored haunts were along it. Mueller took the Quick-Slow Stairs, and glanced into the ravine, but there was no one there. He slowed to a walk near the Tumbling Stream, but saw only a pair of late season deer drinking downstream. The Heart's Curve, Little Stone, and Aerie were likewise abandoned. Not so much as a boot print or dusting of pipe ash to mark that someone had been there.

Mueller was sweating by the time he returned to the lodge. Elkins glanced up from the sofa where he was reading a dog-eared book with a broken spine. He pursed his lips, but went back to reading when Mueller didn't say anything. Elsa stuck her head out of the kitchen.

"Breakfast is almost ready," she said, when she saw it was Mueller.

"I'll be down in a moment," Mueller said, pushing himself up the stairs. He showered, put on fresh clothes, and slid into his traditional seat at the head of the table by the time Elkins had finished pouring his coffee.

"Isinglass won't be joining us, I take it?" Elkins said, adding a dash of sugar to his cup before sipping.

"I didn't see him," Mueller said, closing his mouth as Elsa brought out a plate of sausages, eggs, and a stack of toast. When she'd gone again, Mueller continued, "Something happened between he and Elsa. I doubt he wants to show his face here right now."

"I won't say I told him so," Elkins said, taking a piece of toast and buttering it. "But I told him so."

Elsa sat at the far end of the table, forked some eggs onto her plate, and took a sausage. They ate quietly for a time, no one remarking on

Isinglass's absence. After Mueller ate two eggs, and decided to indulge in a piece of toast, he frowned.

"Has anyone seen our guest?" Mueller asked.

"I spoke to Mr. Kerner just after you left," Elsa said. "He said he was still tired from his journey, but I ran a shower for him, and told him I'd set aside some breakfast if he wasn't feeling up to joining us."

"Man spends a lot of time in bed," Elkins said, chewing. "Then again, I suppose he didn't come here to see the sights."

"He has a bad heart," Elsa said, frowning at Elkins. "He came here for quiet, and to relax."

"Well, there is plenty of that," Mueller said, taking a swallow of water. "Thank you for breakfast, Elsa. Shall I help you clean up?"

"There's no need," she said, standing and gathering the dishes. "I won't be doing it for much longer."

The day was quiet after that. Elkins drifted to the armchair near the window. Mueller busied himself tidying his quarters, and when that was finished, wandered through the kitchen to plan for dinner. Elsa took Kerner his meal, and said he was feeling better, but probably wouldn't be up for joining them until tomorrow. Night began creeping down from the peak, and there was neither sight nor sound of Isinglass.

"I wager he hiked down to the Golden Rose," Elkins said, closing his book as the last of the light finally faded. "And gotten himself good and drunk."

"I'll take that wager," Mueller said as he set the table. Elsa had begged off, saying she had packing to finish. "But you have to take the half-track down tomorrow morning to haul him out of his cups if he isn't back on his own."

"As you say." Elkins clapped Mueller on the shoulder, smiling. "You worry too much, Stephen. Mark my words, all will be well soon."

The next morning, Mueller woke to the smell of bacon and coffee. He splashed some water on his face, dressed, and came downstairs. Elsa was in the kitchen, her hair tied back in a tight braid. She didn't even glance up as Mueller walked in, merely pushed a mug of coffee toward him. It was black and strong, which was precisely how he preferred it.

"Will you be eating before, or after you take the Peak?" Elsa asked.

"After, I think," Mueller said, sipping the scalding brew. "It would be a shame if I got halfway down the trail, and found my stomach rebelling."

Elsa gave him the ghost of a smile, and shook her head. Mueller quietly finished his coffee, washed the mug, and set it in the rack to dry.

"One last thing," Mueller said before he stepped outside once more. "When Elkins gets up, remind him to go to town."

Elsa nodded, flipping several slices of bacon. Mueller paused for a moment, looking for something else to say. When nothing came, he stepped out onto the porch, and headed for the Peak View Trail.

The Lover's Hike was a lowland oval meant for strolling. The Peak View Trail, by contrast, made you earn its views. There were no gradual slopes or soft bends in its trails. Rather, you had to contend with steep grades, sharp turns, and the slowly increasing pressure that felt like a fist around your lungs. Mueller kept his pace steady, though, even if he was gasping by the time he finally reached the overlook. With his wind coming thin, and his sides aching like he'd been punched, Mueller put his hands behind his head and drank as much of the cold air as his lungs would take.

The mountain rolled away below him, and between the thick boughs of the evergreens he could see the narrow paths people had trodden for centuries. He could also see where the dirt roads turned to pavement, and all the advances of the modern age began to truly take hold. From his vantage, Mueller could see the spark lights, and the haze of exhaust fumes that hung over the little town in the shadow of the mountain. He could even smell its scent, faint but still present, on the wind out of the south. It made him think of astringent soaps, the clatter of scalpels, and the stink of blood. The perfume of progress.

Once the aches faded from his calves, and he could breathe easily again, Mueller turned his steps back the way he'd come. Though it was downhill, returning to the head of the path was more difficult, if anything. Still, Mueller felt a rush of strength and exhilaration as he descended back to the lodge. By the time he climbed the stairs to the porch, he was soaked through with sweat, panting for breath, and grinning like a fool. Inside it was quiet, and when he glanced out the front window Mueller saw the half-track was gone.

"They left about an hour ago," Kerner said, close enough behind Mueller to make him start. When he turned, he saw Kerner standing near the front desk. He wore a cable-knit sweater beneath a threadbare bathrobe. He still had on his glasses, and his hands were tucked awkwardly into the robe's pockets.

"They?" Mueller said, surprised.

"Mr. Elkins had an errand in town," Kerner said. "Elsa told me she was going with him. I had the impression she may not be returning?"

"Today was her last day," Mueller said. "Still, I won't begrudge her leaving a little early. Especially under the circumstances."

"What circumstances are those?" Kerner asked, tilting his head. It made him look like an inquisitive bird, and for a moment Mueller recalled his earlier reminiscences. The steel grip of a syringe, the pressure of a mask across his face, and the wet, surprisingly slick, feel of blood across his hands. Mueller shook his head, then laughed when he remembered Kerner couldn't see him.

"I'm not one to tell tales out of school," Mueller said. "Are you feeling better?"

"I am, yes," Kerner said, the corners of his mustache twitching as he smiled. "My constitution is not what it was. But I think I've adjusted well enough to the fresh air."

"Can I do anything for you?" Mueller asked. "The radio won't pick up much, but we have some music. Do you enjoy opera?"

"I've developed an appreciation for several things I once would have found distasteful," Kerner said. He walked with sure steps, touched the sofa, then made himself comfortable. "While I wouldn't mind the music, I would much prefer to talk. Voices are my only companions, these days, so I enjoy spending time with them when I can."

"Well, I will do what I can," Mueller said, sitting down in the easy chair near the fire.

They talked. First about unimportant things, like the weather, what travel was like, and the progression that had been made by the highways and rails across the country. Then, once they'd exhausted the everyday, they spoke of the important. Mueller about how he and the others had left both the war and medicine behind them, retreating to a place away from the grinding gears and belching smoke of the modern machine society was becoming. Kerner spoke of his declining health, his adjustment to his new life, and his decision to try getting away from the very same thunder and grind that had driven Mueller into the mountain's bosom. They talked until the day had grown purple, and the only light came from the crackling fire.

"Something wrong?" Kerner asked, tilting his head once more.

"I expected the others back by now," Mueller said, frowning at the door. "Though I wouldn't be surprised if they were pouring what's left of the day into a set of tumblers."

Kerner smiled at that, showing a flash of white teeth behind his beard. "Speaking of spirits, would you happen to have any of last night's wine left? I'm afraid my throat's begun to go dry."

"Of course," Mueller said, standing and stretching. "It was Elkins' vintage, but I doubt he'd begrudge us a bottle."

Mueller crossed to Elkins door, and found it unlocked. When he flipped on the light, though, he started. There was a huddled shape under the dark, wool blanket. There was a smell, too. A wet, cloying, metallic odor that Mueller knew, but wouldn't face.

"Elkins," Mueller said, stepping closer to the bed. "Elkins, are you all right?"

Mueller pulled back the blanket, and gaped at what lay beneath. Elkins stared up at him, his lips drawn back over his teeth in a stiff, silent snarl. His eyes were wide open, dry and glassy with death. A thick, wide slit ran up the side of his neck, and blood had pooled across his pillow, and beneath his neck. Worst of all, though, were his hands. They were missing, the stumps of his wrists raw and awful in the glare of the bare, electric bulbs. They'd been cut through with surgical precision.

Fear and anger both crowded into Mueller's throat, each trying to reach his tongue before the other. He stepped back slowly, sucking corrupted air through his nose. Then something pinched the side of his neck, and a chill shot through his veins. Mueller tried to spin, but his foot tangled in Elkin's discarded rifle sling. He fell, one arm twisted beneath him, his head smacking into the floor. Mueller saw stars, and before he could rise again the stars winked out, leaving him floating in darkness.

The world returned on a slowly rising tide. Music caressed Mueller's ears, faint at first, but growing clearer as he came back to himself. There was a throbbing ache in his head, and a numbness in his neck. He tried to touch them, but his hands wouldn't move. Ropes creaked, and he felt bands of pressure across his chest, his wrists, his legs, and even his forehead. Off to his right, water splashed, followed by a long, slow scrape of a razor against skin. Mueller opened his eyes, and groaned as the light from the chandelier pierced his eyes. He tried to squirm, but he was tightly bound to the dining room table.

"You're awake earlier than I expected," Kerner said, dipping his razor into a bowl of water. He faced the mirror on the wall, then smoothed the foam from his upper lip. Once it was bare, he stroked the razor just beneath his chin. "Must be all that clean living."

"Who are you?" Mueller asked, forcing the question past parched lips.

Kerner turned, and looked at Mueller. Kerner's shirt was unbuttoned, revealing a chest seamed with thick scars. He no longer wore his blind man's glasses, and Mueller stared into a pair of intense blue eyes. He knew those eyes... he had last seen them in Isinglass's face before his trip into the woods with Elsa. Kerner smiled, and Mueller flinched back from him.

"Ah, I see you have answered your own question, Major Mueller," the man who was not Johann Kerner said. He set his razor aside, and that was when Mueller realized he was not still wearing his leather gloves. At the end of his wrists, attached by a smooth bead of fresh skin like a weld, were Elkins' strong, steady hands. "I'm flattered you remember me at all."

"They told me you died," Mueller said.

"I did, for a time," Abel Braun said. He touched the side of Mueller's neck, taking his pulse with his stolen fingers. "Jutta was the one who put the sedative in my veins. And she was the one who woke me up, once I'd been thrown in the pits with all your other failures."

The front door opened, and footsteps rang. Elsa walked in, with a leather bag under her arm. She set it aside, and embraced Abel. They kissed, and it was in that moment Mueller realized what a fool he'd been. All she'd done was dye her hair, and spend some time in the sun... but he had never truly paid attention to the surgical nurses who'd assisted during their procedures. His mind had been too much on the work. Work that had produced miraculous successes, but at the cost of their souls.

"You were whole!" Mueller shouted, flexing against his bonds. "Alive!"

"For a time, I was," Abel agreed. Jutta opened the bag, and took out several tools. She laid them on a serving tray, the steel gleaming. "But your salve was not yet complete, then."

"We would have healed you, once it was," Mueller protested.

"Easy words to say now," Abel said, looking down into Mueller's face. "Did you heal the others, once you finally had your miracle balm?"

Mueller's mouth opened, but he said nothing. All he could see were the fields of dead men beneath their stained sheets. Outflung hands, broken feet, and twisted necks. The wounded who had been brought to them to test their miraculous surgeon's paste. Their balm, as they'd called it, that would heal any wound. All the men who had been left tied to their tables, straining toward the doctors, begging them to make the pain go away. Pain the surgeons had planted in them, and then never taken back. Mueller closed his mouth, and Abel patted his face.

"I didn't think so," he said. "It should comfort you to know that at least one man your knife crippled will reap the benefits of your butcher's labor."

Abel stepped past Jutta, and took out a stainless steel container. Pressurized, and maintained by an internal mechanism, it hissed and ticked as Abel set it on the sideboard. He stroked it fondly, the way a man might pet a favored cat.

"How did you get that?" Mueller asked.

"It wasn't easy," Abel said. "But a dead man can do a great many things, if he's determined. And though my eyes withered and fell from my sockets, my hands grew hard as stone, and my heart grew weak as an old man's, my determination never faltered. Once I found where your balm was being produced, it was simply a matter of finding someone's price."

Jutta set her tray of precision blades down on the sideboard as well. She lifted a pair of butcher's scissors, and cut away Mueller's shirt. The cold metal made gooseflesh break out on his skin.

"Please," Mueller said. The word was clear, calm, and dignified. "Not while I'm awake?"

"I'm sorry, Major, but you know as well as I do that sedatives can foul the healing process once the balm is applied to a fresh organ." Abel pressed a leather belt between Mueller's teeth. He held out his hand, and Jutta placed a scalpel in it. "Be strong. It will all be over soon."

Mueller bit down, determined not to cry out. When he failed, Jutta took a moment to set a record on the gramophone, and let the music drown out his cries. Before the record had ended, Abel took the scissors, snipped, and lifted his prize from Mueller's chest. The bloody jewel that was the centerpiece of life itself. Abel set the heart in a steel cooking tray, and coughed. He half-fell against the table, blinking away dark spots in his vision. Jutta cut the ropes, and grunted as she shoved Mueller's body off the table. He fell in a heap, legs and arms splayed haphazardly. Abel rolled onto the table, collapsing flat on his back.

"Quickly," he said, panting. "Remember, just follow the patterns."

Jutta kissed Abel fiercely, then pressed the belt against his lips. He bit down, closed his eyes, and gripped the edge of the table. His heart was in her hands, now... then again, it always had been.

Jungle Moon

"What the hell was their problem?" Stephanie asked. The girl was barely seventeen years old, but the blond waitress had her hands on her hips like an old housewife as she glared out the front windows of the diner. In the distance the roar of motorcycles was fading down the highway.

"Not everyone needs a reason to be mean, Steph," Mac said. The owner of the diner, as well as its chief cook, Mac was a big guy. Dressed in his cook's whites, with the edge of a tattoo sticking out from under his shirt sleeve, Mac was just on the other side of fifty. His eyes, gray and hard as stone, said he'd seen a lot in those years as they watched the retreating tail lights.

"Still," Stephanie said, tossing her head like an unbroken horse. There had been four of them, young punks in leather jackets with no helmets, all of them riding foreign-looking bikes. They'd been loud and rude, demanding coffee and dinner. Stephanie had served them, and when they'd finished they all got up and tromped out. Their boots on the tile had reminded Mac of the parade grounds when the brass had been on site; extra loud, so they knew you meant every step. "You should have taught 'em some manners, Mac."

"You can't teach some guys, Steph," Mac told the girl. Mac lit his cigar, puffing the cheap roll into life. Blue smoke leaked from his mouth as he locked the doors. On the other side of the glass Mac could see the small, wooden pillar he'd set in the concrete like a doorstop. It was an intricately carved thing, covered in faces and eyes, open mouths, and ghostly bodies sucked into a hurricane. The wood was still wet from the last guy, the leader of the group, who'd unzipped his jeans and taken a leak all over it.

"Then you should have called the cops or something," Stephanie said as she washed the dishes, pausing to pop a stick of gum between her lips. "They come in here, eat all that food, break the glasses, skip out on the check, and, and..."

"Why don't you leave those dishes Steph?" Mac said, gesturing with one hand towards the stools at the counter. "How about a piece of pie?"

Stephanie stopped and stared at Mac, her brows drawn down. She'd been on enough late night drives to know a distraction when she heard one, but Stephanie dried off her hands and stepped away from the deep sink.

"Did you make the pie Mac?" She asked. Mac snorted.

"You think I'd put something in that case I didn't make, Steph?" Mac asked as he stepped towards the rotating dessert stand. "Let's see, we've got cherry, blueberry, apple-"

"Throw some ice cream on that apple and I'm sold," Stephanie said. She eased a hip onto a stool and rested her elbows on the counter while she looked at Mac. Mac took a knife, cut a slice of pie and eased it out onto a plate with a smooth dexterity his big hands didn't seem capable of. Scooping some ice cream onto the side, he garnished the pie with just a sprinkle of powdered sugar.

"Bon apetit," Mac said as he took another pull on his cigar, the stubby tip winking like a cherry bruise.

"I thought you quit smoking Mac?" Stephanie asked in between bites of her pie.

Mac took his cigar out of his mouth, and looked at it like he wasn't quite sure how it got in his mouth. Then he looked out at the front doors. The night was full and thick; the sort of dark that only came in the desert, and he could see little drops of dew forming on the windows as they sweated in the night. A mist had started to form; vapors rising like the ghosts of the day's heat. In his mind's eye Mac saw the kid in charge of the gang, the one with the Japanese bike. He pictured how the veins had pulsed in his paper thin skin, and how the eyes were sunk back in the caverns of his skull. Mac remembered the way the kid's hands jerked, and how his lips had pulled back to show yellow teeth. He saw the pock marks up and down his arm. It had been a long time since Mac had seen tracks like that. A long time since he'd smelled the desperation of addicts mixing in with the heady, exotic scents that came from the jungle.

"I did, Steph," Mac said as he took another pull on his smoke. "But I think we almost died tonight, and it's a tradition."

"Died?" Stephanie asked, the single word a confused grunt around the thick, syrupy fruit she was chewing. Mac nodded.

"And I'm gonna tell you a story," Mac said. "That's why I figured I'd give you the pie. Keep your questions behind your teeth while you ate."

"Is there a girl in your story Mac?" Stephanie asked before putting another mixed forkful of ice cream and pie into her mouth. Mac just smiled. The expression looked diseased, like there was something rotting just beneath the surface.

"Yeah," Mac said quietly as he sucked smoke. It tasted like the one time he'd been in the bush, when they'd actually had to call in a dust-off. His only trip out into the shit of the war, and Mac was glad every day for that. "There's a girl in this story. A real, live romance."

"Good," Stephanie said as she swallowed. "Does it have a happy ending?"

Mac looked like he hadn't heard the second question. His gaze was fixed on some point over Stephanie's shoulder, his eyes unfocused like a camera that had slipped a strap; the reel playing over and over again behind dark lenses, but showing nothing. Finally Mac stubbed out his cigar in an ash tray. It had been clean, and new; just like Mac, when he'd worn a younger man's skin.

"I was stationed in Vietnam during the war," Mac began. "The army told me that I was a machine gunner, which was sorta nice. I was a big kid, and the sixty cal wasn't all that heavy, all things considered. It was all that walking and trudging that took it out of ya while you tried to breathe the water that passed for air over there."

Mac stopped, shaking his head slowly as if he'd started going down the wrong path. Like the false start of an old diesel engine when it kicks into life just long enough to blow the smoke off of everything before it falls quiet again. Mac leaned his big arms on the counter and looked at Stephanie. She was watching him, chewing quietly.

"I did one patrol in the jungle," Mac continued. "After that I never went out into it again."

"Why not?" Stephanie asked. Her eyes were curious, and Mac could almost hear her thinking. There would be plenty of questions, and that was good. They had time.

"It wasn't because of anything really important. When we all got back to the medical camp that we called a base, all of us stinking to high heaven and covered in bug bites, they were a few guys short at the chow hall," Mac said. "So since I knew which knob did what on a stove, I hopped in and started helping out. Pretty soon nobody was grumbling anymore, and some of the guys were actually asking for seconds. That's pretty impressive, considering what army food usually tastes like."

"But you're a great cook, Mac," Stephanie protested. Mac shrugged.

"Yeah, thanks kid." He said, thumbing his crooked nose and sniffing a little bit. "Anyway, that was what the brass said, too. We had a light bird, a lieutenant colonel, stationed at the pit we'd stopped at. When our three weeks of being back were up, a guy showed up with a brand new sixty and a big, scared grin on his face. Guy's name was Patterson, and he was taking my spot in the unit."

Mac could still see Patterson's face. He looked about six chin whiskers short of seventeen, and had probably never used anything more complicated than a hoe. There was a hearty smattering of Ohio in his speech when he told Mac he was taking his spot. They had all looked at Mac with that same expression in their eyes; a dash of anxiety with a pinch of resignation. The last thing they wanted was a green heavy weapons guy, but what could they do? Orders were orders, so they all said their goodbyes and Mac watched as they loaded up in the chopper and shipped out into the bush. That was when he'd reported for his new duty in the kitchen.

"So I showed up at the mess tent, and started work at my new job," Mac continued. "I was just a grunt, but my folks had been in restaurants on the east coast so I knew my way around the place."

Outside the mist had grown thicker, and it was rising up like a wave. It reminded Mac of the way the jungle fog would reach out for the little camp they'd made. Like the country knew there was something wrong, some sort of invader, and it was trying to isolate them before it devoured them whole. That mist felt heavy, and it made your skin tighten up with gooseflesh no matter how hot it was. It was like if you reached out it might bite you. The thousand heads of Vietnam, all ready to snap at you with ghostly gunfire, or hidden booby traps that seemed to spring out of the very earth. Ancient mysteries and modern technology alike made it clear to the outsiders they weren't wanted.

"For the first month or two it was just routine as usual," Mac said. He took out a dish rag and wiped the counter top, even though it wasn't dirty. "Show up in the morning, cook breakfast. Switch out shift, and get a different guy to cook lunch. Then we switched back, and got to work on dinner. It was simple, easy, and boring as hell."

"Boring?" Stephanie asked. Her eyes sparkled in a way that Mac recognized; it was the look that a few kids always got when they heard old war stories. He was willing to bet that Stephanie got a similar look when her history teacher talked about the two world wars. Keen to know more about all that adventure, but only eager because she was looking back through time rather than waist-deep in the past. "But you were in *Vietnam!*"

"Yeah, but it's different behind the wire," Mac said. He tossed the cloth into the sink, and it made a wet, slapping sound. "When you're sleeping in a bunker or a tent with mosquito nets, and you know there's guys out there watching the night with machine guns and hand grenades, it's a lot harder to really be afraid. It's like you can see the war, when the casualties come in mostly, but it stops at the barbed wire. Like no matter what kinds of ghost powers Charlie was supposed to have, he couldn't make it into our hooches."

"Oh," Stephanie said. She stared down at her plate, picking at her pie. It was mostly gone, but she started hunting for bits of crust in the soup of syrup and melted ice cream.

"Anyway, after my first week there we were running low on kitchen supplies. Just standard stuff like rice, potatoes, bread, all that. The next morning I stepped into the mess tent, and there were four-" Mac stopped for a moment, frowning. The old words had almost come back to him. It was a habit he'd tried to break, especially once he was back in the states. "There were these four people from a village up the way. They were all dressed in loose clothes, with straw hats on their heads. I nearly shit myself when I walked in on 'em."

"Who were they?" Stephanie asked, the question exploding out of her. Mac held up a hand, a half smile on his face.

"Don't get your hopes up kid, I told you this is a love story, right?" Mac asked. "So I reach for my gun, and remembered I didn't have it, just as I noticed that Briar, the chief cook, was talking with the old man of the group. Stacked in the corner were some fresh loaves of bread, some sacks of rice, and a bunch of other stuff. Briar was talking in Vietnamese, and I guessed they were haggling over prices. After a few minutes they shook hands, and Briar traded them some stuff we had in spades but weren't using. Flour, a bit of table salt, stuff the locals had a hard time coming by."

"Yeah, but who *were* they?" Stephanie asked again. Mac frowned at her, and Stephanie lowered her head. There was a flush creeping up her neck.

"They were just some villagers trying to get some things they needed," Mac said. He picked up the old Ka-Bar knife that he'd won from a Marine in a game of cards, and peeled some potatoes. The action was repetitive, simple, and Mac's hands took to it easily. The steady strokes of the blade kept time with his voice, setting a pace to his story. "They were just a family, like anybody else. An old papa-san, his son and daughter-in-law, and their daughter, Shin Me."

"Wait a minute," Stephanie said. "You knew her name but no one else's. Is she the girl you were talking about?"

"Anybody ever tell you you're a bright kid, Steph?" He kept skinning the potato, dropping the nude spud into a bowl, and grabbing another. It was like he was talking about the weather, and not about a woman he'd known in the long ago and far away. "She was nineteen years old that summer. She had thick black hair, and her eyes shined like someone had spilled stars in them. She spoke English, too. As they were leaving, I told Briar that I thought she was cute. Shin Me turned at the door and winked at me, then told me thank you."

Stephanie laughed at that, and Mac laughed a little, too. He hadn't been that much older than Stephanie was now when that happened; a thought Mac pushed out of the way to a place where the light from his single bulb of self reflection didn't reach.

"To be fair, I said something a lot worse than how cute she was," Mac amended, tossing the other potato into the bowl. Mac rolled his broad shoulders and looked down at his hands, one still holding the old knife. "I'd been in country too long, I guess. Or maybe it was just the army, but either way that wasn't how my mom raised me to talk. Especially not to a woman. So I stewed about it for a little while, maybe two weeks. Long enough for our supplies to start running a little low again. Just like I figured, Shin Me and her family came back, this time with a cart and a mule."

"How did they manage to grow that much stuff?" Stephanie asked. Her plate was mostly clean, except for a few crumbs and a single dollop of whipped cream.

"That part comes later Steph, just listen all right?" Mac said, turning on the faucet, rinsing the tubers. "So I wait until the haggling's all done and whatnot, then I step outside to help with the stuff. I lift it up, and look over at Shin Me. I told her I was sorry for what I'd said before, and asked her to forgive me for it. I never could speak Vietnamese worth a damn. I tried like son of a bitch for two weeks just to learn how to say I'm sorry, but my mouth wouldn't do it. So I figured that even if the language was wrong, the words should still be right."

"That was sweet, Mac," Stephanie said. "I wish that guys at my school knew to do that."

"That was sort of the reaction I got out of Shin Me," Mac said, tossing the peeled remnants into the trash, and putting the potatoes in a tray at the bottom of the fridge. "She didn't really say much else to me that day, but she stayed close. Sort of like she was looking me over, trying to figure me out. Just far enough away that I couldn't touch her, but still close enough that I could smell her."

Mac was silent for a long moment as the memories flooded back to him. He smelled jasmine and lotus on Shin Me's skin, mixed with that indefinable aroma of fresh, clean sweat. His eyes were drawn by the mist outside. It was thick now, cutting off sight of the world beyond the windows; devil's smoke reaching for the lights in the lot. Mac swallowed hard, and tore himself back to the present.

"After they left, it was back to business as usual. Just humping sacks of spuds and grain, mixing up beans and corn, cooking up hash, and all the other shit that Briar could think to give me and the boys to do," Mac continued. "The guy was a shitty cook, but he knew how to run a tight ship. As soon as I started in the mess tent he backed off and watched the big picture. Getting the little shit right, that became my job."

"So you got a promotion?" Stephanie asked, leaning her forearms on the table the same way she did when she flirted or tried to get extra tips. Mac had never told her just what rank he'd had in the army, and she'd always been curious to know. Mac coughed, busying himself with his rag again.

"A Vietnam desk job was what we called it," Mac replied as he wiped sweat from his face. "I got all the responsibility of being the second-in-command at the mess tent when I was on-duty, including extra hours and scheduling, but no shiny bar to put on my collar, and no more pay to bank even if I was doing twice the workload I should have had some days."

"You should have complained to somebody, Mac," Stephanie said. "Briar's superior, or commander, or whatever. If you were doing the work, then you should have gotten the rank for it."

Mac looked at Stephanie for a long moment with eyes that were half-amused and half-flat. It was as if the girl had said something that crossed an important, cultural boundary, but since she didn't know that boundary was there, it was more funny than insulting. Mac leaned his big forearms on the counter top and looked at Stephanie quietly for a few more moments.

"What?" Stephanie asked.

"You want to hear this story or not, kid?" Mac asked her. Stephanie colored again, and she looked like she was about to say something before she swallowed it, scooped up the last of her whipped cream, and put it in her mouth. Mac nodded his approval. "I was in country for a long damn time. Guys who were cooks or file clerks, even supply officers, we didn't get the same concern that the guys in the bush did. The people back home, they wanted their boys to be safe and sound after they spent their tour fighting. But those of us who stayed in bunkers and tents with machine guns nests and choppers, all of us who stayed in the rear, we weren't so big a risk when it came to public opinion. So we were just sort of left there. Or I was, at least. But I didn't mind much. After a while Briar got sent home, and then I got his spot. Rank and all."

"Good," Stephanie said.

"And of course, I got to deal with all the problems that had been Briar's responsibility," Mac said, continuing on as if Stephanie hadn't said anything. "And the chief problem that we had was resupply. We had a lot of guys in our little camp, and we had to get all of them three squares a day. With choppers sometimes making it in, and sometimes not, we had to improvise sometimes."

"Like with Shin Me's family?" Stephanie asked.

"Yeah," Mac answered. "It seemed that Shin Me's grandpa was the local go-to guy if you needed something. So we traded with them. I didn't mind much. Since I couldn't speak Vietnamese, Shin Me had to translate for her old pop whenever they'd come into the camp. So I got to see a lot of her."

Stephanie snickered a little bit, but she tried to hide it behind her hand. Mac smiled, and there was that strange something in his expression again. It was like the taste you got when you bit a ripe orange, but deep down rot was creeping through the fruit.

"I was halfway through my second tour when I got some decent leave time," Mac said. "I could have gone back to Saigon or somewhere, but I decided to stay right where I was."

"Did you ask out Shin Me?" Stephanie asked. The girl was practically bouncing in her seat at the prospect of the romantic element finally coming to the forefront of the story. Mac looked back out towards the misty windows, and for a while said nothing.

"Yeah, I asked her," Mac said. "Shin Me looked at me kinda funny for a minute when I did. It was like I could see her trying to change the sounds around to make sense of them in her own head. Then she just smiled and took my arm. Apparently I was being invited home as the guest of honor."

"She thought you'd asked her to *marry* you!?" Stephanie asked incredulously. Mac just shook his head impatiently.

"Steph, stop interrupting me or I'm never gonna finish this thing," Mac said. The big cook settled back down, fingers plucking a toothpick from a bowl on the counter. Mac rolled the stick between his teeth, chewing at it. "No, she didn't misunderstand me. But I went to her home, a decent-sized place compared to a lot of the villages. Her mama set out quite a feast, and Shin Me held up my part of the conversation, translating for both sides. All in all, it was a pretty nice night. One of the best I can remember having over there."

Mac crossed the room, tugging the cords to close the blinds. After a few minutes, once all the windows had been covered, he sat down on a stool next to Stephanie, took a deep breath and picked up right where he'd left off.

"It was the first of a lot of nights for us. When I got leave, I went out to Shin Me's place. It got to the point that I could find it in the dark if I wanted to," Mac said. "And I wanted to, a few of those nights."

"You snuck out past the guards, and the barbed wire, and to Shin Me's place?" Stephanie asked. Her voice was barely a whisper, amazed that the old man she made sandwiches with during the day had once been so young and gutsy. Or so romantic.

"Yeah, I did," Mac said. "It wasn't too hard really. We were a camp, not a base. Because of that there wasn't really any kind of strict discipline inside unless you were on guard duty. All I had to do was give the guy on gate the heads up, and he'd let me through. Maybe keep an eye out for me about when I said I'd be back. Getting away from the base was the easy part."

"What was the hard part?" Stephanie giggled. Mac gave her a stern look, but when you're seventeen, you're seventeen. Mac chuckled a bit; kids hadn't really changed all that much, no matter what the old timers said about them.

"Getting past Shin Me's old grandpa," Mac said. "That man slept like a cat, and he had ears that were just about as good. We had our close calls, but no one ever said anything when I'd come over in the daytime."

Mac smiled as he thought back, lips quirking up at the corners. Stephanie felt in that moment that if she looked at him hard enough that she might see a young GI, with his brown crew cut and smooth face that hadn't been ravaged by time and memories yet. Mac shook his head, and as he did the illusion of his younger self vanished.

"It was really good just spending time at that house," Mac continued, wiping at his eyes as if there was something in them. "I'd help with the pigs, work on the roof. There was even one night that I cooked for them. It made the whole family laugh, but everyone liked what I made. It was exotic, Shin Me's dad said. I remember that really well."

"So... what happened?" Stephanie asked after several moments of silence from Mac. "Did you get reassigned, or something?"

"No," Mac said softly. He wiped his eyes again, but when he turned and looked at Stephanie, his gaze was clear and hard. Soldier's eyes. "Shin Me died."

"What?" Stephanie asked, her voice shooting out as if she'd been punched in the stomach. The girl took several deep breaths, throwing her head back as if she was winded by the words Mac had spoken. "What happened? Was is the Viet Cong? Did they find out that her family was trading with the enemy, or something?"

"No," Mac said. "It was one of our guys who got her."

"Well... was it a mistake?" Stephanie asked. "Did she surprise someone on a trail, or something?"

There was a pleading tone in the girl's voice, and Mac could hear it ringing like a gong in a choir room. Stephanie didn't want to believe that bad things happened this close to the end of a story. Mac felt something cold slide around in his guts when he thought about that night. For just a moment he considered lying to Stephanie. Considered telling her that it was a random thing; a freak accident that had taken Shin Me out of this story. Maybe a land mine, or a stray bullet from a firefight she had nothing to do with. But that wouldn't be the truth, and if Mac lied to Stephanie it would be like lying to himself. It would be like letting a little bit of that lie into his heart and his soul. Vietnam had taught Mac never to lie to himself, if it had taught him nothing else.

"It wasn't an accident," Mac said. "I did it."

Silence hung in the room, filling it with a cold, oppressive dampness. Stephanie stared at him, her mind whirling. She was trying to put what she knew about Mac, and about the story he'd told her so far, together with the statement he'd just made. Once she'd exhausted every excuse she could possibly think of Stephanie asked the question that she didn't want the answer to, but had to have anyway.

"Why, Mac?" She asked. Mac took a deep breath, and fancied he could smell the cool, water scent of the mist that was pressing up against the windows behind the blinds.

"It was late one night when Shin Me came to the camp," Mac began. "The moon was high, no mistaking her at all. All the guys at the watch posts knew her by sight, if not by name. It was a small camp, and word got around when one of the guys started to see a local girl, so they let her in without thinking about it. She said she was coming to surprise me when they asked, and they didn't have a reason not to believe her."

"But why did she-" Stephanie began, but her eyes went wide before she could finish. The answer had come to her. She closed her mouth, her teeth clicking softly.

"Shin Me didn't come to my bunk at all," Mac said. His voice was softer now, and Stephanie had to lean forward on her stool to catch his words. "She went directly to the mess tent. There was no one around, so whatever it was she'd been about to do wouldn't have been good."

"About to do?" Stephanie whispered. Mac nodded and wiped his nose with one, large thumb.

"I couldn't sleep that night. Something about the heat I guess, I just never got used to it," Mac said. "So I was out walking around, and I passed one of the guys who'd let Shin Me in. He winked at me and asked how my night had been. Once I knew that Shin Me was in the camp, I checked my bunk to make sure I hadn't missed her. When she wasn't there, I went to the mess tent."

Mac stopped suddenly. The sound that he made when he tried to speak sounded like his tongue had tried to choke him. He cleared his throat, and tried again.

"Before I could even get a look at what was going on, Shin Me stabbed me right here," Mac said, holding up his shirt to reveal a deep, grooved a scar along his abdomen. "It was a paring knife, otherwise she would have hurt me a lot worse. When she saw it was me, Shin Me smiled. It was a nasty kind of smile. It made me think of kids that went into the jungle, and came back a little too loose in their own skin."

Mac shivered as he remembered the look on Shin Me's face, tucking his shirt back down. She was like something out of a kid's bogeyman story, her black hair tangled, and her eyes sunk back in her head. The girl's skin had been scratched like she'd slept nervously, and there was a tightness in her mouth and the corners of her eyes that Mac had seen before. He remembered what she'd said to him then. They were words that he'd never forget.

"Shin Me said that she hated me, and that she'd always hated me," Mac whispered. "That she'd only pretended to love me because she wanted to get in here, and kill all the soldiers. To poison their food through me. I was just a tool to her, meant to be used and thrown away. She told me that I'd polluted her, and that she hated me for that more than anything."

"So..." Stephanie said, her voice trailing off into something that wasn't quite a question and wasn't quite a statement. It was the sound of a steam engine running out of power at the end of a bridge to nowhere. The only punctuation that can ever follow a true war story.

"So," Mac echoed. "Briar had left me his old sidearm when he left, and I always wore it. Even when I went out on walks. It was just a habit, but one that I never broke."

Something crashed outside the diner; a metal fist punching into one of the light poles. The pole shimmied, casting crazed, dancing shadows along the blocked windows. Stephanie jumped, dashing to the front doors, but even with the parking lot lit by the other flood lights, all she could see was a world of swirling quicksilver. Stephanie pressed her face against the glass doors, trying to see out into the shrouded night.

"There's something out there Mac," she said.

"Leave it be, Steph," Mac said. His voice was soft, and strangely incurious; a parent warning a child away from a stove they've reached for a thousand times. "Just leave it be."

Stephanie kept staring out into the swirling mist, her face practically pushed against the glass. Then she saw something; a dark, shambling shape stumbling toward the door. Stephanie felt her throat knot up, a scream trying to claw its way onto her tongue a she watched it come closer.

The figure lost its balance, and fell against the door. It was a man, streaked with blood and filthy sweat. He raised his head like it weighed a hundred pounds, staring into the glass with wide, dark eyes that were sunken, and scared.

"Mac!" Stephanie called out, her hand reaching for the door's lock. "It's that guy from earlier! He's been hurt!"

Before Stephanie could open the door, Mac's big hand overwhelmed her smaller fingers. His touch was gentle, but firm as he pulled her hand away from the lock. Stephanie turned and looked up at Mac. He was watching the figure outside. It was the leader of the little gang who'd been causing trouble earlier. The one with the Japanese bike, and the infected tracks. Blood welled from a cut across his forehead, running down the side of his face. His eyes were aware, though, and Mac looked into those eyes. Made himself look into them.

"Help!" The wounded man croaked. The young punk slammed his palm against the window, the force of the limb's weight making a light slap against the glass. He held his hand there a moment, then looked over his shoulder as if he'd heard something. With his bravado washed away with blood and pain, he looked impossibly young. He began to tremble. He turned away from the mist, and looked through the door at Mac and Stephanie. He was crying, the tears dripping off his nose and mixing with his blood on the concrete. *Help me* he mouthed, unable to even summon words.

"Mac," Stephanie pleaded, unable to take her eyes away from the boy. "Please... open the door."

"Leave it be, Steph," Mac said. "Just leave it be."

The words had barely left Mac's mouth when something happened outside. Swirls of mist wrapped around the boy. They grasped his wrists and arms, his waist, squeezed his thighs, and caressed his face. The desperation peaked in his face, and for just a moment it seemed that the eddies of fog that whipped around him weren't just bits of ground cloud. They were long, bony fingers. The light that danced through the mist lit hundreds, thousands of pin prick, yellow eyes. They looked at the boy for a moment tightening their ephemeral grip on him. Then the mist yanked him away.

The boy flew, clutching at the wooden pole. His eyes bulged, his tongue spilling from his open mouth. Tendrils of mist pulled at his fingers, loosening his grip. He screamed, and it was the cry of a terrified child finding out that monsters were real. The scream only lived for a moment before it, like its owner, was swallowed up entirely by the mist. Mac slowly unwrapped his fingers from Stephanie's hand. She took slow, dreamy steps back, unable to look away from the window.

"Mac," Stephanie said, her voice wavering and watery. "We've got to do something. Call the cops or... or..."

"It won't do any good," Mac said. He stared out the door for an eternal moment, his big hands at his sides. In that moment, he looked like a man who could tell Atlas a thing or two about burdens. "It would be like how I tried to tell the brass that Shin Me's family had nothing to do with what she'd tried to do. Lacing rat poison in the rations, I mean, not stabbing me."

Mac put his hand up against the glass, covering the bloody hand print. Slowly, Mac let his hand fall back down again.

"No one listened to me, and I was mostly in and out of surgery for the next week or two anyway," Mac said. He didn't turn to look at Stephanie, but he stared out the windows, talking to the night outside like he was telling a bed time story. "By the time I was up and about, I was told that Shin Me's whole family had been killed. There was a term that they used for what happened, something that made it look like they hadn't been involved, but it was just a fancy name for bullshit. The brass wanted to make a point, and they wanted everyone who knew that family to understand what would happen if someone else tried what Shin Me had.."

"Mac," Stephanie managed, her voice a raw whisper. Her eyes were wide and afraid as she stared at her boss's broad back. Mac rubbed at the scar on his side through the thin shirt like it was a worry stone.

"When I got back to my bunk, I found a package waiting for me," Mac said. "It was that staff out there, all wrapped up with a note in Vietnamese. It took me a while, but I finally got somebody to translate it for me."

"What did it say?" Stephanie asked. Mac didn't answer at first, and Stephanie was about to repeat her question when he started talking again.

"It wasn't signed, but I think it was from Shin Me's grandpa," Mac said. "It said, 'Though we're no longer with you here, we shall watch out for you. Keep this with you as a little piece of Vietnam. It will protect you better than Shin Me did your child.'"

Mac turned away from the doors like a man twice his age. He ran a finger through the melted ice cream on Stephanie's plate, licking it clean like it was some kind of ritual. Mac turned his face away, but when he spoke the tears kept off his face were in his words.

"The mist's cleared up now, Steph," he said. "It should be okay to drive yourself home. I'll call the cops, report the bike crash. Tell them the rider's gone."

Stephanie moved slowly, as if worried the world might come apart all around her. She took her coat down off the hook she'd set it on what felt like a century ago, and slid it on. Each step across the checkerboard floor made her think of a childhood rhyme, and though she could feel the rhythm of it in her mind she couldn't remember the words. When she reached the door Stephanie saw that the bloody hand print was gone. So was the mist. The night outside was warm, and a layer of dew had covered everything. As she touched the door handle, she heard Mac mumble to himself.

"None of us came back from there alone," Mac muttered. "We all brought our ghosts home with us."

Stephanie turned, but all she could see was Mac's back, his head slumped in his hands. His shoulders jerked as he cried noiselessly. Stephanie unlocked the door, and stepped into the night. She walked hurriedly to her car, tennis shoes slapping against the wet blacktop. She didn't look back, but if she had she might have seen the imprint left in the dew on the door; a small, barely formed hand drawn in dampness, as if it had rested against the pane for a long, long time. A little hand trying with all its might to reach across that threshold to its daddy.

Nerves

Dr. Kristin Pierce was buttoning up her coat to leave for the day, when her door opened and Carla burst in. One of the intake nurses, Carla was in her mid-forties, and she was unflappable. When Kristin saw the look on her face, though, she felt her end-of-the-day relief curdle. Kristin didn't have to ask, but she did anyway.

"What is it Carla?"

"Dr. Pierce, I know you were on your way out the door, but there's..." Carla trailed off, half glancing over her shoulder. "There's a man who wants to see you."

"Uh-huh," Kristin said as she pinched the bridge of her nose. It was raining outside, and the pressure from the coming storm was squeezing her head like a vise. She didn't need this stress on top of the barometric beating she was taking. Kristin let out a long breath, her nostrils flaring. "Is it an emergency?"

"I can't say," Carla said, her lips pressed together. Kristin had only been at the 5th Street Clinic for six months, but even in that time she'd learned to read her co-workers well enough. Before Carla could open her mouth again, Kristin finished the thought for her.

"But you've got a feeling?" Kristin asked. Carla nodded her head. The last time Carla had told her she'd had one of her feelings, it turned out that the guy who'd come in had severe paranoid schizophrenia and had nearly gone to where he used to work and killed everyone because his dead father was telling him to. Kristin unbuttoned her coat, and hung it back on the tree. "All right Carla, show him in."

"You might want to brace yourself." Carla said. "This guy... he's one of the dirty ones."

"Thanks," Kristin said, already groaning inwardly as she uncapped two air fresheners that she kept on her desk. She hoped it would be enough. She had enough time to pour a fresh cup of coffee and get out a pad of yellow paper before her door opened again, and a man came in.

He was a wreck; barely more than a stringy scarecrow belted into an over-sized raincoat with a stained, floppy hat on his head. He shuffled in slowly, and Kristin could smell a hint of him even over her wall of fresh scent. He reeked of old liquor, and of a wet dog just come in from the rain. He sat slowly in the chair opposite her desk, his thin, spidery hands swollen at the knuckles and black at the fingertips. Kristin got up and shut the door, holding her breath till she sat down again.

"Dr. Pierce?" The man asked her in a rough rasp.

"Yes," Kristin replied. "You needed to see me, Mr...?"

"Call me Butcher," he said. Kristin had to strain to hear him. Nothing moved other than his mouth, his chest barely rising enough to draw fresh air

164

when he spoke.

"Well then, Mr. Butcher," Kristin said, including a title. Homeless people were so often ignored that she found giving them common respect was enough to bring some of them to tears. She hoped that didn't happen here... she wanted to get this over quickly. "What can I do for you?"

"I tried to find a priest," Butcher said, his jaw working as if he was chewing on the words. "But none of them had the time to hear my story. I haven't told it to anyone, and I don't think there's much time left."

"I'll listen," Kristin said, giving Butcher a smile she doubted he could see. He was slumped in the chair with the brim of his hat hiding the upper half of his face. He looked like a dead man left there like some practical joke in particularly poor taste.

"But you won't believe," Butcher said. He was silent for a moment, then he nodded his head slowly. It looked like even such a simple movement took all of his effort. "Maybe listening will be enough."

Kristin didn't say anything; she said she would listen, and so she began in earnest. For several minutes the only thing to listen to was the sound of rain dripping off Butcher's hat; the fat, dirty drops splashing with metronomic slaps in his lap. Then Butcher began to speak carefully, as if his voice was a fragile thing made of glass.

"I would like to begin by saying that I am not on any medication, nor do I have any conditions that have impaired my reasoning," Butcher said. "In fact, given my current state of being, I'd say that I'm still remarkably sane."

Kristin said nothing, letting Butcher sort out his own thoughts. She picked up her pen, and Butcher snorted a laugh. His lips drew up spasmodically, revealing yellowing teeth and blackened gums. He reached into his coat, and took out a flask. He scrabbled at the spout, his stiff fingers clumsy as he tried to open it.

"Don't bother writing it down," Butcher said as he hooked his fingernails into the groove and pried the top open. "You aren't going to believe it, and even if you do, no one else will."

Kristin didn't argue with him. She set her pen back down, and folded her hands like an attentive school girl. If she hadn't, she likely would have taken to massaging her head again. The ache was becoming more noticeable already, and Kristin had a feeling that it was going to get a lot worse before it got better. Butcher tilted his flask up, drinking slowly.

"Two weeks ago I was working out of the country," Butcher said, trying to spin the top back onto his flask as he spoke. His tongue, wet and flaccid, slurred slightly, slithered over his scabby lips like a blind worm. "You've heard the reports on the news? Civilian contractors involved in torture, bringing in drugs and techniques that the army can't, or won't, use to prisons and gulags, things like that?"

"I've heard, yes," Kristin said. She hadn't really paid that much attention, but she didn't want Butcher to try to explain it to her, so she agreed. She'd pick up the train of his thoughts eventually.

"It's only the tip of the iceberg," Butcher said. "There's parts of the government doing things that you don't know about, and that I wish I didn't know about. Things that would make a person think they were staring straight into hell. One of those things is something called Purgatory."

"And what is purgatory?" Kristin asked, taking a sip of her coffee. It was just hot enough not to burn her tongue, and that was good. She had to try to focus on the positives before her patience ran out.

"I was a researcher in the medical field," Butcher said as if Kristin hadn't spoken. "I accepted a contract through an organization I won't name. They probably don't exist anymore anyway, and who controlled them I don't even want to guess at."

"What did they hire you to do?" Kristin asked. Butcher paused for a moment, and Kristin could see his neck tense as he swallowed. He cleared his throat, coughing something up in the process.

"I was told I'd be administering medical aid to prisoners of war, and recording the field data for the interrogation methods being used as part of a study to prepare the results for the military. The process was exhaustive. Only American citizens were considered for the position, with an extensive background check, school records back to kindergarten, and an exhaustive essay that boiled down to whether or not the end justified the means." Butcher unscrewed the cap of his flask again. "I don't know what they were looking for, but I passed."

Kristin watched Butcher as he spoke, combing over his movements and body language. He was completely still except for necessary movements. His legs didn't move, and his hands rested except when he was drinking. Kristin didn't even know if his eyes were open, or if he was talking to the empty space behind his closed lids.

"I was given several days to get my affairs in order," Butcher said. "Find a cleaning lady to come in and spruce up my apartment once a month, inform my landlord I'd be gone for a long time, but that he could expect a regular check from me. Then I was given a plane ticket, and told not to bring anything of my own with me, because I wouldn't be needing any of it where I was going."

"And where did you go?" Kristin asked once Butcher had fallen silent again. He didn't stir for a moment, then his arm raised and he drank, swallowing hard. Most drunks that Kristin had seen at the clinic had trouble keeping the bottle away from their lips. Butcher looked to be having trouble getting it down. She hoped that he wouldn't have any trouble keeping it down.

"Not too far from here," Butcher said cryptically. "I was being set up on a small base that catered to unusual methods of interrogation. That's all I'm willing to tell you."

"All right," Kristin said as she leaned back in her chair. Beneath the desk she massaged the space between her thumb and forefinger. A nervous habit that she'd had ever since she had to give presentations when she was finishing her undergrad degree. "Go on."

"It appeared to be a mostly civilian operation when I arrived," Butcher said. "Guys in loose khakis and Polo shirts. There were a few soldiers scattered around for security, but it was the eggheads and the inquisitors running the show."

Kristin tried to focus, but Butcher's smell kept wafting toward her as he talked. The man's scent was stagnant and earthy; the kind of thing that might be okay, if you could ever get used to the rankness of it. It was a dumpster smell; the kind where rotting meat was lurking beneath the surface scents of wet cardboard and old curry spices. Kristin took a drink of her coffee; it was going cold, but the smell of it inside the cup was enough to save her nose.

"They started me off from day one doing my observation work," Butcher said. There was a slight tremor in his voice as he spoke, and he tried to swallow again. "I put on a white lab coat and a button down shirt, got a clipboard, and was told to observe and report."

"And what did you observe?" Kristin asked, swallowing hard herself as the cold coffee tried to stick in her throat.

"Monsters at work," Butcher whispered. He lifted his flask again, and Butcher gritted his teeth in what might have been a grin. His lips peeled back again, like the skin of a rotting orange. "Pulling fingernails using a pair of pliers is effective, but predictable. The folks at this place were a lot more creative than that. More so than anyone should ever be."

"Creative how?" Kristin asked. She watched Butcher carefully for his reaction to the question. Delusions by their very nature were very similar to dreams. Generalities were easy, but when details were asked for they tended to dissipate like castles made of smoke.

"All sorts of things," Butcher replied. "Electricity was a common one. Running a pulse along the floor or a chair and forcing the prisoner to drink water. That way when he finally let go and pissed himself, the voltage would have a pathway. There were mind games, too. Guys using the Koran as rolling papers to light up fat cigars, or to start fires in the heat. There were all kinds of things they did. It took me three months just to watch their 'conventional' techniques and catalog them all."

Butcher's head dipped further as he stared into his lap like a naughty child, waiting for grown up judgment. He slid his flask, still open, back into his pocket. With exaggerated care Butcher tried to lace his fingers together. His swollen knuckles and arthritic, clawed fingers didn't want to obey. He was clearly a man in pain, and Kristin wondered just what else was in his confession that would release that pain. She also wondered whether or not that confession was real, or just the moonshine of lunacy pickling Butcher's brain.

"It was edging on towards the end of the summer when they brought out the experimental procedure," Butcher said. His voice was fading like a bad radio signal, and Kristin leaned forward to hear him better, ignoring the rotten smell stroking a fingertip around her nostrils. "It was kept in thick syringes big enough to be used on horses. They were old-fashioned and glass sided, with steel plungers. What was in them didn't look any more threatening than water. Or plague. It's only in movies and books where weapons look like weapons. What was in those syringes could as easily have been a booster shot, if they hadn't been so goddamn big."

"But it wasn't, was it?" Kristin asked. Butcher shook his head slowly.

"They called it Purgatory, named after that place between heaven and hell that can seem like an eternity all its own," Butcher said. "It was a special additive that had been developed by a US pharmaceutical company. Its purpose, or so they said, was to keep nerve endings responsive and electricity flowing through the body, even during the event of extreme trauma. Applied to someone who was being tortured, it heightened their sensitivity, and kept them feeling long after they normally would have stopped."

Kristin wished she'd thought to turn on the voice recorder. Butcher told his story so calmly, and he genuinely didn't seem to care whether or not she believed him. That was unusual in her experience. More common were the lost men and women, whether they wore rags or riches, that just wanted someone to understand. Someone to tell them what was happening. Butcher was giving a confession, and as soon as Kristin realized that she felt a spark of unease grow in her belly. A spark that led her fingers to rest a little closer to the red button underneath her desk that would inform the orderlies that she needed help.

"There were dozens of subjects in the experiment. More than a hundred by the time the true properties of Purgatory were discovered," Butcher continued, unmindful of Kristin's shifting. "They'd brought in a fresh interrogator, someone who hadn't learned the ropes yet. He went too far, and his prisoner had to be taken away by medical personnel. He died."

As Butcher spoke those last two words, he was wracked by shivers. Kristin watched as he doubled over, almost falling in on himself. She reached down to a small cooler for a bottle of water, cracked the seal and put it on the corner of her desk. Butcher took it and drank. He drained half of the bottle, then lowered his hands to his lap, cupping the bottle like a child that didn't want to drop his cup.

"I had to see for myself what had happened to the man that the new fish had killed before I'd believe it," Butcher said. "When I got to the infirmary he was sitting up in his bed, hands clasped to his chest and praying."

"I thought you said he was dead?" Kristin asked. Butcher nodded his head.

"No pulse, cooling body temperature, unresponsive pupils," Butcher said. "He'd even emptied his bowels in the screaming room. He was dead as democracy, but there he was praying to god with everything he had, and begging for his merciful lord to end the pain he felt."

Kristin fell silent. Butcher hadn't shifted his position, moved his head, or even tapped his foot. She was beginning to work through possible diagnoses in her mind.

"When the guys in charge heard, they immediately inoculated all the prisoners with Purgatory," Butcher said. "Once they'd waited long enough for the effects to take hold, every prisoner was brought to the mess hall, the biggest room in the entire facility. They were put in a line, and the prime subject, the dead man who'd tried to talk to god, was brought before them. His fingernails were still gone, and the trauma to his chest was very evident. His ribs had been broken badly enough you could watch them move when he walked."

Butcher paused, his voice cracking slightly. He raised the water bottle, limbs trembling, and drank greedily again. Once the bottle was entirely drained, he dropped his hands to his lap again. They fell bonelessly, slapping against his dirty pants. He raised his head slightly, eyes still taking shelter behind the tattered brim of his hat.

"The head of the facility shot the man in the back of the skull," Butcher said. "Nine millimeter hollow point. It destroyed his face, and it sprayed wet meat over the floor like an impressionist painting. The dead man screamed through the empty hole. He was blind, and it hurt... it hurt so much."

Butcher put the empty bottle on the corner of Kristin's desk. Kristin could see small bugs, white and fat, crawling over the surface of the bottle where Butcher had gripped it. Some of them were inside, squirming along the curves. She felt her stomach clench, and thought she might be sick, but she clamped her jaw shut and refused to allow it. The feeling passed. She looked back at Butcher, forcing her eyes away from the insects.

"It got the reaction the facility head wanted," Butcher said, a short, harsh sound like a vomiting dog coming out of him. Kristin realized it was a laugh. "The prisoners panicked. Some fell to their knees and prayed. Some pissed themselves. Others... they just stared at what they were seeing. They didn't want to believe it, but there it was, screaming and writhing on the floor right in front of them. An unholy miracle painted in martyr's blood."

Butcher swallowed hard, and Kristin saw one of his teeth wriggling in its socket. The stink was getting worse. Kristin's throat clenched again, as if her lungs would rather go without air that allow that miasma into them. She wanted to say something, but before she could get the breath to, Butcher continued his bizarre narrative.

"And like any cluster fuck, pretty soon everyone was getting sloppy," Butcher said. "They figured that if the prisoners couldn't die, then why bother trying to keep them alive? So pretty soon the first victim was joined by others. Dozens of others. There were some who'd had their skulls caved in, some who'd been cut to ribbons and bled out, others who'd lost limbs, though only their trunk kept moving around."

"Mr. Butcher," Kristin tried to interrupt him. When she spoke, Butcher raised his head, and Kristin fell silent. For the first time she got a good look at his face. His visage was long and stretched, pulled taught like a two dollar Halloween mask over the bones. His nose had been splashed by the water, and a stream of dirt ran off of it. It took a moment for Kristin to realize it was makeup foundation. There were patches of it all along his cheeks and forehead where the stuff had run off, revealing open sores, a few of which moved unnaturally. As if more of the fat, pale bugs were worming their way into his flesh. But the worst were his eyes. Butcher's eyes were empty and flat, cloudy like cheap glass. There were flecks of blood in them, and the pupils were wide and staring, swallowing up the sickly yellow orbs like a nightmare staring into the endless dark. It was the face of a man who had been given a glimpse of hell, and who knew with certainty that he was going back there for a much longer stay.

"The hate those men suffered was incredible," Butcher said softly. "The brutality unspeakable. It didn't matter if they were terrorists or civilians, innocent or guilty; what was done in those screaming rooms turned them into inhuman things."

Butcher's tongue flicked out over his lips, and Kristin could saw it was gray, turning black around the edges. It was swollen and dry, and it rasped as Butcher kept speaking.

"What happened next wasn't really a surprise. Every action has an equal and opposite reaction," Butcher said, his eyes unblinking. "We didn't know how long the dead men would walk. They didn't eat or sleep, just sat there, stared at the walls and screamed or whimpered. So when all of them were found in their cells, slumped over and unmoving, doctors were called in to examine them. No pulses of course, and no eye reactions. The doctors declared that they'd finally given up the ghost. But they hadn't."

Butcher leaned forward in his chair, and Kristin leaned back away from him. Her lips pulled back in an unconscious snarl. She was transfixed by Butcher's eyes. Those dead, damned eyes that held her like a butterfly pinned to a cork board.

"That night that all the dead men stopped playing their game," Butcher said. "There were a few soldiers guarding the facility, but guns are no use against men who can't die. Men for whom pain is such a constant that it becomes meaningless. A bare handful of them killed everyone. Everyone but me."

"W-why?" Kristin mumbled. Her lips were numb, and the gloss that coated them tasted like wax.

"They needed a messenger," Butcher said. "They chose me because they all knew I'd been sent there to record and observe. To turn their lives into numbers, and to tell the masters what had happened. They let me live because I had never harmed any of them, and this would have happened whether or not I'd ever been there."

"They set you free?" Kristin asked. Her voice was small and soft, the sound of a child wondering if the fairy tale would have a happy ending. "They let you go?"

Again Butcher barked that harsh, sharp laugh. He sounded like a man choking on broken glass.

"They didn't set me free... they just gave me an extended sentence," Butcher whispered. "They held me down and pumped my veins full of the last dose of Purgatory. Then they put me in a boat. As a farewell gift they gave me an oar, and a gun with a single bullet. They said that it didn't matter if I used it or not, since I'd bring the message home anyway."

Kristin swallowed hard, and her mind scrambled for purchase like it was going over a cliff. She was trying to reach for a theory, a handhold, or even an inconsistency, but the look in Butcher's face, and that horrid stench... Kristin knew how the story ended.

"Did you?" Kristin asked. The question could have been about the gun, about the message, or about whether or not Butcher had started rowing that tiny boat, hoping someone would find him before heat, thirst, and hunger would make that bullet look like his best friend. Butcher smiled, his lips splitting, and peeled off his hat. It came with the sound of a tearing scab.

"I made it five days before I couldn't take it anymore," Butcher said.

Kristin's eyes widened, and tears of revulsion and terror spilled over her cheeks as she put a hand to her mouth. The top of Butcher's head was gone. Sharp, ugly fragments of bone jutted out around the hole in his crown, and gummy tracts of blood covered the putrescent scalp. Crawling through what was left of his brains were colonies of fat, white maggots that made a sound like meat being put through a grinder. She thought desperately of a study partner she'd had who always turned up her nose at her headaches, and informed Kristin that the brain had no pain sensing nerve endings.

"I put the gun in my mouth so I wouldn't miss... but it still hurts," Butcher said. "The pain has nothing to do with my body, or with dying. The prisoners claimed that they could feel their soul being tied to their flesh. And they were right."

Butcher put his hat back on his head, covering the seething corruption that had taken root in what he'd hoped would be his way out. He stood, creaking and jerking like an ungainly puppet. Kristin felt like a little girl who'd curled up with her grandmother to watch their favorite shows, only realizing after the credits rolled that the old lady wasn't breathing anymore.

"It's what makes the nerve endings so sensitive," Butcher said. After a long moment, he smiled again; an almost beatific expression on the ravaged face with the humanity running away in filthy tears. It revealed a mind that had gone to rot, and a soul being eaten by corruption. "This is what it feels like to be god."

Then without a word the man who'd called himself Butcher opened the door, and walked out. He went back through the waiting room filled with pain and suffering, and he understood it all better than anyone would have believed. He was a devil among the damned.

Happily Ever After

The rain was cold as it slid down Rachel's neck. She laughed, and ran with her arms spread out wide like a child finally free from a formal event; her legs pumping as water spotted her dress and dampened her hair. Peter's footsteps pounded on the pavement behind her, and his laughter joined hers as they pelted through the thickening downpour.

A car sped past, and water spumed up in a wave that barely missed the two of them. Peter leaped forward, overtaking her as he raced up the front stairs, sheltering under the building's overhang. A moment later Rachel threw herself into his arms.

"So much for a long, romantic walk," Rachel managed, the echoes of her earlier laughter still clinging to her voice as she caught her breath.

"So much," Peter said, panting. He looked into her face, and something burned in his eyes. Bright pinpricks that drew her in, leaving her helpless. Then Peter leaned forward, and kissed Rachel softly. They both tasted like rain and wind, with a hint of fire in the depths. Rachel broke the kiss and tried to look serious.

"Hey now," she said. "I didn't come back to your place for that, Peter."

"I know that," Peter said. He looked slightly embarrassed, flushing hard. Rachel smiled at him, and leaned up on the balls of her feet to kiss Peter's cheek. Despite its chastity, there was a promise in that gesture. He smiled at her, and for a moment it was like the sun coming out. Then he opened the door, and held it for her.

"Thank you," Rachel said as she stepped past. The hallway was dim, but there were stairs that led up, and stairs that led down. Peter shut the door behind her and smiled, brushing the small of Rachel's back.

"My place is upstairs," Peter whispered. The building smelled of age in the way that a well cared for library did; all hardwoods and leather, with a hint of dust. Rachel couldn't help but smile as she mounted the steps, her fingers slipping along the carved oak handrail. She could feel Peter behind her, nearly close enough to touch, his warmth radiating through the chill that was starting to slip into her skin.

The stairs ended at an intricately carved door with a heavy lock that looked like something out of a fairy tale, especially in the half-light of the streetlamps filtering in through the windows. Peter carefully stepped around her, and drew an old-fashioned key from his jacket pocket. He unlocked the door, and stepped into the darkness beyond. A moment later, soft, white light spilled from globe lamps along the walls. The floor inside Peter's place was polished wood, and there were thick carpets laid down under the leather furniture. The walls were brick, and in the center of the far wall there was a fireplace, its wide mouth already open and filled with wood. It had the close air of a lived-in cabin, mixed with the old-world charm of a country study.

"It's not much," Peter said with a smile as he closed the door behind Rachel. "But it's home."

"It's amazing!" Rachel said, stepping forward and trying to look everywhere at once. She felt her legs tangle in themselves, and then she was falling. Peter was there to catch her though, and as he held her it was Rachel's turn to blush. He smiled and lifted her up easily, steadying her while holding her close.

"Careful now," he said, leaning down and kissing her temple. "You didn't come here for that either, love."

Rachel's blush grew hotter, and she squeezed Peter in something that wasn't quite a hug before she let him go. Peter stepped around the sofa and bent down near the fireplace, striking a match. He added some kindling from a stack of nearby newspapers that had been ravaged by scissors, making sure the blaze got going.

"There now," Peter said. He stood and closed the grate, a steel fan in the shape of a peacock's tail, before he turned towards Rachel. "That should be enough to warm us up, and dry us off a bit."

Rachel kicked off her shoes, and padded to the fireplace. In soft light, with the smell of wood smoke and the crackling heat of the fire, she felt almost as if she was in one of her Sunday books. The sort of over-thumbed paperbacks that featured fantasies painted in garish color on the front, and that sold for less than a dollar on the discount rack. Peter's soft blue eyes seemed to dance in the light of the fire, and it was like gazing into a wishing pond. His dark hair fell damp across his forehead, and when he showed his smile again there was something creeping in around the edges that was more than the boyish charm that had made Rachel's heart flutter throughout their first date.

"I hope that run through the rain didn't change your mind on dessert, love?" Peter asked, turning a statement into a question. Rachel laughed, and shook her head, her wet hair flying.

"No, but it had better be worth all the effort," She said, barely containing a giggle. Peter just winked at her and grinned.

"You can tell me once you've tried it," He said, vanishing through a nearby archway. "It's my home recipe."

Rachel sat down on the thick carpet to watch the fire. The flames were beginning to dance over the logs, the tinder curling and charring as heat wafted over her skin. Gradually she felt her goose flesh fading, and a powerful urge to lay down like a cat and just enjoy the warmth. She was about to do just that, when Peter returned, holding two plates.

"Bon Apetite" Peter said, holding out one of the plates to Rachel. Rachel took the plate, and looked at the single, thick slice of pie on it. There was a large dollop of cream on top, and it smelled of the familiar, childish temptation of the sweet. Peter folded himself down till he was sitting cross legged, half facing the fire and half facing Rachel. Then he picked up his fork, and began to eat his pumpkin pie. Rachel did likewise, and her eyes widened at the taste. She chewed slowly, savoring the rich, spicy flavor before she swallowed.

"This is really good," Rachel said.

"It's the Cool Whip," Peter said, his face serious. He managed to hold that expression for all of three seconds before his face broke into another of his wide, pleased smiles. They ate in silence for a time, just enjoying the fire and the pie. Rachel was down to a smidgen of crust, and Peter was just scooping up the last of his cream when Rachel spoke again.

"Your parents really named you Peter Peterson?" Rachel asked. Peter just nodded his head, affecting a great, heaving sigh.

"I'm sure they thought it was a great idea at the time," Peter said.

"And you just served up pumpkin pie?" Rachel asked, her eyebrow raising slightly.

"Consider it a mark of how much I trust you by the end of a first date," Peter said, waving his clotted fork at Rachel. "Usually I only do this at family parties, or when I've been dating someone for a while."

Rachel just smiled at Peter as he put the fork in his mouth to finish the last bite before setting his plate aside. His lips were smeared with cream, and Rachel laughed. She leaned forward and slipped her fingertip along the rim of Peter's lips. Then with a small, teasing smile, she put her finger in her mouth and sucked the melting cream off of it.

"Did you get it all?" Peter asked, his voice a little thicker than it had been only a moment before.

"Let me check," Rachel said. She got up onto her knees and leaned forward, gently running her tongue over his bottom lip. Peter leaned forward, his lips parting as he kissed her again. Rachel groaned into the kiss, closing her eyes as she tasted the sweet cinnamon and cream mixed with the deeper, richer taste of the man beneath it. Peter broke the kiss, and smiled at her. That same mischief she'd glimpsed throughout the night burned more strongly in his eyes, now.

"Did you get it all that time?" he asked, voice practically purring.

"I think so," Rachel answered, kissing Peter again. The second kiss wasn't as long as the first had been, but it was enough to send both of them into motion like a starting pistol. Within moments they were on the floor, tasting each other, hands groping slowly at first, then faster as passions grew and overflowed. Then Peter stopped, his breath coming in sharp gasps against Rachel's neck. Rachel kissed his cheek softly, her fingers gentle as they stroked his shoulders.

"What's wrong Peter?" she whispered. He raised his head and met her eyes, holding her gaze. There was an expression that Rachel couldn't quite read flickering on his face. It was a ghost in the firelight; there one moment, and gone the next, never there long enough for her to be sure of what she saw.

"Are you sure?" Peter asked. Rachel smiled, and in case that smile wasn't answer enough, she kissed him again with her arms around his neck. She raised her hips against him, making sure to leave no doubt in either or their minds.

"Yes!" Rachel breathed into Peter's ear. She felt his arms around her, lifting her up off the ground, his lips finding hers and devouring her cries.

"Then let's do it properly," Peter said.

He released Rachel, but only to close the front of the fireplace. The light continued to dance through the glass as Peter took her hand, leading Rachel down a dark hallway. The polished boards were cool beneath her feet, and Rachel clung to Peter's hand like he was a guide leading her to another world. A world she'd dreamed about, but had never imagined would be real. Not for her, anyway. She caught glimpses of other rooms through several open doors; the normal transformed into the fantastic by her pounding heart and the half light from beyond the windows. At the end of the hall Peter opened a door, and light blossomed from behind it.

The room was papered in soft, dark drapes, and in the center of it stood a four-post bed whose ebony wood was offset by red sheets. Heavy, round lights like something from a by-gone and gilded age burned in the corners of the room. There were no clothes on the floor, no pictures on the walls or stuffed in cluttered frames. It was like a scene from a movie, or out of a dream where the mundane concerns of comfort or practicality held no sway. Rachel only looked for a moment, though, before Peter's hands were on her again, lifting her up off the ground and carrying her into that strange, beautiful room.

"Peter!" Rachel gasped as he set her down on her feet once more. He just smiled and kissed her again; a quick kiss that closed her lips rather than opening them.

"Shh," Peter whispered, his fingers sliding through Rachel's damp hair. His touch, warm and sinuous, slipped teasingly over her neck, tugging the straps of Rachel's dress away to reveal more of her soft, creamy skin. His mouth followed his fingers, lighting fires that banished the damp chill of the rain to nothing but a memory. Soon Peter had taken a knee at Rachel's feet like Lancelot, while she stood over him, stripped of everything but her skin and the desire that quivered inside it. Rachel gasped as Peter began to slowly kiss his way up her body, lingering at her thighs, the seat of her pleasure, and then again on her breasts, lavishing them with attention before his mouth found its way to hers again.

"Now then," Rachel said with a breathy gasp as she broke the kiss, her fingers on the buttons of Peter's shirt. "My turn."

Peter stared at her for a moment, his muscles locked. He held her eyes, his face blank as a mask with two empty holes in it. Then life bled back into him, and he slowly relaxed as she pulled away his shirt to reveal his broad, muscular chest. Rachel ran her hands down, pulling away his belt, and then kneeling down before him as she stripped him as nude as she was. Peter's breath was sharp, groaning as Rachel leaned forward to taste him. By the time she stood again Peter's breath came in deep, rushing moans and a fire had been lit inside of him. He clutched Rachel to him as his breathing evened out, laying her gently on the bed.

The rain began to increase its beat, like an audience at the coliseum scenting blood on the sands. Thunder rolled louder, and strokes of lightning lit the dim room in a harsh brightness that seemed to add an extra sensuousness to the dimness that followed. Peter looked down into Rachel's face, brushing hair from her forehead. He slipped into her as his lips met hers, and Rachel let out a throaty moan like an alley cat's purr. She clutched Peter tightly to her, tying not to scream. It had been so long. As the thrusts continued, though Peter drew the music of passion from her lips, even as he stayed silent. He was the musician, and she his instrument to play till the song had come to its end.

Rachel didn't know how long they made love, or how many times she'd had her world obliterated by one orgasm after another, but when Peter finally pulled himself from her, she felt loose and hot, fulfilled and satiated in ways that she couldn't quite describe. She stretched, her body boneless as she rolled onto her side, laying her head on Peter's shoulder. She could smell the musky scent of sex mixed with the clean sweat that still lingered on Peter's skin. It was a thrilling scent, and it made Rachel smile as she closed her eyes, her hands refusing to stop touching him in case it turned out to be nothing more than a dream after all.

"So," Peter said as he raised himself up on one elbow, half turning to look at Rachel. "What do you think?"

"Mmm... about what?" Rachel asked, her voice still low and husky.

"Your ad said you were looking for your happy ending," Peter said with a grin. "Did you get what you were after, Rachel?"

"Yes," Rachel said as she craned her neck to kiss Peter's lips, tasting him once more as she shivered. "I definitely think that I did."

Peter kissed her back softly, combing his fingers through her hair. His touch was soft, gentle as he pulled back, his fingertips just barely teasing her neck as he smiled. Rachel saw there were tears in Peter's eyes, and her heart ached just a bit. She wondered what it was that he was holding inside him, and if she was going to see it. Wondered if he'd chosen her to show his true self to.

"Good," Peter whispered. Rachel watched as he closed his eyes, those tears spilling off his lashes like trees shedding dew. She watched, for a long moment unable to say or do anything. She was just about to reach out to Peter, tell him it was all right, when he opened his eyes. The sweet man she'd spent the evening with was gone, now. That darting thing had come out of hiding, and Rachel stared into its gaze, paralyzed.

Peter cupped her chin, staring into Rachel through the holes in his mask. Just before she could pull away, Peter's shoulders and neck tightened, the powerful muscles bunching and coiling like a striking serpent. Rachel's gaze spun out of control, and somewhere she heard a vicious, snapping sound. She felt suddenly light headed, and her eyes closed. Rachel opened her mouth to mutter something, maybe to ask a question, but her tongue tasted like old pennies. She felt drool running down her chin, but her hand didn't move when she tried to wipe it away. Her lips quirked as if she'd thought of something funny to say, then went slack. Lightning flashed, and Rachel's eyes were two glass marbles in the sudden flare.

The thing that wore Peter like a skin opened its eyes and looked down at Rachel. She looked so sad now; a soft woman who'd never been able to chase her dreams, lying at the end of a broken rainbow. He hoped that, somehow, she'd felt happy towards the end of it. That she'd gotten that fairy tale she'd wanted. There were no happy endings, that's what he'd said to her over dinner. There were only stories that someone had stopped telling before the truly awful things happened. She'd almost caught on then, a clever little heroine that almost stayed on the path. Almost.

Peter stood, his hands tender as he arranged Rachel on the bed. He could smell her already, the flesh cooling as breath departed, and the mess that had been made when death had claimed her. The reaper always left chaff behind, and it was the devil's work itself to keep it cleaned up. Peter grunted, wrapping Rachel in the sheets he'd bought for that night, and he left her there in her own little bower.

Peter stepped off of the stage he'd set, shedding pieces of his persona as he went. He padded down the stairs to the door with three locks. He retrieved the secret keys from their bolt hole, opened the door, and walked through to a room that was hot with the dragon's breath of an old-fashioned boiler. A room that smelled of the dank aroma of a den. The scents comforted him as he walked blind into the corner, turning on the shower and scrubbing away the visage he'd worked so hard to cultivate. He felt like he had in the rain earlier; the anticipation making shudders slide through his bones as the cold thing in his guts thrashed in its cage. It could always smell when a meal was close.

Peter crawled into his own bed, striking dirty matches and lighting the candles on the side tables. They sputtered and flickered, dancing in the red light that revealed the stacks of newspapers along the sides of the dirty mattress. Scissors, old and streaked with rust, sat on top of the nearest pile. Peter dialed the number from the latest clipping he'd found earlier that day, smiling that wide smile that showed all of his teeth as he read the small want ad over again. A single white female, 29 years old, who was just looking for her Prince Charming. Lightning flashed outside, making his eyes and teeth glow bright and hot in the darkness as he left his message in a voice gone soft with chalk. The wolf in sheep's clothing hung up the phone, and waited.

ABOUT THE AUTHOR

Neal Litherland resides in Northwest Indiana, a stone's throw away from Chicago. A novelist, short story writer, and RPG designer, The Rejects marks his third release where his work hasn't shared the stage with other contributors. For more of his work check out the pulp fantasy novel *Crier's Knife*, as well as the steampunk noir collection *New Avalon: Love and Loss in The City of Steam*.

Made in the USA
Middletown, DE
24 September 2022

11147257R00111